W9-AHH-000

YA
HIL

01/13

Russell Library
123 Broad Street
Middletown, CT 06457

ERASING TIME

ERASING TIME

C.J. HILL

 KATHERINE TEGEN BOOKS
An Imprint of HarperCollins Publishers

Katherine Tegen Books is an imprint of HarperCollinsPublishers.

Erasing Time
Copyright © 2012 by C. J. Hill
All rights reserved. Printed in the United States of America.
No part of this book may be used or reproduced in any manner whatsoever
without written permission except in the case of brief quotations embodied
in critical articles and reviews. For information address HarperCollins
Children's Books, a division of HarperCollins Publishers,
10 East 53rd Street, New York, NY 10022.
www.epicreads.com

Library of Congress Cataloging-in-Publication Data
Hill, C. J.
Erasing time / C. J. Hill. — 1st ed.
    p. cm.
Summary: Eighteen-year-old twins Taylor and Sheridan are pulled into
the future and must find a way to stop the evil government from using the
time machine again.
    ISBN 978-0-06-212392-3 (trade bdg.)
    [1. Time travel—Fiction. 2. Government, Resistance to—Fiction.
3. Sisters—Fiction. 4. Twins—Fiction. 5. Science fiction.] I. Title.
PZ7.H547687Er 2012   2011044624
[Fic]—dc23   CIP
                                                                         AC

Typography by Carla Weise
    12 13 14 15 16 CG/RRDH 10 9 8 7 6 5 4 3 2 1
❖
First Edition

ERASING TIME

chapterhapter
1

It was as good a day as any to plan treason.

Echo's hands moved over the computer control panels in a quick rhythm until an aerial picture of Traventon appeared on the screen. He enlarged the wilderness that bordered the domed city, searching for any sign of a path. In order to escape from the city, he needed to find a safe route—the route others took when they fled.

The date code on the picture said it was eighteen years old. From before the war with Chicago. Had the area changed since then? It might have.

If Echo could find the encoded site where the government kept recent pictures, he could splice into it. But that would be dangerous. It was illegal to do unauthorized searches. The Information Department kept track of the government sites, and the more important the data was, the harder it was to search it undetected. No point in taking risks he didn't have to take. People had been given memory washes for less. Anyway, a recent picture might not help him any more than this one. People had been escaping from the city for decades, so if a trail existed, he might be able to see it in this picture too.

A massive forest spread out to the east of the city, greener next to the river that supplied the city's water. Toward the west, the vegetation became sparse and interspersed with brown and gray rock. The deep shadows indicated height, although whether they showed hills or mountains, Echo couldn't tell. To the north of the dome was the scattered wreckage of the old city: Denver, destroyed in the raids of the twenty-third century. When Echo was a baby, his father had gone there with an archaeological team to rummage through the rubble for artifacts. But that had been nearly two decades ago, before the vikers became such a danger. Now the wilderness was so infested with the criminal bands that no one was allowed outside the city walls unless they had a good reason and a strong weapon.

Echo had a laser box hidden in a false compartment in his closet. It was one more secret, one more danger that he wouldn't have thought himself capable of a few months ago.

He went back to studying the photo and the dome that had always been his home. He didn't want to leave his father, his friends—everything—but if he stayed, the Dakine would kill him. He only had weeks, days maybe, before assassins came for him. The secret society didn't waste time on trials or the sort of bureaucracy that made the government so slow. They just hunted you down.

Echo rotated the picture on the computer screen, hoping a different perspective would show him something—some clue as to which way people went when they left Traventon. The most logical route was along the river. It would provide travelers water if they had disinfectors with them.

Echo zoomed in on the river. He didn't have a disinfector, but he had another advantage. He had access to historical documents. He knew that before disinfectors, people boiled water to make it safe. It had been easy enough for him to compile a solar-powered heat coil.

The best direction to go would be south. It was warmer. He'd gleaned this fact from historical documents too: stories he'd read about cowboys riding across dry, dusty lands and women who sat in the shade fanning themselves. There was also something called cacti, which were sharp and painful but not fast moving, so he ought to be able to avoid those.

Whether any of the southern cities would risk taking him in was another matter. He had computer skills worth paying for, but no way to convince anyone he wasn't a spy.

The door to the Wordlab slid open, drawing Echo's attention away from the computer. He expected to see one of the wordsmiths coming in. Instead, two black-clad Enforcers strode into the room.

Echo's hands jerked to a stop on the control panel. It was treason to try to leave the city, and he had an aerial picture of Traventon on his computer, the dome of the city in full view. Would it look too suspicious to close out the screen, or was it better to make up an excuse—pretend he was doing some sort of authorized research?

He sat frozen in his chair, undecided, caught in his own panic. The Enforcers walked toward him, their faces barely visible through their helmet shields. It was impossible to read their expressions. Did they already know? Just before the men reached his desk, Echo ran his fingers over the keyboard. It wasn't subtle, but the photo of Traventon disappeared from his screen.

He put on a disinterested expression.

"Echo Monterro?" one of the men asked.

"Yes."

"We're here to escort you to the Scicenter. Jeth's request."

So they didn't know what he'd been researching, hadn't been tracking his activities. Echo relaxed in his chair. "Why does my father want me at the Scicenter?"

The man simply motioned toward the door.

Echo didn't ask for more information. It wasn't wise to question Enforcers. He stood and walked awkwardly between them to the door.

Echo had been to the Scicenter before, usually to get age dating on an artifact or to get virus sweeps on something the Histocenter had borrowed from another city's archaic collection. This time the Enforcers took him past the main floors to the restricted section on the fourth floor. They strode down a wide hallway, then turned into a narrow one. It led to a room with LAB 15 inscribed on the door.

When the door slid open, it took Echo a moment to find Jeth. His father was one of about ten men, most of whom were either huddled around computer terminals or congregated in front of a large machine. It stood at least four meters high and

4

had cables trailing from its top and a glass cubicle sticking out of the middle, like an elevator that had been fused to a short building.

Jeth was off to one side, regarding the structure warily.

Echo walked away from the Enforcers and joined him. "This seems like a fun gathering. We've got a roomful of scientists, Enforcers, and a huge, scary-looking machine." His gaze circled the room again. "Why exactly are we here?"

"Probably for nothing." Jeth kept staring at the machine. "I doubt it will work. It's just the government's latest way to deplete the city's funds." He shook his head with the same resignation he used whenever he talked about taxes. "They call it the Time Strainer. They're trying to retrieve a man from the early twenty-first century."

Echo's gaze snapped back to the machine. "That's impossible."

Jeth nodded. "I'm sure the scientists got generous salaries anyway."

Echo stared at the jutting angles of the crystal booth—a booth, he realized, that was waiting for an occupant. Time waves had been a topic of scientific discussion for years, but he couldn't believe the government had been so reckless that they'd actually built a machine. Had they even considered the possible consequences?

Well, they had considered one consequence at least. The scientists knew they would need help communicating with someone from so long ago. Jeth was one of Traverton's senior historians and a wordsmith as well. Echo had just finished his apprenticeship in the same studies. The two of them could translate the old speech.

The scientists walked back and forth between the booth and the nearby control screen, bristling with nervous energy—except for one man. He stood by the control screen with his arms folded. His long black-and-gray-striped hair framed a serious, scowling face. He surveyed the rest of the men with irritation.

So he was probably in charge.

And then Echo realized who the man was. Carver Helix. The science chairman himself.

The title *science chairman* was a misnomer, since Helix was more government official than scientist. But still, the fact that he was here meant this was an important project. "Who do they plan to take from the past?" Echo asked.

"A scientist," Jeth said. "Tyler Sherwood."

Echo didn't say anything else; the implications of this machine kept multiplying in his mind. If this Time Strainer worked, would the government be able to pull anyone from any time into this room? World leaders? Inventors? Enemies?

They would alter history whether they meant to or not. And they probably meant to. Echo stood by the crystal chamber, waited, and desperately hoped it wouldn't work.

chapter chapter

2

Learning physics, Sheridan decided, wasn't a necessary part of a fulfilling life. It required you to remember all sorts of laws. Not rules, not suggestions. Laws. Like high school didn't already have enough things you had to remember. Besides, Sheridan wanted to become an English professor, and they never used physics.

She sat down on her bed and picked up a pencil, feeling like a martyr while she waited for her sister, Taylor, to start her tutoring session.

Taylor wasn't in any hurry. She stood in front of the mirror applying smoky eye shadow to her eyelids.

"So," Sheridan said, "this is all going to make sense after you explain it?"

Taylor tilted her head, surveying her work. "Physics always

makes sense. Your ability to comprehend it is another matter."

Sheridan rolled her eyes. *Physics always makes sense.* She and Taylor were identical twins, but their similarities stopped with their looks and their birth date. Taylor had leapfrogged over school grades, had graduated high school at age thirteen and college at sixteen. She was now working on a doctoral program in particle physics at UT while Sheridan and every other eighteen-year-old in Knoxville, Tennessee, were plowing through their senior year. So having Taylor for a twin was enough to make anyone feel stupid, even when she didn't spout off glib little statements about how easy physics was.

"If it made perfect sense," Sheridan said, "it wouldn't have taken so many years for people to discover it. I mean, how long did civilization exist before that apple dropped on Newton's head?"

Taylor didn't answer. She finished with her makeup and ran a hand through her strawberry-blond hair, unsure whether she was pleased with it.

Their natural hair color was a coppery red, but Taylor had abandoned it last year. She kept saying she wanted to be an *individual*, which basically meant she tried to look as little like Sheridan as possible. Sheridan's hair was long and straight, so Taylor's hair was bleached, layered, and wavy. Sheridan wore glasses, so Taylor wore colored contacts that turned her hazel eyes green. Sheridan only used a little makeup, so Taylor put on so much foundation, you would have thought freckles were a sin.

Taylor had a date tonight. A stealth one, because their parents didn't allow them to go out with guys who were in their twenties. In Taylor's defense, that was hard to avoid since she was in graduate school. She didn't meet a whole lot of teens.

Their parents also wanted to thoroughly interview any guys who asked Taylor or Sheridan out. This was probably because their father was a minister. Years of counseling teens with raging hormones had made him cautious about anyone who might talk to, socialize with, or in any way touch his daughters.

"Where are you going tonight?" Sheridan asked.

Taylor picked up some red lipstick and brushed it across her mouth. "Movie."

"You'll get caught." Knoxville wasn't a small town, but somehow it was small enough that things got back to their parents.

"Nah, it's one of those artsy foreign films on campus. I won't see anyone who knows Dad and Mom. However . . ." She turned and cast a smile at Sheridan. "I told Mom that the two of us were going, so I need you to come to campus with me. You can hang out at the library while I'm with Mason."

Sheridan tapped the end of her pencil against her lips and gazed at the ceiling. "Let me think about the benefits of spending all evening at a library and then possibly ending up grounded. . . . Nope, nothing's coming to me."

"I'll help you with your homework."

Taylor used to do that without expecting payment in return. Sheridan shut her physics book with a thud.

Taylor didn't notice. She took Sheridan's new denim jacket from the closet and slipped it on, covering a top that was tighter and lower cut than their parents would have liked. "Or if you'd rather, I'll do your physics homework for a week."

Which wasn't the point. Sheridan wanted to understand

the homework, not cheat. Still, she hated fighting with Taylor. Taylor had a memory that held not only an unnatural amount of scientific minutia, but also grudges.

"Fine," Sheridan said, flipping her book open again. "I'll go. Just explain Newton's third law. I don't care what my teacher says—a chair doesn't push back when you sit on it."

Taylor flopped down on the bed. "Yes, it does. For every action there is an equal and opposite reaction, even sitting on a chair."

"I've been sitting on chairs all of my life, and not once has one ever pushed back."

Taylor didn't answer. Instead she looked, with a startled expression, over at the corner of the room. Sheridan turned to see a small ball of light floating halfway between the floor and the ceiling. It twirled in on itself, like water flowing down a drain.

"What's that?" Sheridan asked.

"I don't know." Taylor stood and walked cautiously toward it.

It must be a reflection, an optical illusion of some kind. Maybe some trick one of their little brothers was playing. Sheridan glanced around, searching for something that could cast light up that way. When her eyes returned to the ball, it had grown. It shimmered, spilling out over itself.

Sheridan left the bed and edged over for a closer look. The light spread out horizontally, pulsing, growing so large, it looked dangerous. Could it be an electric field from a broken wire somewhere? The bright afterglow made it hard to see anything.

Sheridan took a step backward, shielding her eyes. "Mom!"

she yelled. "Something weird is happening in my room!"

Taylor stood transfixed. Her hair lifted from her shoulders, and sparks pinged off her fingertips. She raised her hand as though to push the light away.

Sheridan grabbed her sister's arm to pull her backward. "Don't touch it!"

Taylor didn't budge, didn't answer.

You weren't ever supposed to touch electric currents. Taylor should know that. Sheridan tried again to yank her sister backward, but instead felt herself being dragged toward the widening crevice of light. Sheridan's hair swished out in front of her, fluttering.

"Mom!" she shouted again, alarm spiraling in her chest. Her mother's footsteps quickened into a run. In another moment she would be here, and everything would be all right.

Sheridan held on to Taylor. The muscles in her arms and legs felt like they were hardening. Sparks flew from her body and twirled away, swallowed into the crack of light. None of this made sense.

Sheridan didn't hear the sound of her door opening. It was swallowed up in a noise like a wave crashing over the room.

"Stop!" her mother called. The word twisted, distorted, broke into a thousand tumbling pieces.

Sheridan wanted to turn and look at her mother, but the light enveloped her, a brilliant electric mouth devouring her and Taylor both. *I'm going to die*, she realized, and didn't have time for another thought before a shock slapped through her, buckling her legs. Then everything went deeply black.

11

chapter ~~hapter~~
3

At first Sheridan sensed nothing. Then, slowly, she heard voices, far away, filtering toward her.

"Two?" someone asked, and then she heard mumbling she couldn't understand.

Sheridan shook her head in an effort to rid herself of the drowsiness that clung to her. She had a sense that time had passed but couldn't tell how much. She opened her eyes, then immediately shut them. Colors blurred together in a kaleidoscope of shapes.

Mumble mumble . . . "Awake," one of the voices said. Or perhaps he said, "A wake." Wasn't that another word for a funeral? Was she dead?

She opened her eyes again. Everything still looked jumbled, dizzy. She raised a hand to her eyes, checking for her glasses.

They were still there. She blinked several times until the colors coalesced, kept the boundaries of their shapes.

She had thought she was lying down, but instead found herself standing—upright and weightless, floating somehow, behind a glass wall. She could have reached out to touch it, but her attention was drawn to the people who stood on the other side watching her.

They looked nothing like angels.

About a dozen men peered back at her. Some had hair that stood straight up in colorful geometric shapes. The rest had long hair colored with strange streaks, stripes, and designs.

Their faces were likewise decorated. Some wore only smudges of color, others looked like they'd painted entire murals on their bodies. Most of the men wore shirts in colors that matched their hair and faces. A couple were dressed in metallic black suits and wore helmets with smoky-colored visors. No one looked very happy.

How odd.

Sheridan blinked some more, hoping this might further change the scene. A man with fierce eyes and black-and-gray-striped hair stepped away from the others. He came toward her, frowning.

Sheridan watched him, trying to keep him in focus. "Apparently, I didn't make it to heaven."

"What?"

It was only then that Sheridan noticed Taylor suspended next to her in the glass booth. She groggily lifted her head and opened her eyes. "Where are we?"

"My first guess is hell, but I'm not sure yet."

The man in front of the wall spoke to them. *"Wet es yerr yama?"* As his lips moved, Sheridan could see his nostrils flaring but couldn't make sense of what he'd said.

"What?" Taylor asked, half slurring the word.

"Yerr yama?" he repeated. *"Wet es yerr yama?"*

What language was he speaking?

Taylor gave a shudder and jolted into wakefulness. She put her hands along the glass wall in front of them, leaning toward it. "Where are we?" Her voice rose sharply, as though just realizing she should be panicking. "Let us out of here!" She hit the wall with the palm of her hand. It made a pointlessly small smacking sound.

The man with the black-and-gray-striped hair turned to the men behind him and motioned a couple of them forward. "Jeth, Echo."

Two men broke away from the group and walked toward the glass wall. The first guy was perhaps only a few years older than Sheridan, with broad shoulders and light-blue hair that grew darker toward his shoulders. A turquoise crescent moon curved around his left eye and down his cheekbone, making his blue eyes stand out with vibrant color.

He studied them with open amazement, his gaze taking in their every detail.

The other man was middle-aged and slightly shorter. Dark-maroon hair receded over a high forehead, and a row of large green dots traveled down his face. He smiled up at them. "I. Am. Jeth. Don't. Be. Afraid." He enunciated each word slowly. "We. Are. Not. Hurting. You."

"We'll be the judge of that," Taylor said. "Get us out of here."

Jeth looked at them blankly. "The judge?"

"Let us out!" Taylor shouted.

Jeth's speech relaxed as though he was finally confident they could hear him. "We have a few questions before you're released. What are your names?"

Taylor kicked the wall, with no better results than when she'd hit it. "Let us out now!"

Sheridan put one hand against the wall's surface, looking for a door out. She didn't see one. They were in some sort of cage, and screaming and kicking wasn't going to help them. "I'm Sheridan Bradford."

A whole roomful of brows furrowed.

"And the other girl with you?" Jeth asked.

Taylor was still kicking the wall, so Sheridan answered for her. "Taylor Bradford."

Now not only did the brows furrow, but heads shook and gazes dropped. Only Jeth and Echo seemed unruffled by the news. Jeth shook his head philosophically, and Echo—although he tried to hide it—smiled.

The men in the background turned to one another, talking in so many different conversations that the room rumbled with noise. The man with the black-and-gray-striped hair marched from one group to the next, spitting out words. He looked like he wanted to hit someone.

Sheridan brought her attention back to Jeth and Echo. "Who are you? Why are we here?"

"You're here," Echo said with a smirk, "because the Time Strainer doesn't work as well as it's supposed to."

Taylor took a break from smacking the walls. "Time

Strainer?" she repeated. "What are you talking about?"

"The year is 2447," Jeth said.

Taylor shook her head, but her eyes grew worried. "Time travel is impossible. It's a scientific fact."

Jeth gave a bemused shrug. "We were surprised too."

This wasn't happening. It was an elaborate prank. Someone had made that big ball of light appear in her room, had brought Taylor and her here, put them in this glass cage, and rigged things so they floated in air like gravity didn't exist. . . .

Oh no.

You couldn't make people float in air. This was real.

They were in the future.

On one hand this was probably better than, say, being dead. Even as fear pushed through Sheridan, pounding in her stomach and making her ears ring, another part of her breathed out the word *opportunity*. Some people dreamed of the future, would give anything to see it, and here she was in it. The future.

She saw a stark white room and a dozen people who looked like clowns who had gone bad.

It was no good being optimistic about this. She didn't want to find out about the future. She wanted to go home.

Jeth was explaining the Time Strainer to Taylor. "The scientists expected it to retrieve a man—Tyler Sherwood—but instead it brought us you." He shook his head. "It's the machine's first use. Obviously it still has some problems."

Taylor had gone so pale, her red lipstick looked like two bright slashes across her mouth. She gaped at the men and didn't speak.

Usually Taylor said whatever she thought, uncensored.

Sheridan was the one who chose her words carefully. But in Taylor's silence, Sheridan found herself stepping into her sister's role. "Problems? What sort of crappy search engine does your machine have? It can make people time travel but it can't tell the difference between a man and two girls?" Her voice rang with accusation. "Like what—it just grabbed the first two people whose names sounded remotely like the right ones?" She rubbed shaking fingers across her temple and took deep breaths. "You're going to make sure this thing is working before you send us back, aren't you?"

She suddenly had visions of ending up in a time and place where people who unexpectedly popped into existence were burned as witches.

Echo sent her an apologetic smile. "We don't run the Time Strainer. We're just here as translators."

Jeth had taken a step to the side of the glass booth to get a better look at her profile. "Judging from your clothes, I'm guessing you came from the early twenty-first century. Am I right about that?"

Sheridan let out a huff of exasperation.

"Late twentieth century perhaps? They were similar in so many ways."

Sheridan glanced at Taylor for direction—for something—but found her sister staring forward with a vacant expression.

Taylor, who'd always been the one to take control of any situation, floated limply in shock. Sheridan grabbed hold of her arm. "My sister is sick," she said. "We need to go home now."

"Don't worry," Jeth said. "The scientists are monitoring your medical information."

As far as Sheridan could tell, the scientists were too busy being chewed out to pay attention to anything else in the room.

Echo must have thought the same thing. He said, "I'll ask if it's all right to release you." He turned and walked to where the man with the gray-and-black-striped hair stood berating the others. Echo spoke to him, motioning toward Taylor. The man spared Taylor a fleeting glance, then turned back to the others and continued his reprimands. It was clear he didn't care what state Taylor was in.

Sheridan tugged on Taylor's arm. "Are you okay?"

Taylor shook her head and shut her eyes. "No," she whispered. "No. No. No. No." Her breathing was too fast, too shallow.

Sheridan turned back to Jeth. "Do something for her."

"We are," he said, then tilted his head. "What you're wearing—this was casual wear, yes?"

Sheridan was about to launch into further protests, this time punctuated by hysterical screams, when a metallic clicking sound echoed through the chamber. A hot breeze swirled around them, and then with a whoosh, she and Taylor dropped to the floor.

Sheridan landed on her feet. Taylor did too, but wobbled. She kept repeating, "No," and each time, the word got softer, like pain was whittling it down. Sheridan held on to her sister to steady her.

Echo and two black-clad men walked toward the booth. When they were close, the front wall slid open. Jeth motioned for Sheridan and Taylor to come forward.

Sheridan hadn't realized how tall everyone was before,

but now that she stood on the ground, she could tell that even the shortest men were over six feet tall. She held on to Taylor tighter, as much for security as to support her. Sheridan noticed another thing about the men. Most of them wore white badges with long rows of numbers on them.

Jeth held out a hand to Taylor. "Come with us."

Taylor didn't seem like she could walk, but Sheridan pulled her forward anyway, and they stumbled out of the glass chamber. The door swished closed behind them. The two black-clad men each raised an arm, holding out dark boxes in their direction.

A gift? Perhaps it was something people needed here in the future. Sheridan warily reached out to take one.

Instead of giving her the box, the man yanked his hand away and barked out something she couldn't understand.

Echo stepped in front of her, shielding her from the man. Meanwhile, Jeth spoke to both the black-clad men in fast, reprimanding words until they lowered their black boxes.

Then Sheridan understood. The boxes weren't gifts; they were weapons.

Taylor went completely limp. She'd fainted. As Sheridan struggled to keep her sister from falling onto the floor, Jeth came over and scooped Taylor up in his arms. He motioned to the room's door with a tilt of his head. "Come."

What choice did she have? She didn't want to stay here with the black-clad men, or the man with the black-and-gray-striped hair who was yelling at everyone. Still, she didn't move. Leaving the Time Strainer would be leaving the link she had with her home, with her own time.

Echo reached over and took her hand. "We'll help Taylor.

Don't worry." He gently pulled Sheridan toward the door. "Come this way."

She looked back at the glass booth one last time, then allowed Echo to guide her out of the room.

chapterhapter
4

The group went into a hallway whose ceiling, walls, and floor
shone like pale glazed marble. Sheridan wondered how people
in the future managed to keep buildings so clean. She glanced
at Jeth's and Echo's shoes. They looked more like bedroom slip-
pers than real footwear.

Well, there you had it. In the future, people assaulted their
hair with color but kept their floors pristine. All those years of
civilization were not wasted.

It occurred to her that she should find out what sorts
of important events were coming. Wars, accidents, natural
disasters—things she could warn people about once she got
back home.

Of course, that would be changing the future, and she'd
read enough sci-fi novels to know people were touchy about

that. Perhaps these men wouldn't let her go back for that reason. Perhaps she already knew too much.

Echo still had hold of her hand. He slowed his pace and let Jeth and Taylor pull farther ahead. "While a med helps your sister," he said in a hushed tone, "one of the Strainer scientists will speak to you. If you can, don't let him know that you're twins."

With Taylor's differing hair, eye color, and makeup, strangers didn't usually pick up on the fact that they were identical twins. Echo had.

"Why?" Sheridan asked.

"Let him believe you're two separate people."

"We *are* two separate people."

"You have the same DNA," Echo said patiently. "To the scientists, that makes you one person. If they think the Time Strainer malfunctioned so badly it brought two different people, maybe they'll hesitate before using it again." He lowered his voice to a whisper, but the intensity in his eyes emphasized his words. "You need to understand—the Time Strainer is dangerous."

"Oh, I understand," she said. "I was the one who was just sucked into a gigantic electric crevice. If you know it's dangerous, why are you helping the scientists with it?"

"I'm not helping them," he said. "I'm helping you understand what they say."

Sheridan glanced at Taylor, worried that if she didn't keep her sister in sight, she might disappear altogether. "What language do the scientists speak?"

"English."

Sheridan considered this. "I'm pretty sure I know English, and they weren't speaking it."

Echo shrugged shoulders broad enough that her high school football team would have loved him. "Language evolves. If someone from Shakespeare's time had visited your day, would he have understood you?"

She supposed not but didn't answer his question. "How come I can understand you?"

"My father and I are wordsmiths—historians who've studied the progression of the English language. I specialize in you."

Her gaze shot to his face, trying to make sense of that. "You . . . you what?"

"I mean, your age," he corrected. "I specialize in the twentieth and twenty-first centuries."

"Oh," she said, relieved. "I was about to be seriously creeped out that there were historians specializing in me."

He gave her a sheepish grin. "There might be some. I can only speak for myself. So far, I've never specialized in Sheridan Bradford."

Jeth stopped in front of a white door, waiting for Echo and Sheridan to catch up. Taylor had opened her eyes and was looking around in confusion.

"You're all right," Sheridan told her. "Well, sort of."

When Echo reached the door, he pushed a button on the wall, and the door slid open to reveal a large room. A bed was set up in the far corner. Instead of a headboard, a large computer monitor perched above the pillow. A cart sat next to the bed, full of things that were probably medical equipment. Two men were in the room. One stood by the cart; the other sat at a shiny black table near the door. Chairs connected to the table with large black bars, so they stood suspended above the ground without legs. She'd seen chairs like that at fast food restaurants.

McDonald's must have set the standard for interior decorating in the future.

Well, that explained everybody's hair anyway.

Echo led Sheridan to the table. She sat down while Jeth helped Taylor into an adjoining chair.

The man who'd been at the cart came toward them, his gaze on Taylor. *"Wet es har kon de-ce-own?"*

Wet es—"What is." She tried to follow the rest of their conversation but caught only a word here and there.

After a few moments of talk, the med went back to the cart, opened a drawer, and took out a syringe with a long needle.

Perhaps these people took their mistakes seriously. Sheridan thought of the dog pound and how the workers put unwanted animals to sleep. Is that what she and Taylor had become, unwanted animals?

She must have gasped, because Echo whispered, "It's all right. The shot is to revive Taylor."

It worked immediately. When Taylor saw the man coming toward her, she jerked upright and screamed. The chairs weren't stationary. Taylor's chair swiveled and slid backward before coming to a stop. She stumbled out of it, backing up with her hands raised in front of her. "Stay away from me!"

Echo went after her. He took hold of her arm but didn't force her to come back to the table. "It's all right," he said in soothing tones. "The med has no reason to hurt you." Jeth also stood but spoke to the med, intercepting him before he reached Taylor.

24

The Strainer scientist still sat at the table, watching Sheridan intently. He leaned forward, ready to go after her if she bolted.

Sheridan stayed seated, glaring back at him.

Whatever Jeth said to the medic, it worked. He retreated to the back of the room, put the needle onto the cart, then leaned against the bed in a bored fashion.

Echo led Taylor back to the table. She sat down, still trembling. Jeth patted her hand like she was a lost child. "You don't need to be frightened."

Too late for that.

The scientist spoke to Jeth, rattling off incomprehensible sentences. When he was done, Jeth turned to Sheridan and Taylor. "How long did you feel you were in stasis before you arrived at our time period?"

"Not long," Sheridan said, unsure who to look at when she answered. "Minutes. Hours maybe."

Jeth relayed her answer to the man, and he asked his next question.

Jeth turned back to her. "Are you experiencing any residual pain?"

"I'm experiencing a lot of residual aggravation," she said. "Because no one will tell me when you're sending us home."

"Pain?" Jeth asked again.

Sheridan lifted her hand, using it to punctuate her words. "Aren't you guys worried about messing around with the past? You could change something important in history."

"Pain?" Jeth asked patiently.

"No," Sheridan said.

Taylor didn't answer. She held her hand to her temple like

she was trying to massage a headache away.

The scientist gave Jeth his next question. "Are you experiencing any cognitive difficulties due to your reconfiguration?"

Did an intense desire to scream at the top of her lungs count?

Echo spoke to his father. "Ask if it's possible to send them back. They should know."

Jeth hesitated, then sighed and gave in. He relayed the question to the scientist.

The two spoke back and forth for a few minutes, and every once in a while Echo asked a question. His blue eyes were intent as he listened, disapproving. A furrow of concern creased his forehead.

It gave Sheridan a tight, twisting feeling in her stomach. Maybe the Time Strainer had malfunctioned so badly, it would take a long time to fix it. She and Taylor exchanged worried glances.

Finally the men finished talking and turned back to the table. Jeth steepled his fingers together. "Back in your time, were you familiar with computers?"

"Yes," Sheridan and Taylor said together.

"You used the search function?"

"Yes," Taylor said, and Sheridan was content to let her speak for both of them. Taylor knew more about computers.

"Imagine time as one big database," Jeth said, "and think of yourself as one word somewhere in a billion-page document. The search function can find that word and pull it out of those billions of pages. That's what the Time Strainer does. It finds a specific life and brings it forward in time." He held up his hand, then let it fall back to the table. "At least it was supposed to. Perhaps the search function on your computer didn't always work correctly. You wanted the word *can* and got the word *scanned* instead. Do you understand?" His gaze bounced between Sheridan and Taylor. "Our scientists don't know why this happened. They're at the Time Strainer right now trying to get the right man."

Well, so much for Echo's hope that the first failure would make the scientists wary of using the machine again. They didn't seem to care who they accidentally zapped into the future. She hoped that next time they got nothing but a swarm of angry bees.

Taylor went back to rubbing her temple. "What will they do if they find him?"

"They'll ask for raises," Echo said, then added, "Actually, they'll probably do that anyway."

Jeth ignored his son. "Tyler Sherwood will help our scientists with biology work."

Sheridan decided to return to her original question. "So when are they going to send us back?"

Jeth's eyebrows drew together, as though he wasn't sure why she hadn't understood his first explanation. He spoke slowly to her. "Back in your time, were you familiar with the freezer?"

"Yes," Sheridan said, and felt reasonably certain she could answer for herself when the machine involved was no longer a computer but a kitchen appliance.

"And sometimes you put vegetables in and saved them for later."

"Yes." Sometimes it had been vegetables, although more often it had been ice cream or frozen pizza.

"When you took a vegetable out later—even much later—it was preserved, just as it had been when you put it in?"

Sheridan nodded.

"But if you had wanted to, you couldn't have returned it to its harvest, could you?"

"No." She choked out the word, and it seemed to take all of her effort, all of her energy.

"Our technology preserved your matter and brought it into the future, but we can't return you to the past."

Sheridan began shaking then, violent tremors she couldn't control. Her family, her time period—everything was gone, erased. In one moment it had disintegrated into dust. She thought of her mother running to her bedroom. Had she seen Taylor and her disappear?

The pain came next. Sheridan felt like her middle was being cut in half. She bent over until her cheek touched the cold, smooth surface of the table.

Taylor said, "Get a blanket for her." Only it sounded far away, and Sheridan wondered why Taylor said it, since blankets wouldn't help anything.

Taylor was saying other things now, very fast, and some of them sounded like swearwords, but that couldn't be right. Taylor didn't swear. Taylor was always in control. Always smart. Which was why Taylor had gone into shock at the beginning of this whole thing. She'd understood what it meant and had gotten her breakdown out of the way so she could be back in control. Now she stood there yelling like she wasn't grieving. As though she hadn't lost everyone in the world too.

The med came toward Sheridan, and he carried not a blanket but a shot. Taylor was still yelling at him, and the words were most definitely swearwords.

Sheridan pushed herself up from her chair and took dizzy steps backward. She wanted to find the scientists and demand they make this right. How could they build a machine that snatched people from their time period without creating a way to put them back?

Echo was beside her even though she hadn't seen him get up from his chair or cross the room. His tone was low and soothing. "It's all right."

He took her hand, but she yanked it away. "This is not all right." She stepped backward from him. "What is your definition of all right, that you could possibly think any of this is all right?" She took another step away. There was nowhere to run, though, no way to escape from what had happened. She was going to cry, sob probably, and she didn't want to.

Echo took her hand again. Instead of leading her back to the table, he pulled her gently into his arms. It was almost an embrace. "The med has no reason to hurt you."

He had said the same thing to Taylor, and this time Sheridan heard what he was actually saying. A phrase of her father's came to mind, and she said it out loud—not as a compliment, but as an accusation. "A lie doesn't sit comfortably on your tongue."

Echo tilted his head down, checking her expression. He had no idea what she meant.

The medic was almost to them. Sheridan tried to break from Echo's grasp. "You didn't say the medic *wouldn't* hurt us, only that he has *no reason* to do it. You know he might, and you don't like lying about it."

She couldn't free herself from Echo's arms. He pulled her closer, holding her in place so the medic could give her the shot.

"I'll do what I can to protect you," Echo whispered into her ear. "I'm not lying about that either."

She felt the prick of pain in her neck and then felt nothing else.

chapter
hapter

5

The second time Sheridan awoke, she didn't open her eyes right away. She kept them closed and listened. Men were talking on the other side of the room.

She struggled to make sense of their accent. They rolled their *r*'s, and the vowels were mixed up, like someone had randomly switched them.

"*Et es batarr theese wa,*" someone said. It is better this way. "*Orra way no et well werrk.*" Something . . . we know it will work.

Another voice said, "*Pues, way no wet te axpact ahora.*" Something, we know what to expect . . . something. What did *orra* mean?

"*Tharr halth es bueno.*" *Bueno* meant "good" in Spanish. The other Spanish words clicked into place in her mind. *Ahora* meant "now." *Pues* was one of those words like *well* that people threw into sentences when they were thinking about what else to say.

A man, angrier than the other two, said, *"Bet et desnt materr ef way kent feend Tylorr Shaerrwood."*

So they still hadn't found Mr. Sherwood. He didn't know how lucky he was.

The voices went on, and she strained to follow them. She could only figure out that the first two men wanted to convince the third man that the experiment wasn't really a failure. Finally Sheridan heard the swish of a door, and then silence.

They'd left.

She opened her eyes and saw Echo sitting on a chair near her head. His bright blue eyes studied her. "Were you able to understand any of it?"

She blinked back at him. "What?"

"I could tell you were awake." He pointed up to a lighted screen above her bed. "When you listen, your brain activity goes way up."

Sheridan sat up and glanced at the screen, at lights that flickered and moved but made no sense.

"How are you feeling?" he asked.

"Kidnapped."

He gave her a sympathetic smile. "Besides that?"

"Fine, I guess." Her grief was still there, strong and throbbing in her heart, but she kept it in check. She didn't want to break down again.

"According to the scientists," he said, "your cells should stabilize soon."

Her gaze snapped back to him. "My cells are unstable?"

He shrugged. "You were a stream of energy for four hundred

years. It takes a while to adjust to being matter again."

She froze, afraid to move in case quick action would cause her to explode.

"You look great, though," Echo said. "I mean, you've reconfigured nicely." He cleared his throat and motioned to the screen. "According to the computer, your health statistics are all good." And then, as though he were offering her a consolation prize, he added, "While you slept, the med devirused you and fixed your vision problem."

Sheridan's hands went to her face. Her glasses were gone. She didn't comment on it. She'd just realized Taylor was nowhere around. "Where's my sister?"

"With Jeth in an Infolab. She's learning about what's happened in the last four centuries."

Still reconfigured then. Sheridan slowly pushed the blanket off her lap. Her muscles seemed to be working properly. "What will happen to us now?"

"We want you to work at the Wordlab with us, but Jeth hasn't proposed the idea yet. He's waiting until the scientists are in a better mood."

Wordlab? She didn't ask what that was. She didn't want Echo to think she had agreed to any of it, didn't feel like being grateful for his help. He wasn't one of the scientists who'd brought her here, but he was a part of the future, and that was enough to make her resent him.

It wasn't logical or fair, but there it was.

Echo didn't notice her silence. He gazed at her like she was a fascinating painting.

Sheridan took a moment to study him back. Despite the

blue hair, he was handsome in a DC Comics sort of way. He had a sort of Superman look to him: square jaw, straight nose, rugged shoulders. But there was also a seriousness about Echo, a depth to his blue eyes that couldn't have been captured in comic book form.

"Do you have any questions?" he asked. "Taylor couldn't ask them fast enough."

Before the medic had given Sheridan the shot, Echo had told her, "I'll do what I can to protect you." Had he meant he'd make sure the medic didn't hurt her? Or maybe he meant the scientists. Did she need protecting from anyone else? Somehow she couldn't bring herself to ask him; not while the resentment was still thick inside her. Instead, she focused on his sleek blue hair. "When did people start color coordinating their hair with their outfits?"

"Fashion changes quickly. But not everyone alters their hair color. Some people keep their born shade."

She reached over and touched the glossy blue moon on Echo's cheek. She expected some of the blue to come off on her fingers. It didn't. It felt exactly like normal skin.

She ran her finger over it again. "Is this a tattoo?"

"A skin dye. It stays on until we use a retracting agent to remove it."

She dropped her hand from his face, suddenly embarrassed to have touched him. "Do women do that to their hair too—dye it, shape it—and paint colors on their faces?"

Echo laughed, and she was somehow surprised that it sounded exactly like a laugh from her time period: warm, deep, and completely human. "Would you expect women to have more moderation? The sex that wore corsets and girdles and plucked their eyebrows out?"

"A simple yes would have done."

"Oh." He was still smiling. "Then, yes." He motioned to the door. "We can go find some women here at the Scicenter if you want to see them."

Seridan shook her head and sighed. What fashion guru had decided that using your face for a coloring book looked good?

When she didn't speak, Echo said, "If you don't have any more questions, then I have one for you." He leaned back in his chair, surveying her again. "In your century, what was it like to be an identical twin?"

It was ironic that his first question was one she'd been asked frequently in her own time period. "It's hard to tell, because I've never been anything else."

Her answer brought another smile to his lips. "I should have asked the question differently. I used to say the same thing to people."

Sheridan straightened. "You're an identical twin?"

"I was," he said. He opened his mouth to say more but didn't. Instead, he swallowed and looked away.

She knew then that his twin had died. Probably recently. She knew because if Taylor had died, she would have felt the same pain she saw flash through his eyes.

She leaned toward him. "I'm sorry." It wasn't a hollow phrase, thrown between them to ward off the awkwardness of silence. She felt it—felt a connection to him through their losses. His twin, her family. Her resentment for him thinned and vanished.

He nodded but didn't elaborate about his brother. "What I

meant to ask was how the rest of your society treated you."

She could have gone on and on about that but knew Echo would understand the longhand for what she said in shorthand. "Growing up, we got lots of attention, which would have been nice except that people also treated us like we were one-half of the same person. Like, in third grade Taylor made some girls angry, and so they got mad at me too by default.

"Sometimes it was hard to share everything. And we're still constantly compared. Taylor's the smart one, the outgoing one, and the daring one." Sheridan didn't say, but mentally added, *The one guys like first.* "I'm the responsible one, the quiet one." *The one who always gets hit up for favors. The one who guys like after Taylor has turned them down.*

Echo took all of this in. "When someone calls Taylor's name, do you turn around?"

"Of course. For most of my life there was a good chance they were really calling me and just couldn't tell which one I was." She gave a sheepish shrug. "Even now that Taylor has completely changed her look, I still do it."

"Do you sometimes know what she'll say before she says it?"

"Yeah, but that's easy. If it's arrogant or snarky, Taylor is going to say it." Sheridan tilted her head. "Do people here in the future still think twins have a mystical psychic bond?" That was one of the annoying things about being a twin. People were always so disappointed to learn she and Taylor couldn't read each other's minds.

"Twins almost never happen," Echo said. "The medical workers prevent it."

That seemed odd. "How?"

He shifted in his seat, hesitated. "People in Traventon want superior children, so the Medcenter specialists select the best genes from the population and use those to create babies. Technicians are only supposed to put single, healthy embryos into women, but they made a mistake in our case."

Sheridan frowned. "Doesn't anyone want to have their children the natural way?"

"And risk having inferior children? No. At age eleven, girls undergo a surgery that prevents accidental reproduction."

Sheridan stifled a gasp. She was long past age eleven. "No one will make me have surgery, will they?"

He looked uncomfortable, which probably meant yes. "The government will decide. They control everything that affects Traventon."

"Everything? What happened to democracy?"

She had asked the question rhetorically. He didn't answer it that way.

"Democracies didn't last long after your time. It was too hard for average people to make decisions about policies. So now the government educates a select group of people and appoints them to positions." He tilted his head at her, questioningly. "You must have seen it happening. Democracy was already declining during your time."

Sheridan wanted to protest this fact but couldn't. She didn't know enough about Congress or the democratic process to tell whether it had been in decline. Which, she realized, might be proof Echo was right.

It couldn't be good that democracy was gone. In fact, it could be very bad.

She felt a prickle of fear, and with it an urgent desire to see her sister. Sheridan got off the bed. "Can we see Taylor now?"

"If that's what you want." Echo stood, took Sheridan's hand, and led her to the door. Perhaps it was customary in this society to hold hands, or perhaps he was afraid she'd run away. Whatever the reason, she was glad for the warmth of his fingers intertwined with hers. It made her feel more secure in this strange place.

They left the room and went down the white hallway. Sheridan's footsteps made a tapping noise against the floor, like a gavel slowly pronouncing a judgment. She wondered how long it would take until everything stopped feeling so surreal, like it was happening to someone else.

She sneaked a glance at Echo's profile. He was tall, handsome, and holding her hand. Definitely surreal.

If he had gone to her high school, what type of person would he have been? Her first thought was: one of the popular jocks, the kind of guy cheerleaders doted on. But the underlying seriousness in Echo's eyes wouldn't let her pin him to that group and leave him there, mindlessly enjoying his adulations.

He had stepped in front of her when the black-clad men had pointed weapons at her. He'd said he would do what he could to protect her—and he didn't even know her.

Echo caught her looking at him, but she didn't turn away like she normally would have. "When you said you'd protect me, who did you mean from?"

"Anyone you need protecting from." He gave her a smile, and it felt like a prize. "Did you have someone in mind already?"

"Yes. Everyone who totes around needles."

He ran his thumb across the back of her hand. "You'll be fine now. No need for more needles."

She was a long way from fine but didn't say so.

"Are you hungry?" he asked. "There's a foodmart here in the Scicenter."

Sheridan shook her head.

He gave her hand a squeeze. "The food isn't bad here. A lot is similar to what you ate."

"I don't think I could eat anything right now."

Echo looked at her for a few more moments—still studying her, she supposed. "They say people in your time kept animals to kill so they could eat their flesh."

And apparently people in 2447 were strict vegetarians.

He was not going to understand the lure of pepperoni or cheeseburgers, or her personal favorite, bacon. She didn't feel like she had the energy to explain protein needs to him, but lies didn't sit easily on her tongue either.

She chose an answer that didn't implicate her. "My family lived on an acre of land, and we had two horses." She hadn't thought to miss them until now, and it hit her with a stab of pain. Breeze and Bolt were gone too. "We also had a dog named Georgie. We never would have eaten any of them, though." Georgie, however, had caused the death of a few stray sparrows, at least one mouse, and whatever it was they put in Alpo.

"Tell me," Echo said, "how many animals from your time period talked?"

Sheridan's gaze darted to his eyes to see if he was joking. He wasn't. "None. Why would you think animals talked?"

"We have documentation—movies, pictures, stories—that

show some animals spoke. . . ." He let the sentence drift off, puzzled.

"Echo," she said, "have you ever tried to talk to an animal?"

"Animals are extinct. The flesh eaters of your time killed them all."

She stopped walking, and his hand pulled away from hers. "No. That can't be right."

"I would have liked to see them," he said, stopping too. "We have programs with computer-generated animals in the Virtual Reality center, but it isn't the same."

Sheridan shook her head—short, quick denials. "People loved animals. We kept them for pets. And we couldn't have killed *all* of them. We tried to get rid of mice and rats, and it was impossible."

"They're all gone," Echo said. "Even the rats."

She folded her arms across her chest. "You're wrong. Just like you're wrong about animals talking. They didn't."

His eyebrows drew together. "We have stories dating back thousands of years. Aesop's fables. 'Little Red Riding Hood.' 'The Three Little Pigs.' Your time period had Bugs Bunny, Winnie-the-Pooh—"

"Those are just children's stories."

"Yes, but adults told them to their children." He cocked his head. "Do you expect me to believe that for generations, across human culture, parents routinely lied to their kids about the communication capabilities of animals?"

"Yes."

He raised a disbelieving eyebrow.

"Oh, come on," she said. "Who would hire three pigs to

work construction jobs? They couldn't hold hammers with their little cloven hooves." She let out a frustrated sigh. It was unbelievable, really, that she was standing here discussing pig careers. "Don't you have any nature shows from our time period? Maybe a *National Geographic* magazine or two?"

Echo took hold of her hand and resumed guiding her down the hall as though it wasn't worth arguing about. "Only the records that were transferred from silicon to holographic memory were preserved over the centuries. Unfortunately, most of your programming was destroyed during the information wars of the twenty-third century."

"Information wars?"

"Attacks on computer systems. When a civilization's internal neural network is destroyed, it's easy to take over. That's why information isn't available to the public anymore. It's too hard to defend. It's lucky we salvaged anything from your time period."

"Wait—what do you mean, information isn't available anymore?"

He wasn't listening, though. His pace slowed to a standstill and he let go of her hand. He looked at her as though the reason for her denials about animals speaking had suddenly become clear to him. "You were one of the flesh eaters, weren't you?"

She nearly denied it. She didn't want to give him the least bit of leverage in the argument. But he might ask Taylor about their eating habits, and then he would think Sheridan was a flesh eater and a liar as well.

She lifted her chin. "Believe whatever you want. Apparently that's what you do regardless." She set off down the hallway, even though she didn't know where she was going. "If the animals are really gone, though, couldn't your scientists have used the Time Strainer to bring some back instead of abducting random people?"

Echo let her walk a few steps, then took hold of her hand to stop her. He put his other hand on a button by a door, opening it, then led her inside.

Rows of computers and chairs filled the room. Taylor and Jeth sat in front of a computer watching something on the screen. Taylor looked up when they walked in, and relief swept over her face. She stood up and gave Sheridan a hug. "I'm so glad you're all right."

Sheridan returned the hug, then pulled away. "Taylor, tell the truth—did animals ever talk?"

"What?" Taylor stared at her, perhaps mentally revising her assessment of Sheridan's health.

"Animals. Did they or didn't they wear clothes and speak English?"

Taylor put her hand across Sheridan's forehead, checking for signs of fever. "Uh . . . no."

Sheridan turned to Echo and gave him a pointed look. "I told you so."

He crossed his arms and walked over to where his father sat, as though standing there reinforced his position. "Two testimonies don't erase the records."

Taylor's gaze slid back and forth between Sheridan and Echo. "What records?"

"'Little Red Riding Hood,'" Sheridan said, "and *Winnie-the-Pooh*."

Jeth leaned back in his chair, considering this. "Perhaps by your period in history, animals chose silence as a sort of resistance."

Taylor held her hand up to interrupt the conversation. "Hello—animals don't talk now, do they?"

"No animals are left," Echo said. "The people of your generation ate them."

Sheridan wrinkled her nose. "Like I would eat a rat."

Taylor went back to her chair and sat down. "If all animals were extinct, the earth's ecosystems would have crashed to the point that they couldn't sustain human life."

"The ecosystems did crash," Echo said. "That's why people live in enclosed cities now—to protect the Agrocenters."

"And pollination happens how?" Taylor asked.

"Done by pollenbots. Miniature droids."

"Right," Taylor said, in the tone she used when she'd decided someone was so delusional there was no point arguing with them. Jeth and Echo didn't know the tone, but Sheridan did and it gave her hope. As long as Taylor doubted Echo's explanation, it wasn't necessarily true.

"How was food produced in your day?" Jeth asked, leaving the subject of the animals' demise behind.

"I don't know much about it," Taylor said. She ran her hand through her hair wearily. "Look, is there—"

Taylor didn't finish. Both Echo and Jeth were glancing about the room with puzzled expressions.

"It's a saying," Taylor said, and her voice sounded tight. "It means, 'Listen.'"

"*Look* means *listen*?" Jeth's eyebrows furrowed together with obvious skepticism.

"Listen," Taylor said slowly, "where are Sheridan and I going to stay?"

Jeth stood up from his chair, stretching. His maroon hair swayed across his shoulders. "I suppose it's time we talked to the scientists about your accommodations." He motioned to Echo. "It's better to ask in person." Then the two of them walked toward the door.

"Don't leave this room," Jeth called over his shoulder. "The scientists wouldn't like you wandering the building un-escorted."

Sheridan didn't care what the scientists liked. Perhaps this was evident in her expression. Echo looked at her and added, "The Enforcers wouldn't like it either."

chapter 6

hapter

Jeth and Echo walked toward Lab Fifteen. Echo waited for his father to say something about the girls being identical twins— the coincidence of it, or the irony. Jeth didn't. Was it possible his father hadn't noticed? Echo decided not to ask. The subject would lead to his brother.

"Taylor and Sheridan are quite beautiful," Jeth said. "I had expected girls from that era to look sickly and weak, malnourished from a constant diet of sugar and fat."

"Historians must be wrong about their diet." Echo didn't say more about their eating habits.

"I suppose we'll find we've miscalculated lots of things," Jeth said. "I expected the girls to be happy to be here, away from the anarchy and danger of their time. Instead they're quite unplugged about it." Jeth mulled this over. "I guess the unknown is always feared."

"They have a different way of thinking about things. It might be hard for them to understand our culture." Echo was midway through this sentence when he realized the mistake he and Jeth had just made.

They hadn't been thinking of the twenty-first-century culture when they left the girls alone in the Infolab. Back in the early twenty-first century, people didn't have crystals implanted in their wrists. They could move around freely without being tracked. The girls were upset about being brought here, and in all probability they had bolted from the room as soon as Jeth and Echo turned the first corner.

"Sangre," Echo swore softly under his breath. At this very moment Sheridan and Taylor were probably wandering around somewhere, untraceable because they had no crystals, trying to . . . but what *would* they try to do?

They couldn't understand the language, had nowhere to go and no way to even activate food dispensers.

And if the wrong people found them . . .

Echo stopped in the hallway. "We should go back and make sure the girls haven't escaped."

"Escaped?" Jeth said the word with disdain. "Where would they escape to?"

"Nowhere, but they don't know that. They don't understand our society."

Jeth and Echo had reached the elevator, and Jeth pushed the button. "I didn't find them stupid. In fact, I was surprised at Taylor's intelligence. She learned the computer functions after seeing me do them only once."

Echo didn't move toward the elevator. "I never said they were stupid. I said they didn't understand." The elevator door opened. Echo remained where he was. "I'm going back."

Jeth stepped into the elevator and waited for Echo to follow. "They ought to have time alone. If one of us stays to guard them, they'll feel like prisoners. It's better to let them know we trust them."

Echo sighed, looked down the hallway, then stepped into the elevator. As he watched the floor numbers change, he told himself he didn't have time to worry about these girls. He had other problems. He had plans to make.

It didn't work. He worried about them anyway, kept thinking about what it would be like to wake up and find yourself uploaded into another century.

A few minutes later, they reached Lab Fifteen. Several scientists were there, going over data at various computer terminals. Jeth headed toward one of the lead scientists, and Echo followed.

The man's name was Anton. Echo remembered him from this morning because of the red slash zigzagging across his face. Those had been popular last year. Half the city had gone around looking like they'd been gouged in some horrible battle. But lately the color red had fallen out of style. Scientists, like wordsmiths, it seemed, didn't keep up with fashion trends. Echo might have been wearing red himself if his brother hadn't been so attentive to fashion cycles.

And now that his brother was gone . . .

Echo felt a sharp pain at the reminder and shook off the thought. It was better not to think of his brother. Every time

Echo's mind wandered in that direction, he felt his concentration, his strength—everything—caving in.

Think about now, he told himself.

Anton scrolled down through equations on the screen without noting the wordsmith's arrival. *"Bien . . . bien . . . bien,"* he muttered. *"Sangre,* if we'd made a mistake, the stabilizer gains would be off phase."

Jeth made a small coughing noise, and Anton looked up. When he saw it was the wordsmiths, he returned his attention to the screen. "Is there a problem with the time riders?"

"No," Jeth said. "They've recovered from their shock and are already adapting."

"Bien."

"We'll need to put them somewhere. Have they been assigned rooms?"

Anton momentarily stopped scrolling. "We'd planned on keeping Tyler Sherwood here at the Scicenter, but nothing flies right the first time you toss it in the air." He straightened, caressing the small of his back with one hand. "We should have planned for a failure. We should have strained someone less important the first time."

Echo glanced at the computer, his eyes taking in the rows of numbers in a casual manner. "You can't find Tyler Sherwood at all?"

Anton frowned and bent toward the screen. "It's not a simple procedure. Helix says we should go back farther in time, where Sherwood's signal is more accessible, but if we took him before he was through making his contribution to science—think of the history implosions that could occur. We only have a *poquito* of time, the smallest of slots to work with. A miscalculation too early could bring us a child." Anton swiped a finger across the monitor, and the screen changed. "We need to pick up Tyler Sherwood's signal toward the end of his life."

"I'm sure you'll accomplish it," Jeth said. "Until then, we'll take the girls to the Histocenter and work with them."

Anton looked around the room, this time lowering his voice and leaning closer to the wordsmiths. "Helix wants us to do a memory wash on them today and erase our mistake altogether, but the rest of us think it's too early for that."

"A memory wash?" Jeth's shoulders sagged as though the air had gone out of him. "That can't be necessary?"

"It's not wise," Anton agreed. "You don't destroy the first experiment just because it didn't work. You study it to find out what went wrong. That's the problem with having government officials in charge of the program. They don't appreciate how science works."

Jeth held up one hand in a gesture of protest. "We have the opportunity to learn about history from the girls. Helix must understand that."

Anton grunted. "Unfortunately, government officials don't appreciate history either."

"Why do a memory wash?" Echo's words came out harsher than he'd intended. "The girls haven't been convicted of any crimes or fanaticisms."

Anton's gaze circled the room again, and he lowered his voice even further. "To keep it a secret. If the public found out about the Time Strainer, it would be one outrage after another. Half of Traventon would be furious we tampered with history, and the other half would be furious we're not using it to bring their favorite rock band back to life."

That, Echo thought, was a generous assessment of the public's reaction. More likely, 80 percent of the people would think only of rock bands. The other 20 percent were Dakine, who would devote themselves to stealing the Time Strainer so they could use it to alter history to their advantage. Hadn't the government officials considered that?

Probably not. Just like they hadn't considered that there were some things a memory wash couldn't fix. Even if the girls' memories were erased, their culture would still be hard-wired into them. They would still speak old-twenties English. They would still have a residual knowledge of how things worked back then and no knowledge of how things worked now. If the scientists didn't consider this beforehand, they'd realize it soon after. And then what would they do with the girls? Terminate them?

"Delay the memory wash," Jeth told Anton. "You might still collect useful information from them. They came from the same period as Tyler Sherwood."

"Yes." Anton said the word slowly, as though he was running intense mathematical equations as he spoke. "That is a peculiar coincidence, isn't it?"

"Think what a freeze it would be," Jeth added, "if you erased their memories and then needed information from them."

Anton nodded in measured agreement. "We'll try to convince Helix not to do the wash until we have Tyler Sherwood here."

Jeth smiled. "I'm sure that won't be long, so we'll study

the girls while we can." As he turned to walk away, he added, "Beep me when you have Tyler Sherwood, and we'll come back to translate."

Anton nodded again, still with the deep-mathematical-equations look on his face. He didn't say good-bye as they left.

Back in the hallway, Jeth set a quick pace to the Infolab. "A memory wash," he said with scorn. "Government officials and scientists have no understanding of the importance of history. None at all."

"It's a good thing that the government works so slowly," Echo said.

"Not slowly enough," Jeth said.

chapter 7

hapter

As soon as Jeth and Echo left the room, Sheridan sank into one of the chairs. She felt overloaded, numb. "Is this really the future?"

Taylor was pacing back and forth in front of the row of computers. "What else could it be?"

"Maybe it's a bad dream—some sort of psychotic nervous breakdown from too much studying."

"Great," Taylor said. "That means I'm the one with the breakdown. You never study."

Sheridan lifted her chin. "I do too. I study all the time."

"You read novels."

"I'm in honors English. That *is* studying."

Taylor sighed and waved her hand in dismissal. "I'm probably in some sort of coma right now, while you're off reading *Wuthering Heights* and eating potato chips." Another sigh. "I should have been an English major. A fat lot of good physics did me."

Neither of them spoke again, but even their silences were full of meaning. Taylor was working things out in her mind, and Sheridan waited for her evaluation.

Taylor kept pacing.

Finally Sheridan prodded her. "Do you think animals are really extinct?"

Taylor turned on her heel and walked back in the other direction. "The chances of a complete extinction are somewhere between not likely and utterly impossible. People couldn't have survived for hundreds of years—even in protected cities—if the rest of earth's ecosystems had been destroyed. Plants, insects, and animals are interdependent, so the fact that there is still oxygen on the planet suggests that to some degree they are still alive."

"Then why do the people here believe—"

"Because it's what their government wants them to believe. They don't want people leaving the city." Taylor stopped pacing and sat down next to Sheridan. She looked like a doctor about to give a patient unpleasant news. "Major plagues swept around the world eight times over the last four centuries. Seventy-five percent of the people died off. Jeth says that's why they do genetic breeding now—to ensure the population is disease resistant."

"Echo told me how they have children," Sheridan said. "It seems wrong."

Taylor didn't comment on its wrongness. "Individual

city-states rule their own people now. Traventon is one of the largest, and it has the habit of racking up huge debts with other cities. When it defaults, it goes to war with its creditor. It has advanced technology, so it's come out on top so far, but that can't go on indefinitely."

Without meaning to, Sheridan gripped the edge of her chair. It sounded like the beginning of a bad list, and she could tell Taylor was holding back information, testing her to see how she dealt with little chunks of misfortune before she handed her the whole thing. "What else?" Sheridan asked.

"Government-appointed chairmen control everything in Traventon, and there's no way to get rid of them. Regular people don't have a vote, don't have weapons, and don't even have access to information. You need a government clearance to own a computer with internet capabilities, and it's illegal to access sites outside your professional needs." She shook her head. "Jeth was so proud of the humane way they treat their criminals. They erase their memories and make them do menial work in the Agrocenter. Which might not be so awful, except that anyone who disagrees with the government is a criminal. No one is even allowed out of the city without permission. I think that's the real reason why all the cities are domed."

Sheridan didn't stop gripping her chair. "We can't stay here."

"We can't go back," Taylor stated flatly.

"We don't know that. We're just taking their word for it." Sheridan stood, turned around the room, and looked for—she didn't know what. All that met her eyes were chairs, desks, and computers. Cold, inanimate objects. "Maybe you could figure out how to make the Time Strainer go backward." As she said the words, she felt the first inklings of hope rise within her. "You're as smart as any of those scientists. I know you are."

Taylor's expression remained rigid. "It isn't that simple. It's not like I can flip a reverse button on the machine."

"Then make it work another way."

Taylor grunted like she always did when she thought something was painfully obvious and she shouldn't have to explain it. "First of all, they'll never let me anywhere near that machine or any of its specifications. Second, even if I studied it, that doesn't mean I could figure out how to work it differently.

"Third, if I came up with an idea for a time machine, I wouldn't have the tools, material, or staff to make it. I mean, I understand the aerodynamic theories behind airplanes, but that doesn't mean I can build one in my spare time.

"And even if the first three issues didn't exist, I wouldn't build a time machine anyway. It's bad enough this society can drag people to the future. I wouldn't want them to be able to insert themselves into the past too." The edge left Taylor's voice, and only resignation remained. "We're stuck here and we'd better learn to deal with it."

Silence followed Taylor's statement. A silence so deep, it penetrated every part of Sheridan. Every hope that had sprung up now withered painfully. She sat back on her chair with a thud.

"On the positive side," Taylor added, "they've got some cool technology here. Like cleaning robots. And a lot of their sites say they're close to finding a cure for aging." She shrugged, looking wary again. "Of course, that might just be an excuse to control people's wages. Everyone has to pay an immortality tax to keep the government's research going."

Sheridan didn't say anything. She didn't have to. Taylor could read Sheridan's silences as well as Sheridan could read Taylor's.

Taylor let out a sigh. "All right. Later, when we know we're safe, I'll try to study their technology to figure out if there's any way to go home. Until then, we need to act happy and not resentful, or we'll find ourselves working in the Agrocenter with no memory of how we got there." She waved her hand encouragingly in Sheridan's direction. "So show some enthusiasm. Smile once in a while. That's all I'm asking."

A few moments later Jeth and Echo returned. Sheridan couldn't smile, but she wasn't screaming, which showed much more enthusiasm than she actually felt.

Jeth and Echo took them to the Histocenter in a beige, egg-shaped car with darkened windows. Instead of seats in rows, one circular seat wrapped around the interior of the car. No one drove. Jeth put his hand on the control panel, spoke the destination, and the car started up and glided slowly along the silver rails that ran down the middle of the streets. The whole thing vaguely reminded Sheridan of an amusement park ride.

A radio automatically came on, and a woman's lilting voice spoke words Sheridan couldn't quite understand.

Echo took a metal tube from his pocket and handed it to his father. Jeth waved it over the control panel, and the voice stopped. "We don't need to listen to city updates right now," he said. "I'd rather talk."

He handed the tube back to his son, then smiled at Taylor and Sheridan. "Don't tell anyone we have a silencer. They're slightly illegal."

Illegal to turn off the radio? Sheridan shot Taylor a look, but Taylor's attention was on Jeth. "Where do the cars get their fuel?"

"The energy grid," Jeth said. "Which mostly relies on solar panels on the dome." He tapped an illuminated city map on the dashboard. "And the car sensors assure that the cars never hit one another."

Which probably wasn't that difficult since the cars only went about twenty miles an hour. Still, Taylor smiled the entire drive, happily asking questions about the car's engineering and the city's energy grid—things Sheridan wouldn't have been interested in even if she understood them.

Sheridan gazed out a window at the passing scenery. The city looked like the inside of some gigantic indoor mall. Instead of grass, beige walkways spread in all directions. Instead of streets, silver railings snaked in between the buildings, supporting endless numbers of identical egg-shaped cars. Where sky should have been, a white opaque material stretched overhead. No sunshine. No stars.

Several of the buildings didn't have outside walls. Sheridan could see into what looked like a toy store, a clothing store, and a furniture store.

After about fifteen minutes, they pulled into a parking building and the car slid into an empty space in a row of identical cars. As Sheridan climbed out, she asked, "How do you keep track of your car when they all look the same?"

"We don't," Echo said. "We use them, then leave them for the next person."

"How wonderfully social," Taylor gushed.

The group started across the parking lot. "But what if you go somewhere," Sheridan said, "and someone takes your car and you're stranded?"

Jeth pointed to the circular button on a metallic box that he wore on his belt. "You signal you need a car on your comlink, and the closest available one comes to you."

"How convenient," Taylor cooed.

They walked inside the building and took an elevator to the seventh floor of the Histocenter. Pictures from history lined the hallways—no, they weren't pictures, they were more like computer screens. The clouds over Egyptian pyramids rolled across the sky. Flags surrounding the Washington Monument blew in the wind. Napoléon's eyes followed them and his chest moved up and down, breathing.

Which was sort of creepy.

When they reached room 72C, Jeth paused before pushing the door button. "You'll like this. We decorated the office with replicas of period pieces in order to create the right atmosphere."

He pushed the button with a flourish, and the door slid open to reveal a room that looked more like a used furniture store than an office. Sofas of different colors lined three walls. An assortment of coffee tables and dressers were scattered between them. Dark and light wood stood together, Victorian next to Western, and mismatched knickknacks perched everywhere.

Another door stood behind the furniture, and Sheridan wondered where it led. Was this overcrowded room the Wordlab, or was this a lobby with the lab behind the door?

They went inside. Sheridan had expected the musty smell of old things, but it had a crisp smell, like clean laundry.

Taylor twirled around, taking in the room. "It's lovely. Almost like being at home."

Jeth proudly pointed out a row of computers that sat on a long desk. "Since historians are part of the intellecturate, we have access to the city's Infolabs."

"How wonderful," Taylor said, and strolled over to a large wooden cabinet with an etched-glass front. Inside, objects were suspended in clear boxes: a cell phone, a watch, a teacup, a computer mouse. "These are antiques now, aren't they?"

"Yes." Jeth joined her at the cabinet, admiring his collection. "We keep the artifacts vacuum sealed so they won't deteriorate. This is my personal collection. Most relics are at the city museum."

Sheridan knew what had caught Taylor's eye. A handgun sat on the middle shelf. "Do they still work?" Taylor asked. "The phone, the mouse . . . the gun?"

"Our technology is incompatible with things from your time. The gun, *pues*, it would need bullets, and they aren't made anymore. We use laser boxes now."

"Oh." Taylor turned from the cabinet as if it didn't matter. "You'll have to take us to the museum sometime." She sent Jeth a dazzling smile. "It will be fascinating to see things from the years we missed."

Taylor made *happy* look easy. Sheridan sank down beside Echo on a plaid couch by the window. She tried to think of some sort of compliment about the room, but before she could, the door to the hallway slid open.

A young woman with long pink-and-lavender-striped hair stepped through. Except for her pink eyebrows and lips, her tanned face was free of makeup, and two dark-brown eyes glanced back and forth between Taylor and Sheridan with excitement.

She carried a large bag, which she dropped onto one of the coffee tables, and then she glided over to the group, as graceful as a dancer. "Are these the time riders?" Her accent didn't quite mimic twenty-first-century English but was close enough to be understandable.

"Sheridan, Taylor"—Jeth gestured toward the newcomer— "this is my wordsmith apprentice, Elise."

The name surprised Sheridan. It was from their time period. But then, names often bridged generations. She would probably run into her share of Marys, Roberts, and Michaels here in the future.

Elise held out her hand to Taylor, as though just remembering it was something people did when meeting.

Taylor shook her hand. "Delighted."

Elise dropped Taylor's hand and glanced around the room. "Really? I thought there was plenty of light in here, but I can brighten it for you."

"Elise," Echo said with a hint of amusement, "in the old twenties *delighted* meant 'happy.'"

"Oh." Elise turned back to Taylor, a blush warming her features. "Then I'm happy you're happy." She fluttered her hand. "You had such strange ways to say things back then. I'll never get them all crooked."

"Straight," Sheridan said.

"Right," Elise said. "I knew the saying had something to do with direction." Still smiling, Elise put her hand across her heart and sighed. "This is so *fantástico*. I wish Joseph could have been here."

The statement brought an immediate silence to the wordsmiths. Echo winced. Jeth frowned, and even Elise, who'd said the sentence, turned somber. Her lips pressed together, and she blinked several times to keep tears from her eyes.

"Joseph was my other son," Jeth said. "He knew the twenty-first century better than any of us. He died a month ago."

"I'm sorry," Sheridan said, and Taylor added, "How hard for you all."

Echo stared at the floor and didn't say anything.

Jeth changed the subject, telling them about the crystals that were implanted in everyone's wrists. While he spoke, he held up his own for them to see. It was about as big as a penny and pulsed red, blood circulating under its surface. A neurochip inside the crystal kept track of him, his assets, and all other personal data. People purchased things by placing their wrists on deduction machines. Money was obsolete.

Sheridan only half listened. It wasn't just Taylor's silences that she could read. She found she could read Echo's too, and his pained silence during all this meant there was something very wrong about Joseph's death.

chapter

8

chapter

As the conversation went on, Sheridan's gaze kept returning to the glass cabinet and the gun. She had never touched a gun in her life, but she wanted that one, wanted to feel less vulnerable. There had to be some way to make bullets. After all, the wordsmiths had replicated furniture and knickknacks from her time period; why not bullets?

During a lull, she said, "I was wondering . . ." then tried to think of a way to ask her question without sounding like she planned on shooting someone.

Everything she thought of sounded suspicious, and now the wordsmiths were all watching her, waiting for her question.

Sheridan shifted in her seat. "I was wondering about the badge on Elise's shirt. What is it?"

The men at the Scicenter had worn them too. White badges,

each with a row of electronic numbers. Sheridan had assumed they were some sort of scientist ID badge, because Jeth and Echo didn't wear them. But then why did Elise have one?

Elise brushed her fingertips across the numbers. "That's my ranking. It's like the way people in your day wore gemstones and animal furs to indicate their social status."

"What?" Sheridan asked.

"No," Echo said, softly correcting Elise. "Gemstones and animal coats were prevalent in the twentieth century. In the twenty-first century, rank was shown by large homes, designer clothing, and expensive cars."

It took a moment for Sheridan to understand. "You mean the numbers tell people how much money you have?"

Taylor clapped her hands together and laughed—genuine laughter this time. "That's the most brilliant thing I've ever heard. Why buy things to prove you're wealthy when you can put your bank account balance on your shirt?"

Elise fidgeted with her badge. "It's not just how many credits you have. The algorithm also factors in your age, health, IQ, job status, how many friends you have, your friends' and family's rankings, and what ratings other people have given you." She peered at her number—602,257—reading it upside down. "Hmm. I'm up fifteen from yesterday."

Echo put his feet up on the coffee table, finally relaxing. "Poor 602,241 through 602,256. They must have had a bad day."

Taylor leaned closer to Elise to look at the badge. "Is that a good rank?"

Elise hesitated, but Echo didn't. "Yes. There are over seven million people in the city."

Elise waved his compliment away. "I'm of prime age and I have a lot of friends. They're generous with their ratings."

Taylor scanned both Echo's and Jeth's shirts. "How come you guys aren't wearing numbers?"

Elise answered before either of them could. "No one expects you to show your rank if you're grieving—but," she added quickly, "their rankings are very good too."

Jeth gave a short, appreciative laugh. "Elise is being kind—which is why she has so many friends. Wordsmith isn't a prestigious job, and I enjoy buying antiques too much to keep my credit balance at an impressive level. But I don't mind. I love my job more than my rank."

Echo didn't comment about his rank, although his expression darkened in a way that made Sheridan assume it wasn't high.

"What a horrible system," she said, feeling for Echo and Jeth so much that she forgot Taylor's advice to sound happy. "You shouldn't judge people by their bank account. Why does anybody go along with it?"

She expected Echo to agree with her, but he only looked at her with curiosity. "Why did the people of your day go along with your system? Excess was success. Why buy things you didn't need, just to show your status?"

"Not everybody did that," Sheridan said. "My family had a ten-year-old minivan and a truck that was held together with bailing wire and hope."

Echo considered this. "You came from a low-ranking family then?"

No. Well, maybe yes, but that hadn't been the point she was

making. Sheridan didn't answer him.

"I don't like the badges," Elise said, straightening hers. "But if you don't wear one, people assume your rank is sewer sludge. It's always the people with ranks in six or seven million who refuse to wear badges for philosophical reasons. Or," she added with a roll of her eyes, "they say they lost their badge. Never believe it when somebody tells you that." She pulled her comlink from her belt. "Which reminds me—I haven't rated my friends today." She busied herself tapping away on the function buttons.

"So," Sheridan said, drawing out the word, "are we going to have to wear badges?" She didn't know why she bothered asking. She already knew the answer.

"Don't worry," Elise said without taking her eyes off her comlink. "You're so interesting, you'll be able to reel in high-ranking friends."

"And until then," Jeth added, "you're stuck with us and will have to answer our questions."

The conversation went on after that, but Sheridan only half listened. She stared out the window and thought about rankings.

Not that long ago, she had complained to her mother about having to drive their beat-up truck to school. A few of the popular girls called it the Garbage Truck, and Sheridan had been afraid it was only one short step until somebody tagged her with the nickname Trashy.

So okay—maybe her society *had* ranked people, but at least they didn't have to wear their status on their shirts like name tags that read, "Hello, My Name Is Loser."

Echo followed Sheridan's gaze out the window to the streets and pavement below. "Our city is much cleaner than the ones you're used to, isn't it?"

Clean yes, but she missed lawns, bushes, and trees. The city was one continuous beige without any green to break it up.

She studied one of the buildings farther down the street. "Why do some buildings have no outside walls?"

"Offices, apartments, and restaurants have walls for privacy. Stores don't. They only use rails for the upper floors to prevent anyone from falling."

Stores without walls? How did they keep people from stealing things? Sheridan decided against asking this question. If she asked about stealing, Echo might think she had a personal interest in the subject. She'd already branded herself as a low-ranking flesh eater. She didn't want to add *thief* to the list.

"What about churches?" she asked. "Where are those?"

"Churches?" Echo said the word as though it had sharp edges. All conversation stopped. Echo and Jeth exchanged pensive looks. "We don't have churches," Jeth said. "Religion was banned ninety years ago in an international treaty on human rights."

His words, although spoken softly, hit Sheridan as if they had actual weight. In her mind's eye she saw her father standing by the chapel door greeting people who came in. He knew each person by name. She couldn't imagine her life, let alone a world, without churches. "Banned?" she breathed out. "Why?"

Jeth's tone indicated that the reason should be self-evident. "Religion promoted divisiveness and oppressed its followers."

The subject was ninety years past arguing, and yet Sheridan

argued it anyway. "No, it didn't."

"Religion," Jeth said with a scoff, "was a compilation of superstition and wishful thinking—which wouldn't have been so bad if its members hadn't been so intent on killing one another."

Sheridan glared at him. She knew Taylor didn't approve. Her sister was sending her wide-eyed pleadings to shut up and sound happy. But Sheridan didn't. "My father was a minister," she said. "The whole point of churches was to help people."

Sheridan waited for Taylor to back her up, to defend their father. Taylor had been drafted into church service projects right alongside the rest of the family. They had served food at the soup kitchen, pulled weeds at the homes of the elderly, collected blankets for the homeless, and raised money for shelters, cancer patients, and whatever organization her father was feeling sorry for at the time.

It wasn't Taylor who spoke; it was Echo. His voice was gentle but firm. A warning. "Religion doesn't exist anymore, and you shouldn't speak of it again. People will think you're intolerant and have violent tendencies."

Elise broke into the conversation, her eyes brimming with sympathy. "Sheridan lost her home today. Don't pry her beliefs away from her too."

The comment brought an immediate change to Jeth. He nodded, and his tone turned coaxing. "We don't mean to upset you. These changes are coming very quickly for you. Relax for now. You can take each new idea slowly—as slowly as you need."

Sheridan let out an exasperated huff. Great. Now they thought she was stupid.

Well, she wasn't. She was a straight-A student in honors classes. The only one who ever made her feel stupid was Taylor, and that wasn't on purpose—it just naturally happened when your twin had the IQ of Einstein.

Sheridan shot Taylor a last pleading glance. *If you won't defend me or Dad, at least defend your convictions.*

Taylor looked away from Sheridan without uttering a word.

Sheridan turned back to the window, stared unseeing out it. Jeth changed the subject to Virtual Reality centers, where people could pretend to be different characters in stories; then Elise told them about dancing parties called darties. Taylor happily asked them questions.

Fine. Let Taylor talk. Apparently she didn't need to take new ideas slowly.

Echo leaned toward Sheridan; his voice was still gentle. "You told me you were the quiet one. I don't think I believe you about that."

"Just wait. I'm going to be really quiet from now on."

He looked up at the ceiling, thinking. "You also said Taylor was the daring one. That doesn't seem right either. It's very daring to profess outlawed beliefs."

But not smart. Taylor was still the smart one.

Echo's gaze returned to Sheridan. "Now I'm not sure how to categorize you."

"I thought you already had plenty of categories for me."

He looked at her quizzically, but she didn't want to elaborate. She turned the topic to him. "What about you?" she asked. "How did you compare to your twin?"

He hesitated, then said, "I'm the lucky one, because I got to meet you."

For a moment she thought he was flirting. Then she decided he probably just meant she was interesting in a historical way. Or maybe he meant he was lucky to be the one alive.

Before she could say anything else, a shrill beeping noise sounded from Jeth's belt. He looked at his comlink. "It's Helix."

"*Sangre*," Echo said. "They must have found Tyler Sherwood."

Sangre. Spanish for "blood." It seemed like an odd swearword to Sheridan. But then, maybe when you didn't believe in a deity, all that was left to swear by was blood.

Jeth stood up and pushed a button on his comlink. Immediately the far wall flickered with light, then turned on like a movie screen. The man with the black-and-gray-striped hair looked out at them.

Jeth walked closer to the wall and in the modern accent asked, "Have you found Tyler Sherwood?"

Helix stiffened, a snarl growing on his face. He said several things that Sheridan didn't understand but that, judging from his tone, were either curses or insults. Then he said, "I'm almost to your office. I'm bringing men to talk to the girls."

This part Sheridan understood perfectly. Helix was coming. And it wasn't to talk. If he wanted to talk, he could do that from the screen. And why bring men?

She couldn't follow the rest of the conversation. Her panic made it too hard to decipher the words. When the call ended, Jeth turned back to the group and used the twenty-first-century accent. "Helix is coming over to talk to you. He'll be here soon."

Sheridan put her hand on Echo's to get his attention. "Is he going to take us somewhere?"

"He didn't say he would."

Jeth clipped his comlink back onto his belt in an unhurried fashion. "You needn't worry. Helix won't hurt you."

Well, that depended on your definition of *hurt*, didn't it? Perhaps he was coming to put one of those crystals in her wrist, or sterilize her, or some equally horrible thing that hadn't come up in casual conversation yet.

Even Taylor, who'd been a continual stream of perky enthusiasm all afternoon, sat quietly on the couch growing pale.

Sheridan let go of Echo's hand and stood up. She knew there was nowhere to run. She probably couldn't find her way out of the building, let alone take up a covert existence in this society. Still, her gaze darted around the room, looking for an escape route.

Taylor stood up too. She walked toward Sheridan wearing a plastered-on smile. "You'll have to forgive Sheridan. She isn't used to the future, and I'm afraid she isn't herself yet."

Elise cocked her head so that her striped ponytail leaned onto her shoulder. "Then who is she now?"

Jeth nodded thoughtfully, almost to himself. "Schizophrenia. It was common in the old twenties."

"I am not schizophrenic!" Sheridan said, probably louder than was necessary.

Taylor took hold of her arm and pulled her a few feet away. To Jeth, she said, "Sheridan will be fine in a minute. I'm going to give her a little pep talk, you know, help her pull herself together."

Elise's eyes narrowed in question. "A pep what?"

"Pull herself together?" Echo asked. "What does that mean?"

Taylor turned back to them, mouth open to explain, but then shook her head instead. "I'm going to talk to Sheridan privately for a minute, okay?"

It wasn't really private. The wordsmiths sat nearby, undoubtedly waiting to see Sheridan do some sort of pulling stunts with her body parts.

Taylor leaned in and gave Sheridan a hug, only it wasn't a hug, it was a way to whisper in her ear. "Could you possibly be acting worse?"

"You're one to talk," Sheridan said, and it wasn't a whisper. She knew that at least Jeth heard her. He frowned in puzzlement as though this, too, was an unfamiliar piece of slang.

"At the rate you're going," Taylor whispered, "we'll both have amnesia by nightfall. Start acting cheerful and unafraid, and whatever you do, don't tell those scientists anything. You remember nothing before you came here."

Sheridan's voice dropped. "I've already said things about the past. If I say I don't remember anything, the wordsmiths will know I'm lying. Then everyone will think I'm a low-ranking, schizophrenic liar."

Taylor sighed in frustration, letting Sheridan know she still wasn't getting the point. "Be as vague as you can about everything. Remember, someone else's life depends on that machine not working."

Taylor released Sheridan from the hug, and they walked back to the couch by the window. "Sheridan feels better now."

Sheridan sat down. She didn't feel better.

"A pep talk," Jeth said. "Wasn't that something cheerleaders did? You two aren't planning on playing football right now, are you?"

Taylor didn't have time to answer. The door slid open, and three men walked into the office, Helix leading the way.

chapter

chapter

9

Helix and his men strode over to the group, every step making Sheridan feel more like a trapped animal. Jeth, Echo, and Elise stood up. Despite his assurances, Jeth wore a tense expression, Elise fiddled with a ring on her finger, and Echo—well, Echo was harder to read. His face was expressionless, but his blue eyes were intense.

A man with a multicolored crew cut unclipped a red cylinder from his belt. It was the size of a cell phone and had a tiny green light circling around its perimeter. He mumbled something to Helix, then stopped in front of Sheridan and Taylor. "Ask them where they were and what was happening right before the Time Strainer brought them here."

Sheridan understood him. It was getting easier the more she heard the accent. Taylor probably understood too, but she shook her head sadly. "We . . . don't . . . understand . . . you."

Jeth gestured at the third man. "He wants to know where you were and what happened right before the Time Strainer brought you here."

"I don't remember," Sheridan said, perhaps too fast.

Taylor got a far-off look on her face. "We were walking across the University of Tennessee campus to study at the library, and then there was this big light, like a lightning bolt. After that, I woke up in the glass case feeling groggy."

Jeth related the answer back to the scientist.

The man folded his arms. "Who else was near? *Gente?* A man *quizá?*"

Gente and *quizá.* Spanish words. *Quizá* meant "perhaps." And *gente* was . . . She couldn't quite put her finger on it.

Jeth said, "Were there any people around you before you came? A man perhaps?"

Gente was "people." Now she remembered.

"I don't remember," Sheridan said, and this time she looked contemplative, for effect.

"There were," Taylor said. "On campus there were always people around. Students, professors, lecturers, all sorts of people."

The man pointed at Taylor. "What was her career?"

Jeth asked the question. Taylor said, "I was in high school. I was planning on studying literature when I got to college. Back in my time, they gave degrees for reading books."

"Did they?" Jeth asked. "How interesting. You'll have to tell me more about the educational process later." Jeth repeated Taylor's answer to the scientists, then asked Sheridan about her career.

"I was a student too," she said.

"What did you study?"

"The normal things. Math, history, English."

Surprise flitted across Jeth's face. "You studied your own language? Do you mean you studied the origination of the English language?"

"Well, no. In English classes we studied literature."

He looked at her blankly. "Then why did they call it English?"

"I don't know. They just did."

Jeth gave a grunt that indicated he didn't believe her, but he repeated the answer to the scientists anyway.

Sheridan fidgeted with her hands, then stopped because she thought it made her look guilty of something. How was it that Taylor could spout off lies without ever being caught, while Sheridan told the truth and was never believed?

The scientist with the crew cut took hold of Sheridan's arm and placed the cylinder on the back of her wrist. It pricked her skin, and she flinched away.

"It's a measurement device," Echo told her. "He's checking your DNA's energy signal."

The crew cut man let go of Sheridan's arm and watched the green circling light on the cylinder. After a few seconds, it flashed a row of symbols. He noted it, then repeated the process on Taylor's arm. When the light flashed the second row of symbols, he scowled. Whatever it meant, he didn't like it.

From behind him, Helix called out, "The readings?"

The scowl dropped from the man's face, and panic swept across his features. By the time he turned to address Helix, however, his face was placid.

"The energy signals are taking longer to stabilize than we anticipated. We should have some good data, but we need to analyze it before we can determine what it means in the context of the Time Strainer. It could be that the girls were standing near the Time Vortex when it opened and were sucked in before it could retrieve Tyler Sherwood. If that was the case, the Time Strainer may have overloaded and closed. It wasn't designed to move multiple people, as it could accidentally intermingle or even scramble DNA." At the mention of DNA, the scientist looked down at his cylinder reading with discomfort.

Sheridan was understanding the accent so well now that her mind was automatically translating the Spanish words, mixing them with the English.

"Or," the scientist went on, "we might have calculated the wrong energy signal for Tyler Sherwood. We were only able to get a partial DNA reading from his papers in the city museum. Or maybe the DNA we thought was his actually belonged to someone else. . . ."

Helix frowned at the scientist, unimpressed by the explanation. "Have your analysis to me by tomorrow. Another failure won't be tolerated." He cast a disdainful look at Sheridan and Taylor, as though they had purposely thrown themselves into the Time Vortex just to vex him; then he turned and went to the door. Jeth accompanied him, asking about the next day's schedule. The scientists trailed after them.

Echo sat back down next to Sheridan, watching the scientists leave. He whispered, "I almost feel sorry for the guy who tested you. He has no clue why his spectral reader gave him the same DNA result on both of you."

Sheridan smiled despite herself and wondered how long it would take him to figure it out.

As Jeth returned to the couches, Taylor picked up a Rubik's Cube from the end table beside her. "They haven't zapped Mr. Sherwood into the future yet?"

"No," Jeth said, sitting down beside her. "They can't find his energy signature in the time stream anymore, and now the machine needs to reboot. They'll make another attempt tomorrow."

Taylor tried to twist one side of the Rubik's Cube. It didn't budge. "What exactly is an energy signature?"

Jeth gave a short laugh. "That's the sort of thing I wasn't able to learn in school. My sons, however, took some science classes before they decided to work with me." He motioned to Echo to explain.

Sheridan didn't remember half the stuff she learned in her science classes, but Echo didn't have to pause to search his memory. "Every atom has a different wavelength, depending on its electrons and their orbits. So the combined atoms in each person's DNA have a unique energy signal. The scientists are probably using energy signals in their search because those don't decay over time. They're constant."

Taylor rotated the Rubik's Cube and tried to twist a different section. It didn't move either. "Why do they want Tyler Sherwood so badly?"

"He put forth theories in your generation that eventually changed the way scientists view matter."

Jeth watched Taylor's apparent attempt to wring the Rubik's Cube but didn't comment on it. "Our instructions are to tell

Mr. Sherwood that he'll work with our scientists to cure aging. He must have done work on regenerating cells."

Taylor returned the untwisting Rubik's Cube to the table. The replica clearly had flaws. "Matter. Energy signals. It sounds terribly complicated. That's why I liked reading novels."

"Ah yes," Jeth said with rising enthusiasm. "You were going to tell me about the educational process."

"What's the point of telling you things," Sheridan asked, remembering their talks about animals and religion with fresh frustration, "when you won't believe what we say?" She didn't mean to look at Echo while she said this. Somehow her gaze slid there anyway. She knew Jeth doubted her, and probably Elise did too, but it bothered her more that Echo didn't believe her.

His blue eyes stared back at her, nearly as vibrant as the crescent moon he wore. He shouldn't have looked like an intellectual. The blue hair that brushed against his broad shoulders should have canceled out any scholarly effect. And yet in the short time she'd known Echo, she could tell he was smart beyond his years. Like Taylor.

"You'll tell us about your lives," Jeth said. "Your experiences don't include everything that took place in your time, though. We've spent so long studying history, we know things about your society and its influences that not even you realize."

Sheridan gestured toward the Rubik's Cube. "By studying pictures of things you obviously don't understand? The sides on that are supposed to move, by the way."

"By studying everything," Echo said. "Especially words."

Jeth leaned toward her intently. "Words are evidence of the past. They leave a trail. Every influence is recorded. For example, we can tell exactly when the Normans conquered England because of the influx of French words into the English language during the eleventh century. We know when a large Hispanic migration to America took place for the same reason. We can discern how people thought by the words they chose, the names they called things. Words always leave a trail."

Jeth stopped suddenly and gave an apologetic smile. "I'm wasting time being a teacher when I should be asking questions. We have so little time together and so much to learn."

As they talked, Sheridan turned Jeth's sentence over in her mind. So little time together? If words left a trail, where did that sentence lead? What did the wordsmiths know that they weren't telling her?

chapter 10
chapter

Echo had seen a hundred pictures of people from the old twenties. He'd studied catalog remnants and magazine remains. When the historical society had held its last Come-in-Costume darty, he'd put on replica 1950s jeans, T-shirt, and tennis shoes and danced the twist. He'd probably done it all wrong. No one had ever seen the complete dance, but that was part of the fun. Making up wild moves.

Anyway, he shouldn't have been fascinated by Sheridan and Taylor's clothes, but he couldn't stop staring at them. Those were *real* jeans. They'd been made in some factory by oppressed workers, then funneled to rich merchants who dictated what the population had to wear. So much history resided in that cloth. More amazing still, Taylor and Sheridan were here, alive.

To memory wash them would be like destroying hieroglyphs

from an ancient Egyptian tomb.

Frustration twined through Echo's chest. While he stayed in the city, he could most likely prevent the girls from getting memory washes. And hadn't he told Sheridan he would protect her? But how long could Echo stay in Traventon before the Dakine turned their attention to him?

Jeth ordered dinner, and the group ate while talking. Echo watched the girls' expressions as he and Jeth asked them questions. He thought their reactions to the questions were nearly as interesting as their answers.

Taylor answered everything happily, asking questions of her own as she did. It was easy to tell she was smart, grasping new concepts and knowledge as soon as they were presented. Still, there was something about her that made Echo suspicious. Perhaps it was that she smiled so frequently, he couldn't tell when she really meant it. If her smile was a pretense, what else was?

Sheridan was the opposite. Every emotion—surprise, frustration, disbelief—appeared in sequence on her face. Her sorrow tugged at him, even when he didn't understand what caused it. During dinner she came close to tears three times— once when Jeth told her that few people chose to marry, once when Elise told her a government literature committee wrote all the novels, and the last time when Jeth mentioned that children were now raised by certified caretakers in government-run learning centers.

As though that were a bad thing.

He had never minded living there. Not really. And he'd seen his parents on weekends. Or at least he'd seen his father. His parents had detached from each other when he was seven, and after that his mother made such a habit of being with different men, he never knew when he would see her or what she would be like.

When he was fifteen, she became infatuated with a military officer and went with him on a defensive action against San Francisco. She never came back. The government said she'd been reassigned to permanent patrol, which meant she was dead. The government didn't like to admit to casualties during any of its wars. They were always reported as being completely successful.

Echo had always felt an unspoken resentment that she'd died that way, that she'd let love pull her into bad choices. But he'd done the same thing. If he hadn't cared so much about Allana, his brother would still be alive.

In that moment, he could picture Allana's features clearly, her gray eyes and her dark-purple lips smiling at him. He remembered the way she wound her arms around his neck and whispered, "How can you two be so different, and yet I have such a hard time deciding who I love best?"

"We're not different," he'd said, and laughed because no one ever accused them of that. They were too similar in their looks and speech for everyone. It was the reason Echo had dyed his hair blue and wore the crescent moon, so people could tell him from Joseph, who had left his hair blond and wore only a small blue star on his cheek.

"You are different," Allana had said, caressing his cheek with her lips. "If you don't realize that, you don't know your brother as well as you think you do."

He pushed the image of Allana away. He never had to

see her again. That was the only good thing to come from the ordeal. Allana was dead too.

Echo blinked, bringing himself back to the present. Jeth was demonstrating the computer functions, explaining that although the intellecturate could access any info sites in the city, Taylor and Sheridan needed to ask him before they researched anything. The government monitored searches, so studying the wrong things could get them into trouble. Sheridan watched Jeth, this time with indignation etched on her face.

Echo liked her. He couldn't help himself. How could he not like someone who was completely genuine, even when it was to her detriment? The way she kept defending her beliefs. The way they mattered to her.

Joseph had been that type of person. At least everyone had thought so. But maybe it never had been true.

He ran his hand through his hair. What kind of person had Joseph really been? It was ironic that he was sitting here thinking about it now and unsure for the first time.

Joseph and Echo. Back when twins weren't such a rarity, it used to be common to name the second one Echo, but it wasn't accurate in their case. Echo had never been Joseph's echo. Never. Echo had always loved life too much to let anyone overshadow him. Echo had been the one who made everyone laugh. Echo had been the one girls were drawn to.

Until Allana.

And then everything changed.

He glanced over at Sheridan. She was sad again, although he'd missed what in the conversation had upset her.

Jeth was showing old family pictures on the computer and

explaining how each couple in Traventon was allowed two children—or at least they would be until aging was cured. Then there would be no need for children. Until then, couples could have one boy and one girl. Nothing upsetting in that statement.

Taylor asked the inevitable question. "Then how come you had two sons?"

Jeth ran his fingertips over a picture of Joseph and Echo when they were toddlers. "Identical twins aren't supposed to happen, but when they do, most people eliminate one of the embryos so they can have a child of each sex. We liked the idea of twins, though. My grandfather was a twin, and he never said it was a bad thing."

"A bad thing?" Taylor asked. "Why would being a twin be a bad thing?"

Jeth's gaze flickered toward Echo, then went back to Taylor. "Everyone told us identical twins would have a confused sense of identity, that they would end up hating each other. But that never happened." Jeth said the words forcefully, almost as though trying to convince himself of this fact. "Joseph and Echo were closer than any siblings I've ever known."

Everyone looked at Echo then. He felt their gazes weighing on him. They expected him to say something, but he couldn't. He couldn't bring himself to say one word, so he nodded mutely, awkwardly.

"I don't think being a twin is a bad thing," Sheridan said, drawing the attention away from him. "Except for when Taylor takes my clothes without asking."

"Hey," Taylor said, "you're lucky that you've always gotten to hang out with someone as cool as me."

Jeth straightened, and his gaze ricocheted back and forth between Taylor and Sheridan. He was finally studying their features instead of just noticing their hair and coloring. "Are you twins? Yes, I see that you are. How incredible! Was it common in your day? Did you ever meet triplets?"

Taylor answered his questions. Sheridan glanced back at Echo, and he could read the emotion on her face. Compassion. She was checking to see if he was all right. He managed a half smile to assure her.

What would become of her here in Traventon? Even if she and Taylor escaped the first memory wash order, they would have to find a way to hide their background or they'd end up with a second order.

Sheridan smiled back at him, a smile so infrequent, he knew it was genuine.

Back in the hallway at the Scicenter, she had asked him who she needed protection from. He hadn't quite been able to tell her the truth, despite her pronouncement that lies didn't sit comfortably on his tongue. The reason lies didn't sit comfortably on his tongue was that there were too many of them. It had turned into a crowded place.

Inwardly, he sighed. He would help Sheridan and Taylor while he could, but even though he wanted to stay and learn everything about the past, a clock was set against him. He knew no more about his future than the girls did about theirs.

chapter 11
chapter

After hours of conversation, Sheridan told the wordsmiths that she wanted to turn in for the night. And then explained that meant she wanted to sleep.

Elise picked up the sack she'd first brought into the room and handed Taylor and Sheridan tooth tablets. They put them in their mouths, and the tablets fizzed their teeth clean. Elise also rubbed tangy-smelling cream onto their hands and arms. "This is sparkle," she said, wiping the excess across Sheridan's neck. "It's cleaning bacteria. Within an hour it will spread across your whole body, eating dead skin, sweat, anything that would make you dirty."

"You don't shower?" Sheridan asked. She wasn't sure she liked the tingling that was crawling up her arms.

"Too much water waste," Jeth said, "and the bacteria can

live up to twenty days per application."

Hungry bacteria. Great. Sheridan managed a smile even though she wanted to scrape the sparkle off her arms.

Elise reached into the bag and handed out pairs of light-blue pajamas. They looked like leggings and tank tops but felt as soft as whipped cream. "They're thermal regulated," she said.

"When you're finished changing," Jeth added, "I'll take your clothes."

Sheridan held the pajamas against her chest while she looked for a place to change. Finally, her gaze returned to the wordsmiths.

"*Pues?*" Jeth said when neither she nor Taylor moved. "Is something wrong with the pajamas?"

"No, but we need a place to change," Sheridan said.

The wordsmiths said nothing for several seconds, then Echo held up one hand as though he'd figured it out. "Privacy," he said. "Men and women didn't disrobe in front of each other in the early twenty-first century."

"Of course," Jeth chimed in. "That was one of their social taboos, wasn't it?" He looked over at Taylor. "You'll have to give me a list of those, and tell me what you know about the meaning and origination of each one."

Taylor nodded weakly at him.

Elise took Sheridan and Taylor to the back room, showed them the bathroom, and explained how to work everything. Then she unrolled a pair of gel beds side by side on the floor. Within a few seconds they grew to normal size, like self-filling air mattresses.

Sheridan changed into her pajamas, feeling a bit awkward

that Elise stood there waiting to take her clothes. At least it wasn't Echo and Jeth.

That was one custom she refused to adopt.

After Elise left, Sheridan took a better look around the room. A desk and computer sat in one corner, but mostly the place looked like an artifact repository. Rows of shelves held vacuum-sealed boxes: a faded Barbie doll, a cracked calculator, a boot, a worn baseball mitt, a water bottle—things she would have thrown into the garbage without a second thought. Now they were museum pieces.

Sheridan lay down on one of the gel beds, and it molded against her body. The cleaning bacteria must have liked the warmth. The tingling grew stronger. "I'm not going to be able to get to sleep," she said. "I have sparkle crawling down my back." She twitched and turned over. "Is it going up your nose?"

Taylor had been sitting on her bed, staring at the shelves and thinking. For the first time in hours her face was devoid of a smile. "We have to get out of this city," she whispered.

Sheridan kept her voice low, in case the wordsmiths were in the other room. "I thought you said we couldn't go back in time."

"We can't," Taylor said, "but we still have to leave Traventon. Once they implant those tracking crystals in our wrists, they'll control our entire lives. I'm not letting some power-hungry and morally depraved government tell me what I can learn, say, and do."

Sheridan propped herself up on an elbow, which immediately sank into the bed. "Where will we go?"

"I don't know, but Traventon isn't the only city on earth. Some of them have to be better."

Sheridan felt the stirrings of hope reviving. Taylor was right. Civilization might be completely different somewhere else. "How can we get out? I thought the government didn't let people leave."

"We'll have to figure out where Traventon is on the map and do some research on the nearby cities. We'll also need to get supplies and find out if there's any way to buy, steal, or make bullets. When we leave, that gun is going with us." Taylor lay down on her side, letting one arm hang off her mattress. "I'm too tired to think about it tonight. I'll work on it tomorrow." She yawned, then pushed the button by her bed that controlled the lights.

A shade rolled down the window, the ceiling light flicked off, and the room went completely dark.

"One more thing," Taylor said. "Try to stick with Echo and keep him away from me."

"Why?"

"I don't want him to figure out what we're planning. It will be easier to fool Jeth. He's not as smart."

Sheridan turned on her side, settling into the bed. "The wordsmiths might not be around tomorrow. If they find Tyler Sherwood, they'll be busy with him."

"I hope not."

"Why?"

"Because Tyler Sherwood didn't work on regenerating cells. He worked on ways to take them apart. If they want him here in the future, it's because they plan on destroying something."

It took Sheridan a moment to process the statement. "I didn't know you knew who Tyler Sherwood was."

But Taylor didn't answer, and after a few seconds Sheridan heard the deep breaths of sleep coming from her bed.

It was harder for Sheridan to sleep. It was too stressful to think about the present and too painful to think about the past. So she imagined herself riding her horse, Breeze, out underneath the sunshine. After a while, she drifted off to the rhythm of hoofbeats.

WHEN SHERIDAN AWOKE, the back room was empty and the lights were set on a dim glow. She got up, stretched, and walked into the main room looking for Taylor. The wordsmiths were nowhere around. Taylor sat perched in front of one the computers looking through some sort of data. Sheridan wondered, but only vaguely, how Taylor had managed to log on.

"Good morning," Sheridan said. As she walked toward the computers, she caught sight of the artifact cabinet. There, hanging in the back like denim flags, were her and Taylor's jeans. They'd been put in among the relics of the past, already sealed in long, clear, air-vacuumed boxes. A closer look revealed their tops were there too, folded and preserved.

Sheridan stared at them blankly. "Okay, that's just wrong."

"I know," Taylor said. "I'm absolutely not giving them my underwear."

Sheridan smoothed a mass of tangles from her hair and padded over to see what her sister was doing. The computer showed an aerial map of a domed city.

"According to a trade website," Taylor said, scrolling toward a river, "the nearest city to Traventon is two hundred ten kilometers—that's about a hundred and thirty miles—away. If we managed to walk fifteen miles a day, it would still take us almost nine days to get there. I'm looking for roads."

"Are you going to get in trouble for doing unauthorized research?"

"Maybe."

On the bottom left side of the monitor, a small box was playing a commercial. It showed a group of women walking past a man. He smiled and spoke to them, but they glanced at his rank badge and turned away, uninterested. A man's voice said, "Tired of your low rank ruining every darty? Want to see how the glams play? We guarantee a two-digit raise for every ten credits you give Rankraisers. Click us. We have happiness spinning your way."

The scene disappeared, replaced by a picture of the city landscape. The lilting voice Sheridan had heard in the car yesterday purred out, "A sacrifice for the city is an investment in tomorrow." Apparently the government had its own commercials. Sheridan wondered if it always used that same caressing voice in its ads. "The city council works on the hard issues, so you can work hard on your rank."

Well, that seemed like a non sequitur.

A different commercial came on. The screen showed a man relaxing on a balcony with two pink-haired women, one on either side. "El Cielo Estates is now open," he said, and raised a glass that looked like a test tube. "Homes for those with numbers under a hundred thousand."

The pink-haired woman on his right turned to the camera with a sultry pout. "Rank has its privileges, and this is one of them."

"Hmm," Sheridan said. "Even Elise couldn't live there."

Taylor didn't take her eyes from the map. "The people here are obsessed with their ranks. I swear, it's all they ever talk about. I wish I had one of Echo's silencers."

A news show came on next. People were debating whether family rank numbers should be taken out of the rank algorithm, and were getting quite passionate about the subject. One side said it wasn't fair to include family rank since a person couldn't control being related to their family. The other side insisted a family's position in society had always affected individuals' ranks.

Yesterday when Sheridan had learned about how things were in Traventon, she'd supposed there was a huge underlying dissatisfaction in the population—a fear of the government, a silent churning desire for change. But this was worse. They didn't care about rights. They only cared about rank.

Sheridan pulled her gaze away from the screen. "Our time period wasn't as bad, was it?"

Taylor let out a grunt. "High schools had valedictorians, orchestras had numbered chairs, authors had bestseller lists, athletes had the Olympics, sports teams had play-offs, and fans routinely shouted, 'We're number one!' Our culture even turned *spelling* into a competition. I'm just kicking myself that I didn't come up with the whole ranking system back in our day. It would have made me rich—which would have given me an awesome rank."

Sheridan leaned forward to better see the map. "You never used to be so cynical."

"Yes, I did." Taylor panned out from the picture so more

area was visible. "You call me cynical every time I don't like a book that you like."

"That's because you always criticize happy endings."

"Exactly my point."

Sheridan surveyed the map. Traventon looked to be in the Colorado area of the nation. "If we're only a hundred and thirty miles away from the nearest city, why can't we hot-wire a car and drive there in a day?"

"The cars only work on the city rails. Besides, the government can track their vehicles and anyone who has a crystal in their wrist. The only advantage we have so far is that they can't track us." Taylor rested her chin against the palm of her hand and sighed. "Of course, fifteen miles a day is assuming the Rocky Mountains aren't blocking our way, and that the weather is good, and that the next city is any better than Traventon." She scrolled across, looking for domes. "It might actually be worse. According to the information on the computer, every other city on the face of the planet is peopled by bloodthirsty hardened criminals."

"Lovely," Sheridan said.

Taylor zoomed in on a spot that turned out to be a lake, not a city. "It's probably propaganda. The Communist countries used to say the same thing about America during the Cold War."

"Is there some way to tell which cities are better?"

Taylor shook her head and scrolled toward Kansas. "All I know for sure is that everyone thinks Jackalville is the worst. They're involved in some sort of brainwashing thing and they want to take over the world."

"Jackalville isn't the city that's a hundred and thirty miles away, is it?"

Taylor magnified a circle of small domed cities with farmland in between them. "No. That's the odd thing. The computer won't tell me where Jackalville is."

The door at the front of the lab slid open. Taylor exited from the map and turned away from the desk as though she'd only been resting on the chair.

Echo strode into the room carrying a bundle of clothing under one arm. He didn't smile at them as he walked over. He dropped the clothes in front of Sheridan then, without a word of greeting, went to one of the computers. He tapped a few buttons, and voices—Sheridan and Taylor's voices—filtered out through the speakers.

"Once they implant those tracking crystals in our wrists, they'll control our entire lives. I'm not letting some power-hungry and morally depraved government tell me what I can learn, say, and do."

"Where will we go?"

"I don't know."

Echo tapped another button, and the voices stopped. He turned to them, and when he spoke, his words were clipped, sharp. "In the future, I wouldn't say anything in this lab that you want to keep secret. And by the way, Jeth isn't stupid; he just isn't suspicious."

Taylor let out a shaky breath. "You recorded us."

"Of course. We're studying your language and time period."

Sheridan swallowed hard. "You should have told us."

Taylor shut her eyes and leaned back in her chair. "We should have known."

Echo turned back to the computer, tapping a few of the buttons. His profile was taut, his motions deliberate. "I've temporarily turned off the record function and I'm deleting the information from last night and—ah, I see you've been on the computer this morning. I'd better hide those searches from the Information Department too." He spent a few more seconds typing, then straightened. "I heard your conversation only because I had a portable and checked the main computer while I bought clothes for you. The others still don't know that you think the government is morally depraved and that you're planning on stealing our gun and fleeing the first chance you get."

Sheridan stood up and took slow steps toward him. "Are you going to stop us?"

He let out a cough of disbelief. "You couldn't survive in this city by yourself, let alone escape from it."

"You could help us."

He raised his eyebrows, amused. "You want *me* to anger the morally depraved government?"

Sheridan reached out and laid one hand across his arm, pleading with him. "You know we don't belong here. There has to be a better place for us."

He shifted away from Sheridan's touch. His gaze slid over to the door and stayed there while he thought. When he finally turned back to Sheridan, his expression was set. "The other wordsmiths will be here soon, so I can't repeat myself. This is what you need to do: get Elise alone—today—and tell her you want to leave the city. She has connections; she knows the DW. They're a slightly insane group, but they're the only ones besides the Dakine and the government who know how to leave the city safely."

"Who are the Dakine?" Taylor interrupted.

"Bad people. That's all you need to know about them. I don't have time to explain everything." He picked up a green jumpsuit from the pile of clothes and handed it to Taylor. "Don't tell Elise I know about her connections, but when you have a plan to leave the city, tell me."

"Why?" Sheridan asked.

He picked up a blue shirt and skirt and handed it to her. "Because I'm coming with you."

Taylor's eyes narrowed in suspicion. "Why?"

"I have reasons."

Taylor's eyes remained narrowed, the questioning look still hung on her face. "How come we can't tell Elise you know about her connections?"

"She doesn't trust me."

Taylor crossed her arms. "But we should?"

He cast another look at the door. "I told you I don't have time to explain everything."

It was a fine time for Taylor to be skeptical—now that Echo had agreed to help them. Sheridan stepped over to Taylor. "He didn't have to tell us about Elise. He could be stopping us instead of helping us." She smiled back at Echo. "You are going to help us, aren't you?"

"Yes."

She kept smiling. He wanted to help them. She adored him.

Taylor stood up from her chair. "Tell me more about the— what did you call them?—the DW."

"Doctor Worshippers. I called them insane. But I'm also calling them our door out."

"People worship doctors now?" Sheridan asked.

Taylor let out a sigh. "I *so* picked the wrong major. Half the people I knew went pre-med, but no, not me."

"Major?" Echo asked. "What does this have to do with the military?"

Sheridan didn't answer. The lab door slid open, and Jeth and Elise walked inside. Jeth held a bowl of rolls and another of fruit slices. Elise carried plates, cups, and silverware. The group sat down for breakfast without another word about leaving the city. The subject, however, was constantly there in Sheridan's mind. Dakine? Doctor Worshippers? How would they get Elise alone?

After breakfast, Taylor asked Jeth to take them on a tour of the city. This was probably her way of staking out an escape route. Jeth agreed without any undue suspicion, though, and even seemed excited to show off Traventon's advances..

Sheridan and Taylor took the clothes Echo had given them and went to the back room to change. Taylor's green jumpsuit had flickering lights that raced around her torso. Sheridan's blue shirt was made of layers of some filmy material that swayed around her arms and legs when she moved, like drifting seaweed.

She puzzled over a group of small holes in the top of her skirt. Decorations? No, they must be for a belt. Everyone here wore belts with small metal boxes on them—the things they used in order to call one another—comlinks.

"So how are we going to . . . ?" Instead of finishing her sentence, Sheridan made a rolling motion with her hand. She wished she and Taylor had one of those secret languages that she'd heard some twins had. "You know . . . ask about . . . ?"

"Don't say it," Taylor said. "Little pitchers have big ears. Or in this case, computers with recorders."

"Right." Sheridan said, and Taylor's phrase gave her an idea. They might not have a secret twin language, but they could still talk in code. "We can't let our guard down," Sheridan said, "but we need to find a time to talk about flying the coop."

Taylor's mouth opened, probably to yell at Sheridan for blurting out their plans, but then she stopped and smiled. She'd remembered that the wordsmiths only had a vague knowledge of twenty-first-century figures of speech. As long as she and Taylor spoke in those, they could speak freely.

"We'll strike when the iron is hot," Taylor said, "but keep things under wraps for now."

Sheridan smoothed down her skirt the best she could. "I won't let the cat out of the bag."

chapter 12

They rode in one of the egg cars through the city streets. Jeth showed them the shopping district, the agro district, and the government central district. They saw buildings that seemed like they came from the twenty-first century and ones that looked like Dr. Seuss had designed them. Beige concrete walkways sprawled everywhere, shadowed by the opaque sky covering. The people strolling around the shops and walkways had hair colors from every shade of a crayon box.

Echo was right about the women; they dressed the most elaborately. Half of them looked like they were decked out with Christmas lights and tiaras. Some sauntered down the walkway with small mechanical pets trotting by their sides, mostly dogs, but there were other shapes too. Sheridan saw a jeweled cat, a giant lizard, a miniature deer, and even a tiny fluffy buffalo whirring and clicking beside their owners.

People had to manufacture their pets now. There was something sad about that.

As they drove, Taylor asked Jeth questions about leaving the city. At least, Sheridan could tell they were questions about leaving. Taylor asked in roundabout ways to hide her purpose. "Is garbage taken outside the city?" "How is fresh air ventilated inside?" "Where does the city get the raw materials to build things?"

Every once in a while Sheridan chimed in with a question she thought might be helpful, but mostly she read the street signs, memorizing them in case she ever had to find her way through the city. The spelling had changed for a lot of words. More of them were spelled phonetically now.

Costal Pas . . . Coastal Pass. Canun Wey . . . Canyon Way. Munora . . . Menorah—like with the candles Jewish people lighted at Hanukkah. That one would be easy to remember.

They turned from Munora onto Isaiah Drive.

Isaiah? As in the prophet Isaiah?

Why had people who banned religion named one of their streets after an Old Testament prophet?

Sheridan looked at Taylor to see if she had noticed the street sign. She hadn't. Taylor was busy talking with Jeth and Elise about how the city pumped water inside.

Sheridan turned to Echo. "Why is this street named Isaiah?"

"It was probably named after some important citizen. Why?"

"Isaiah was a prophet, a religious figure."

He shrugged. "A lot of names had religious origins, but

everyone has forgotten them now. They're just names to us."

Jeth pushed a button on the control panel to slow the car, an indication he was about to turn tour guide. "We're entering an education district. Hopefully we'll see some children out with their caretakers."

A minute later they did. A dozen children tromped down a walkway, lined up like ducklings following their mother. A woman walked in front of the line, another brought up the rear. As the car drove by, Sheridan saw that the woman in the back wore a long black dress with a white circular collar. More surprising, she had a wimple on her head.

Sheridan took hold of Taylor's arm. "Look at that woman. She's a nun."

Taylor looked. So did the wordsmiths.

It was then Sheridan realized it wasn't a wimple at all. The woman had long black hair and had dyed the portion of her hair around her forehead white.

Taylor figured it out the same time Sheridan did. "It's just coincidence," she said, although she didn't sound positive.

Could it be coincidence that a woman dyed her hair to look like a wimple and wore a dress that looked like a habit? Was that sort of thing allowed in a city that had banned religion ninety years ago?

"What did you call that woman?" Jeth asked.

"A none," Taylor said. "You know, like the number zero. It means someone who's not that smart." Apparently Taylor didn't want another conversation on religion.

"Oh." Jeth craned his neck for a second look. "She seemed competent to me."

"I'm sure she is," Taylor said.

"You're sure she's competent?" Sheridan asked. "Or you're sure she's a nun?"

Taylor gazed out the window again, but the woman was no longer visible. "Hold your tongue for now. We'll go over it at length later."

Jeth cocked his head. "What?"

Taylor waved a hand as though it wasn't important enough to repeat. "Tell me about the material that covers the city. How does it withstand the rain and snow beating down on it year after year?"

Jeth told her about it, but Sheridan tuned them out and kept looking at the city, searching for anyone else who didn't fit in.

Maybe it was just coincidence, a use of black and white in a pattern that had long ago lost its significance. Then again, the early Christians had had to hide who they were. Perhaps that was the case for all religions now.

Sheridan scanned every sign, every building they went past. Now that she was looking, she noticed other things. A shop that had a line of stars over the door: six-sided stars—a Jewish symbol. On the next street, she saw a woman with a red dot between her eyes like Hindu women wore. Could those symbols have survived without the religions that utilized them?

The car was heading toward the edge of the city because Taylor had insisted on seeing the walls. She told Jeth she wanted to see how they were built.

Sheridan moved closer to Echo. "What happened to the religious people when the government outlawed religion?"

Echo shifted in his seat. She could tell he felt awkward talking to her about it. "The government gave them three days to either renounce their beliefs and take an oath of loyalty to the government or to leave the city. Most of them renounced their beliefs. They couldn't survive outside the city without food or any place to go."

"And the ones who didn't renounce?"

"They left to build their own city. I've forgotten the name. Tolerance or maybe Assistance. Something they didn't think the other cities had."

"Where is it?" The words tumbled out of Sheridan's mouth too quickly, and she didn't give him time to answer. "Can we contact them?"

Echo paused, consolation softening his voice. "It's gone. If cities aren't controlled carefully, they turn unstable. Before long, they're destroyed either from the inside or the outside. A city like that . . ." He trailed off, leaving his assessment unfinished.

"A city like that didn't have a chance because it was founded by violent fanatics?" she supplied.

"It disappeared off the newsfeeds before I was born."

Sheridan sat back stiffly in her seat. "It isn't gone." Her words were firm; her convictions were less so. The different religions had put aside their differences for long enough to build a city, but could they have maintained the peace for ninety years?

Echo shook his head and smiled as though she intrigued him. "And you accused me of believing whatever I wanted regardless of the facts. Aren't you doing the same?"

"I suppose we have something in common," she said.

He laughed, and his eyes turned warm. He was gorgeous

when he smiled like that. He even made that ridiculous blue moon look good.

She wondered what he thought of her and then put the idea out of her mind. If he was going to be interested in somebody, it was bound to be Taylor. Brilliant, blond, outgoing Taylor. Still, as they talked, Sheridan let herself imagine what it would be like to catch Echo's attention—if his smile was just for her. If his blue eyes lit up when they saw her. If she could ease the sadness he felt from losing his brother.

When the car reached the street's end, everyone got out. Taylor, Jeth, and Elise headed toward the large, humming, gray walls. Jeth had already started explaining how the solar panels worked.

Echo slipped his hand around Sheridan's and pulled her in a different direction. "You can see the walls along this way too."

She let him lead her away but looked back over her shoulder. "Shouldn't we stay with the others?"

He gave her hand a squeeze as he took her farther away. "Don't you remember? Taylor asked you to keep me away from her."

Sheridan walked beside him, trying not to think about how natural it felt to hold his hand. "That was only so you wouldn't figure out what she's doing. You already know."

"Oh. Well, maybe I just want to be alone with you."

Was he flirting with her? The thought made her heartbeat speed. But then, he probably had some reason for wanting to be alone with her that he hadn't disclosed. After all, he thought she was a low-ranking flesh eater.

They kept walking until a large support beam stood between

them and the others. Then Echo slowed to a stop.

Sheridan felt nervous, awkward. She hardly knew what to say to guys from her own time period, let alone this one. When Echo didn't immediately speak, she let go of his hand and stepped toward the city wall. It stretched upward as far as she could see. Gray sloping panels vibrated and smelled of something old and worn, like the inside of her grandparents' boat.

She reached out to touch the wall. "Why do the walls hum?"

Echo took hold of her arm and pulled her back. "Don't touch it," he said. "There's a force field. Unless you're authorized, the wall sends out a shock."

Sheridan took another step backward and peered at the wall from a safer distance. She and Taylor couldn't scale it or cut into it. Would it be possible to break through the concrete on the ground and dig underneath it?

Echo pulled Sheridan toward him, drawing her attention away from the wall. There wasn't much space between him and her now, and it was hard for Sheridan not to notice how well defined Echo's muscles were. What did guys do to work out in the future?

"I have something for you," he whispered. He took a piece of paper from his shirt pocket. Slowly, as though he held a great secret, he slipped the paper into her hand.

She flipped it over. It could have been the front of a Christmas card. The picture showed Santa Claus with a child perched on one knee.

"Don't let anyone see it," Echo said, leaning in. "After yesterday, *pues*, you were so sad. I thought it would make you feel better to have a picture of the god you worship."

Her gaze went from the picture to his eyes. "Echo, this is Santa Claus."

"I know, and you can't imagine the techneloops I had to craft to access a site with that image."

She forced down a smile. "That's so thoughtful. Really. But Santa Claus isn't God. No one worshipped him—well, not unless you count retailers in general or children on Christmas Day."

Echo's brows drew together, puzzled. "You celebrated his birth every year. The birth of your savior."

"That was Jesus Christ, not Santa Claus."

Echo nodded. "An omniscient god who rewarded the good and punished the bad with coal."

"No, actually, Santa Claus and God are completely different."

He frowned. "But we have references—"

"And your interpretation of those references is wrong." She looked down at the picture in her hands again. "Maybe you can't understand history unless you understand everything that happened in a culture at the time. Maybe it's all just guesses about what went on in the past."

She put the picture into her skirt pocket and smiled at him. "Thanks for giving me this, though. It was sweet of you to try and make me feel better. Sometime when we have more time, I'll explain religion to you."

Echo's expression clouded, and she knew he was still deciding whether to believe her about Santa Claus. Instead of asking more questions, he said, "I'll try to arrange a time for you to be alone with Elise today. Remember to ask her about leaving the city."

"I'm not likely to forget." Sheridan looked back in the direction the others were but couldn't see anything past the support beam. "Maybe Taylor is already working on it. I bet she sends Jeth over to get us."

"And Jeth will wonder why I've taken you off alone." Echo reached for her hand, threading her fingers through his. "We'll have to come up with a believable reason."

He pulled her closer, and Sheridan found it hard to breathe. When she spoke, her voice was uneven. "What do you mean?"

He reached out and touched a strand of her hair, holding it between his fingers like it was something delicate. "Is this your born color?"

"Yes, and the freckles are natural too. I wouldn't have put them on my face otherwise."

"I like your freckles." He dropped the strand of hair and ran a finger across the trail of freckles on the bridge of her nose. "They were top fashion three years ago. Everyone wore them."

"Just my luck. I missed being beautiful by three years."

His finger made a slow line down her cheek. It was the smallest of touches and made her skin tingle. "You haven't missed anything. You're beautiful right now."

Her heart doubled its speed. Echo was definitely flirting, but did he mean any of it? Perhaps he was testing her, studying the male and female interactions of the twenty-first century. Or perhaps flirting was a casual thing people did in the future, and she was about to show herself as being very awkward at the pastime.

She should put an end to this until she figured out what it meant.

And she would. She would tell Echo it was time they returned to the others.

"Do you remember," Echo said, his words a soft lull, "when I told you I didn't specialize in Sheridan Bradford?"

"Yes."

"I've changed my mind about that." He bent his head lower. Slowly. Still giving her a choice to move away if she wanted.

She didn't move. She shut her eyes and let his lips come down on hers.

Kissing had not changed in four centuries.

Sheridan leaned into Echo, slid her hands up his chest until they met behind his neck. A voice somewhere in her mind said, *This is a mistake*. But then another voice countered, *What does it matter now that everything you knew is gone?* All that was left of her world were artifacts in vacuum-sealed boxes. It felt comforting to have someone's arms around her. It made her feel like she wasn't quite alone, like things could be normal again.

Echo ran one hand up her back until it rested against the nape of her neck. His fingers twined through her hair and he leaned in closer.

The voice, the one that steadily repeated, *This is a mistake*, got loud enough that Sheridan pulled away from Echo.

As she did, she heard Jeth say, "There you are."

Sheridan felt her face blush bright red. Not only Jeth, but Elise and Taylor stood nearby. Three pairs of eyes watched her—Jeth's amused, Taylor's surprised, and Elise's—well, Elise's features were drawn together in tight lines. Was that anger or disappointment?

Echo took hold of Sheridan's elbow and propelled her forward. When he spoke, his tone sounded only a little forced, like it was a small thing to be caught kissing a girl he'd only known for a day and a half. "You're done seeing the walls?"

Jeth nodded, smiling. "I thought we could go to a foodmart for lunch. As long as the girls don't talk to anyone, the scientists shouldn't mind if they're out in public." He gestured at Taylor's long sleeves. "No one will even notice they haven't got crystals." Then he smiled again.

He was too pleased by this, just as Elise was too annoyed. Elise's glare was practically burning holes into the side of Echo's head, and Sheridan wasn't sure what any of it meant.

Why in the world had she let Echo kiss her in the first place?

Well, she knew why. The guy was gorgeous and she was practically all alone in the world. Vulnerable.

It was simply a fluke, and she wouldn't let it happen again. From now on she would have a policy that she would refrain from kissing any guy until she knew enough about him to discern his natural hair color.

The group continued walking back to the car. Taylor strolled along beside Sheridan and Echo at an unhurried pace. "So," she said to Sheridan, "have you lost your marbles or are you simply pulling the wool over someone's eyes? Come clean. . . ."

Sheridan blinked in embarrassed surprise, then remembered that only she understood. "It was spur-of-the-moment."

"Great. While I'm brainstorming on making tracks, you're going off the deep end."

Sheridan rolled her eyes at Taylor. "Chill. We'll chew the fat later."

"Oh, there won't be much fat at lunch," Jeth called over. "We eat a healthy diet now. What were you saying about wool and spurs, though? Is that a reference to cowboys?"

"We're just making small talk," Sheridan said.

"Small talk?" Jeth repeated. "How interesting. Do you also have big talk?"

Taylor shook her head. "No, but in our day we had big talkers. We also had people who shot off their mouths."

Jeth considered this. "That sounds painful."

"Only to the people listening," Taylor said, and drifted off to talk to Jeth and Elise.

Echo took Sheridan's hand again, weaving his fingers through hers.

It didn't mean anything. He'd been holding her hand since she'd arrived in the future. It was a custom of theirs. Only he'd never held hands with Taylor or Elise.

She thought about this while she wondered if Echo's kiss had meant anything to him.

Some things never changed. Four centuries had gone by, and she still didn't understand guys.

chapter chapter
13

Echo sat in the foodmart trying to concentrate on the menu items instead of thinking about everything that had just gone wrong.

Kissing Sheridan had been a mistake.

Enjoyable as far as mistakes went, but still a mistake.

Echo had been so sure Jeth would come by himself to get them. After all, Taylor needed to talk to Elise, and Taylor had been manipulating the entire trip. Had it been too much to expect that she would have found a way send Jeth alone? He was supposed to see Echo and Sheridan together so that when Echo left Traventon with the girls, Jeth would assume it was an act of infatuation. He'd think Echo cared too much about Sheridan to risk losing her to memory washes. Jeth would understand, even though it would hurt him to lose his second son.

Or perhaps it would be a relief.

Since the funeral, every time Jeth had looked at Echo, there had been a small accusation in his gaze, a hurt that indicated Jeth knew more than he wanted to.

Things weren't supposed to turn out that way.

When Echo and Joseph were children, and it was Jeth's turn to pick them up at the caretaker center, he always greeted them with a hug. It generally took Jeth a few minutes before he could tell who was Echo and who was Joseph, but it didn't matter. He was excited to see both of them. Jeth always stopped on the way home and bought them candy swirls even if the caretakers reported bad behavior during the week.

Those days seemed impossibly far away now. The hug, the candy, the feeling that anything he'd done wrong didn't matter.

Now it all mattered.

Echo had only wanted Jeth's happiness. He knew Jeth needed family with him. It had been a conscious choice. Echo had chosen which brother would live.

And now here he was, sitting in this foodmart making plans to leave anyway. The thought caused a sharp pain in his chest, but he didn't flinch. He had lived with pain like a second skin since his brother's death.

Echo glanced across the table at the others. Sheridan and Taylor were both reading their medical data. Whenever someone sat down at a foodmart, the table lit up with their weight, body fat percentage, heart rate, and blood pressure.

"That is totally amazing," Taylor said.

"That is totally going to keep me from ordering dessert," Sheridan added.

"Don't worry," Jeth assured her. "If your fat percentage goes too high, you can pay to have a med remove some of it." He patted his stomach. "It's slightly illegal, but we all do it."

Taylor turned her attention to a waitress who was placing food on one of the tables. "With all your advances, you still have waiters?"

"It's a matter of work policy," Jeth explained. "Everyone must work, so there must be work for everyone, even if that means some people have jobs that could be automated."

Sheridan looked at Echo for the first time since they'd sat down. "If there are no animals, how can the menu have chicken parmesan, chicken pasta, and shrimp pizza?"

"It's bioamino protein," he said. "They grow it in the agrodistrict. The meat titles just indicate the flavor."

Taylor squinted at the pictures on the menu. "What do you use in place of dairy products?" Before anyone could answer she said, "Oh, you have almond milk."

Sheridan smirked. "It must be hard to milk an almond."

"Not really," Taylor said. "They have tiny milking machines they attach to the almonds' udders."

Jeth laughed. It had been a long time since Echo had seen his father laugh so easily.

Elise, however, stared at the menu screen with unmoving eyes. She wasn't reading but thinking, and Echo knew about what.

She wasn't happy to see Echo and Sheridan together. Perhaps now Elise wouldn't trust any of them. If she thought Sheridan and Echo were attached, if she suspected Sheridan would tell Echo things, Elise wouldn't tell her anything.

How was Echo supposed to fix that?

Then there was Sheridan herself. She'd been unusually quiet on the way to the foodmart, and every time Echo looked over at her, she blushed and glanced away.

He hadn't thought there were any old-twenties taboos about kissing in public. It was done on a regular basis in the entertainment from that era. But perhaps he was wrong about that, the way Sheridan kept telling him he was wrong about everything else.

Next time he kissed her, he'd have to make sure they were someplace private.

Assuming, of course, there was a next time. Assuming the scientists didn't call to say they had a fix on Tyler Sherwood and completely ruin his plans.

As this thought passed through his mind, Echo's comlink beeped. He sat motionless, feeling like his breath had been sucked from his body.

"It's not the scientists," Jeth said, guessing at his worry. "They would have beeped me, not you."

Echo slid his comlink into a computer that perched on the side of the table. The menu vanished, and two young men appeared on the screen. Caesar had bronze hair and spiked metallic eyebrows sticking up over his eyes like a row of teeth. Next to him was Geno, whose short-cropped hair stood up in purple rows. It matched his lips, which had been decoratively split in several places.

"Echo!" Caesar crooned from the computer. "Where are you shoveling? We stopped by your site, but you weren't there."

"I'm at a foodmart," Echo said flatly. "I'm working with my father."

"Work?" Geno asked. "As I see the event, you're sitting with two beautiful girls."

"Three," Caesar said. "Don't forget Elise."

Geno grinned, making the scars on his mouth stretch. "I'd never want to forget Elise."

Elise pursed her lips and pushed her chair farther away from the table to be out of the two men's sight.

Caesar smiled, leaning forward a bit, looking around the foodmart. "When do we get to darty with your new friends, Echo?"

"I don't do darties anymore," Echo said.

"Doesn't have to be a darty then," Caesar said. "We just want to meet them. They look interesting."

They looked useful, he meant. Echo gritted his teeth together. Somehow Caesar knew about Taylor and Sheridan. How did the Dakine always learn things so quickly?

Caesar's gaze traveled from Taylor to Sheridan, and then back to Echo. "I give it odds they'd like to jump with us."

Which meant the Dakine was determined to have them, and Echo knew why. Sheridan and Taylor were the only two Traventon residents not in their infancy who didn't have crystal implants. The Dakine could send them anywhere undetected, and if the girls were inadvertently killed in the process, *pues,* what did that matter to the Dakine?

Echo put his hand on his comlink, ready to pull it from the computer. "I need to turn off my comlink so everyone can order lunch."

"We'll beep you later," Geno said.

"Really soon," Caesar said, then added with a cryptic smile,

"You can't keep filed away forever, you know. It isn't good for you."

Echo unplugged his comlink without saying good-bye and shoved it into his belt. The menu returned to the computer screen, and he stared at it unseeing.

Jeth leaned over and touched Echo's arm. In his normal voice, not the one with the old-twenties accent, he said, "Caesar's right. You've been much too solemn lately. Joseph wouldn't want that. You need to go out again. See your friends. Perhaps the next time the girls need a break from our research, you could beep—"

Elise leaned over the table and cut him off. "Don't even consider it, Echo. You're not taking the time riders to those filthy shadlers."

"Elise!" Jeth gave her a look of reproof, but she kept her gaze locked on Echo, her eyes sizzling with anger.

She knew. Somehow she knew Caesar and Geno were with the Dakine.

But how?

A feeling of dread crept up Echo's skin. Perhaps she knew because she was Dakine herself.

He pushed away the thought. Elise had connections to the Doctor Worshippers, and those two groups were as opposite as could be. The DW's motto was Freedom of Knowledge, Speech, and Belief. Every once in a while they draped banners with that phrase from the sides of buildings. Sometimes they cut into city program feeds demanding more citizen rights, telling the public they deserved them. They met in secret groups to pass on knowledge and talk of their beliefs.

The Dakine had a different sort of motto: Power to the Dakine, and Death to Anyone Who Got in Their Way. They didn't have to make banners with those words or put them in city program feeds. Every assassination they ordered proclaimed their message. The Enforcers couldn't stop Dakine, and no one else dared to try.

Elise turned away from Echo and went back to reading the menu.

She couldn't be a Dakine member. She was too gentle, too good. But then, he'd been wrong before. He couldn't rule out anyone again.

A memory of Allana pressed into his mind. There she was, walking hand in hand with him toward her building, sending him pouting looks in an attempt to convince him to come home with her. He'd refused because he kept thinking how attached his brother was to her. And Allana would tell him about it. Probably with glee. She'd made a game of playing him and his brother against each other. She stirred up a competition between them and presented herself as the prize. "Eventually I'd like to be exclusive . . . with someone," she would whisper into his ear before she kissed him.

He knew she was whispering the same thing to his brother.

The rivalry shouldn't have happened. Echo had had enough girls orbiting around him. He hadn't needed Allana at all, even if she was beautiful, even if she was the daughter of the chairman of trade. Except for one unfortunate thing. Echo had really cared for her.

Joseph had always loved his studies, his work, too much to be distracted by social rounds. But Allana had had a talent for knowing what was important to guys. She invited Joseph to places of culture, introduced him to head educators, even convinced her father to trade with New Seattle for their archaeology display so that Joseph could touch artifacts from the nineteenth century with his own hands.

Allana hadn't needed such grand endeavors to capture Echo. She'd just played on his ego. He had been an effortless target.

So there he and Allana had been on the street, she gently pulling at his hands and sending him sultry looks, while he stood in front of her building, refusing to go in, but not leaving to go home either.

How had they even started talking about the Dakine? One would think he'd remember the details of such a life-changing conversation. But he didn't. He only remembered Allana's upturned face, half laughing, even though every word that came out of her mouth was completely serious.

"You'd be surprised at how far incircutrated the Dakine are. They're in all professions, even the government."

He had shrugged. "No surprise there. The government never had any integrity to begin with."

She should have gotten a little upset then. She should have at least defended her father. Instead she said, "Integrity is such a weighty item. It's easier to live without it."

"What a great philosophy," he said. "We'd all be happier if the Dakine ran the city." Even saying the word Dakine felt dangerous, felt wrong, and he pulled Allana closer so that their voices would be lower.

She wound her arms around his neck, her bright silver

hair tumbling off her shoulders as she looked up at him. "They practically run the city already. They're everywhere. People you know, people you work with, people you trust."

"Not people *I* work with. Most of the people I work with are my family."

"It's sweet that you're so naive." She ran her hand up his arm. "But really, when will you click onto reality?"

"Echo . . ." Elise cut into his thoughts. He was not on that street but back in the foodmart with all gazes on him.

"Are you going to order?" Elise asked.

"Are you all right?" Jeth added.

"Yes." No. Maybe he still wasn't seeing reality. Maybe he couldn't be sure of Elise. For all he knew, she didn't want Caesar and Geno to get hold of Sheridan and Taylor because her branch of the Dakine had plans for them instead.

Echo punched in his food order and knew he wouldn't be able to finish it.

He had thought that when the time came, when they actually had the supplies to leave the city, he'd be able to convince Elise to trust him. Now he wondered if he could trust her.

chapter 14

chapter

As soon as they got back to the wordsmiths' office, Jeth's comlink beeped. Sheridan stared at it and felt prickles of fear.

"No cause to worry," Jeth said, detaching it from his belt. "The scientists are probably checking to make sure you're still functioning well, no cellular destabilization happening."

"The restaurant table said we were fine," Sheridan offered. She walked over to a couch and pretended she wasn't listening to his conversation.

He pushed a button, and the wall turned into a picture screen. The scientist with the red lightning bolt running down his cheek sat half slumped at a desk. His eyes were glassy, like he hadn't slept for a while.

Jeth walked up to the wall. "Do you have a fix on Tyler Sherwood's signal?"

The man winced. "Tyler Sherwood's signal has all but disappeared from the time line. The science chairman is afraid our attempt to strain Sherwood inadvertently killed him." The man ran his hand over his forehead. "So the mayor has forbidden us to retrieve anyone else until he's reviewed the program. He's half convinced we're running assassinations on important historical figures."

Jeth shook his head sympathetically. "Unfortunate."

"Enforcers will come to your office tomorrow night to take the girls. Mayor's orders. Make sure they're ready."

Jeth nodded. "Of course."

Every muscle in Sheridan's body grew tense. What were the Enforcers going to do with them? She glanced at Echo. He was watching the wall screen, listening. She told herself not to panic. Echo had just kissed her. He wouldn't have done that and then, say, let someone shoot her.

She looked out the window and forced her expression to remain neutral. If the wordsmiths knew she could understand them, she wouldn't be able to eavesdrop on them anymore.

The call ended, and Jeth walked over to the computer and paused the recording function. In his modern accent, he spoke to Echo. "You can delete the order?"

"Of course."

Jeth then turned to the girls and spoke in their accent. "I need to explain something to you." He cleared his throat and looked from Taylor to Sheridan uncomfortably. "The scientists feel you'd function better in our society if you had no memory of your old one. They've ordered memory washes for you."

Sheridan's heart lurched in her chest. They were going to

take her memory. She would wake up somewhere with no clue to her identity except for a picture in her pocket of an unknown jolly fat man in red. She'd probably spend the rest of her days searching for Santa Claus in hopes he could tell her who she was.

"Fortunately," Jeth went on, "Echo has some splicing abilities." He put his hand on his son's shoulder. "Both of my boys had the sight for computigating. They could have been programmers—would have been the finest in the city. But they wanted to work with their father. Best compliment of my life."

Echo's bright blue eyes fixed on Sheridan. His words were soft, calming. "I should be able to cut into the Scicenter's program and delete the memory wash order before it goes to the schedulers."

Taylor's foot jiggled up and down the way it did when she was nervous. She scanned the room, thinking. "And if you can't?"

"Then Enforcers will come tomorrow night and take you to a Medcenter for surgery. If you fight them, you'll be shot. But," Echo added, "you don't need to worry. I can remove the order."

Taylor's foot kept jiggling.

Echo sent Sheridan a questioning gaze. "You trust me, don't you?"

She hesitated only a moment, then nodded.

He smiled back at her, and it felt like a second kiss, delivering the same warmth.

Echo talked with Jeth for a bit longer, discussing the best way to return to the Scicenter so that he could splice into its mainframe.

Taylor tapped her foot into Sheridan's. "Maybe we should just make a break for it."

Sheridan gave a subtle shake of her head. "We'd be biting off more than we can chew. We need to look before we leap, or something could hit the fan. We have a lead to follow before we make like a banana and split."

Elise looked back and forth between them. "Are you still hungry? Sometimes I can't understand what you say."

Taylor and Sheridan simultaneously shook their heads. Neither spoke again.

Jeth and Echo had moved to the cabinet and were deciding on an artifact to take to the Scicenter for dating. They needed an excuse to get near a Scicenter computer.

Sheridan watched them, wondering about memory washes. Did they erase a person's personality, their intelligence? It would be a shame if Taylor lost her intelligence. Taylor's mind was something special, something rare.

And then Sheridan realized why the Time Strainer had brought them here. She should have known all along, and it was probably just luck that the scientists hadn't figured it out too.

She turned to Taylor, her voice nearly a whisper. "Back home, you used a pen name, didn't you?"

Taylor flushed, didn't answer.

How many times had Sheridan seen her sister typing papers about physics theories? Papers not only for class, but for physics journals as well. "You got caught red-handed," Sheridan went on. "They just don't know your hands are red yet."

Taylor whispered, "Mum's the word."

"I won't spill the beans." To show they were united,

Sheridan reached over and gave her sister's hand a squeeze. Really, Taylor should have told Sheridan her secret at the beginning. Sheridan wouldn't have told anyone that Taylor was really Tyler Sherwood.

chapter ~~hapter~~

15

After Jeth and Echo left, Elise went over to the computer and skimmed her hand across the control panel. "Echo isn't the only one who can force a computer malfunction. This will give us fifteen minutes to talk before the recorder cycles round again." She turned away from the computer and plunked down on the overstuffed floral couch. Her dark eyes were pensive underneath her pink eyebrows. As she looked at Sheridan, she wound a lavender strand of hair around her finger. "I know I don't understand all the male and female customs of your culture, but what sort of relationship do you expect with Echo now?"

Taylor smirked, folded her arms, and dropped down onto the couch next to Elise. "Yes, do tell, Sheridan. What is your future with Mr. Blue Moon?"

Sheridan's cheeks grew hot, and she sat down stiffly on the

leatherlike couch across from them. It was one thing to feel you had acted foolishly; it was another to be openly questioned about it. "I don't know. It's hard to think of the future when I might be dragged away by Enforcers tomorrow."

Elise fluttered a hand in Sheridan's direction, waving away her statement. "You don't need to worry. Echo will erase it. He has a way of manipulating things—and people—to his benefit."

Taylor turned to Elise and in a confidential tone said, "I always wait until the second date to kiss a guy."

Sheridan ignored Taylor. "Do you think Echo kissed me to manipulate me—that it didn't matter to him?"

Elise made a scoffing noise. "I don't think kissing has ever mattered to Echo."

Sheridan felt numb, used. She didn't know what to say, so she said nothing.

Taylor cocked her head at Elise, surveying her. The teasing faded from her tone. "You don't like Echo, do you?"

"Not anymore."

"But you used to?" Taylor asked. "Did you two date?"

"Echo and me?" Elise shook her head. "If I had dated either of them, it would have been Joseph. Joseph was more like me." Her voice caught as though she couldn't say his name without sadness. "Echo has always been too spun for me."

"Spun?" Sheridan asked. "What does *spun* mean?"

"It means he spins from girl to girl," Elise said.

"Oh, how nice," Taylor said to Sheridan with pointed emphasis. "You were his latest stop."

And for all Sheridan knew, by tomorrow Echo would be ready to spin to someone else. Perhaps to Taylor.

"It isn't that Echo is bad," Elise went on. "He just made the wrong friends and got wrapped up in a bad situation. He's always been so reckless. And it's like that saying from your time: the reckless never stay wreck-less for long."

"We never said that," Taylor said. "It's catchy though."

"You didn't say that?" Elise's eyebrows dipped. "I must be mixing up my centuries."

Sheridan's mind was still back on Echo spinning away from her. "Does Echo date lots of girls?"

"He used to," Elise said, "but he changed after Allana's death, after Joseph's—he doesn't go anywhere now. Doesn't match up at all."

Which was a relief. Only Sheridan shouldn't be relieved that Echo didn't date when it meant he was still grieving his brother's death. Or perhaps it meant he was finally ready to stop spinning, that his kiss meant something. "Who's Allana?"

Elise ran one hand across a printed rose on the couch cushion. It was faded to nearly a tan color. "She was one of Echo's girlfriends. His favorite. The only problem was, she preferred Joseph." Elise's fingers momentarily stopped their track across the petals. "Or maybe she didn't. Maybe Joseph just presented more of a challenge for her. Anyway, Echo didn't like it. Girls always loved him best. He was the better dresser, better dancer, better flirter. He knows how to splice the compulocks at the Virtual Reality center to get more entertainment time. He's so smart with computers and is always doing such stupid things with them."

Elise gave a wan smile, one that only thinly veiled the sadness behind it. "I used to hate it when people compared

Echo and Joseph, and now I'm doing it. *Pues*, they were wrong about Echo. Everyone said he was the smarter one because he could computigate so easily. But Joseph was smarter. He was just smarter in a gentler way. He never saw the faults in people. Especially not in his brother. He couldn't figure out what Echo had become."

Sheridan felt each word in the pit of her stomach. "What had Echo become?"

Elise stared down at the couch, then glanced over at the door. "Maybe I shouldn't say. I'm only guessing, and I might be wrong. It's a heavy thing to accuse anyone of."

Sheridan waited, not breathing. She knew she was supposed to steer the conversation to the Doctor Worshippers and leaving the city, but she wanted to hear Elise's accusations—not in order to hear Echo's faults. In order to figure out how she should feel toward him.

Elise continued, her voice lower and faster. "Allana was here in the office waiting for Joseph the day before her death. I heard her talking with one of her friends on the computer. She didn't see me come in, although it probably wouldn't have mattered if she had. She was so arrogant about everything. She told her friend, 'I've decided on Joseph.'

"And her friend said, 'But has he decided on you?'

"Allana leaned back in her chair like she was planning on napping in it and said, 'I can overcome his concerns.'

"When her friend asked, 'Aren't you worried that Echo will be angry?' Allana just laughed. I guess she thought that since her father was the chairman of trade, nothing bad would ever touch her."

Elise shut her eyes, swallowed hard. "The next night Joseph and Allana were both murdered. Joseph was shot not far from here, on Plymouth Street. Now every time I go past there, I think of it."

Sheridan couldn't speak. The horror gripped at her throat until she was incapable of sound.

"You think Echo killed them?" Taylor asked.

"Oh, it wasn't Echo," Elise said. "He was walking with Joseph at the time. But it might as well have been him. His group did it. It was their usual type of execution."

"His group?" Taylor repeated.

Elise lowered her voice. "It isn't good to speak of them."

"The Dakine," Sheridan said dully.

Elise's eyes grew wide. In a cracking whisper she said, "You know of them? How?"

Taylor and Sheridan exchanged a look, but neither answered. Was it better to keep Echo's secret or expose him? Who did they trust now? They had trusted Echo and found out he might have been involved in a double murder.

Elise's lips drew into a tight line. "Echo told you about the Dakine, didn't he? What did he say—that they're a stellar organization?"

Sheridan hesitated, still reluctant to betray Echo. "He said they were bad people. That's all."

Elise grunted. "*Pues*, he told the truth about that. They run crime groups. If you have enough credits, you can buy anything from them, from pleasure drugs to city council rulings. People know the Dakine are dangerous. But no one does anything to stop them. Half the people are afraid, and the other half go to the Dakine for fat-reduction treatments." Elise looked from Sheridan to Taylor emphatically. "Stay away from all of it."

Taylor folded her hands calmly in her lap. "Echo also told us you knew people who could help us get out of the city—the DW."

Elise stood up so fast, it looked like she'd been jabbed. One hand flew to her chest, and her jaw went slack. "Why would he tell you that?" and then after several quick breaths, "How did he know?"

Taylor stood up too, as though to help Elise in case she tipped over, but as quickly as Elise had stood up, she sank back down onto the couch. "Joseph," she said weakly. "I told Joseph. He promised he'd never tell anyone." She blinked several times and wrapped her arms across her chest, holding on to herself. "I should have known he wouldn't keep it from Echo. Now I've endangered people. What else does he know?"

"I'm not sure," Sheridan said. "He just told us you had connections to the DW, and that they could help us get out of Traventon."

Taylor sat down beside Elise again. "He wants us to make plans with you and then tell him what they are. Don't worry, though. We won't tell him anything."

Elise leaned back against the couch and shut her eyes. "He's planning some sort of trap for me."

"Would he do that?" Sheridan asked. "Is he really so . . . ?" The sentence dropped from her mouth, unfinished. She was afraid she knew the answer. Echo had been kind to her and kissed her. Was she naive enough to think that meant he could be trusted? How simple she must seem to him, how easy to deceive.

"We'll tell him he was wrong," Taylor said. "We'll tell him you don't know anything about the Doctor Worshippers."

Elise's lips trembled. "He won't believe you. I'll have to leave now, myself."

Taylor reached out and put one hand on Elise's arm. "You can take us with you."

Elise didn't answer right away. Her expression grew vacant. She was already far away, planning things and going over options. "I need to talk to some people. I need to explain to them, to ask them for help." Her voice faded to a whisper. "It isn't an easy thing. You need to have three days of provisions before you start out. Three days. You can't get three days of food from a dispenser. They've got compulocks on them. They track everything you buy."

"Could Echo get around the compulocks?" Sheridan asked.

Elise shot Sheridan a severe look. "Echo can't know about this. He doesn't want to help you. The Dakine hate the Worshippers. They're the only ones who won't bend to Dakine power."

Taylor glanced at the door. "Echo is expecting us to tell him some sort of plan. We'll pretend we're going to let him know, and then after he's given us food, we'll give him the slip."

"The slip?" Elise repeated. "We'll give him underwear?"

"We'll leave without him," Sheridan clarified.

Elise bit her lip. Her words came out in a hurried rush. "It's dangerous to admit to anything. And if something went wrong . . . If he insisted on knowing names or places before he helped . . . I have to consider everything." She looked down at the time flashing on the top of her comlink. "I need to talk to someone. I'll go now while I'm certain Echo isn't tracking me." She stood up, took two steps toward the door, then turned around.

"My mind is frozen. When Echo and Jeth come back, they'll wonder why I've left you here alone. I can't go now."

"You went to get us more clothing," Taylor supplied. "We wanted to try the new fashions, so you went to get us things."

Elise shook her head, making pink and lavender shimmers. "You'll have to come with me for them to believe that story. But you can't come, because even if we left them a message telling them we'd gone shopping, they'd most likely track my crystal and see we weren't in a fashion district. Then they'd know."

Taylor stood. "I'll go with you. Sheridan will stay here because . . ." Taylor waved her hand in Sheridan's direction as though this helped with the excuse. "She doesn't like shopping and doesn't need to try anything on, because anything that fits me will fit her too. She'll keep Jeth and Echo busy so they won't have the time to check on us. And we'll really have to come back with some clothing to make our alibi believable."

Elise nodded and walked quickly toward the door. Even panicked, she glided so that her soft shoes hardly made a sound.

Taylor turned to Sheridan. "Whatever you do, don't let them track Elise. And listen to some feeds on the computer while we're gone. We need to work on our accents if we want to blend in."

Sheridan glanced at the monitor. "I don't know how to work the computers."

Taylor sighed, walked back over to a computer, and typed on the control panel. "They're simple once you're logged in. Just say or type in what you want it to do." She headed toward the door again. "You can listen to news stories."

Before Sheridan could ask anything else, the door swished closed behind Taylor and Elise. Sheridan stood for a moment in the silence, then slowly sat down.

She looked over the keyboard. The computer wouldn't understand her accent, but most of the symbols were familiar. She could figure out how to make it work. She had to figure it out, because she knew exactly what she wanted the computer to do: find information about Joseph's and Allana's deaths.

chapter
16

"Show me information about the murder of Joseph . . ." Sheridan let her hands rest on the desk. It had taken an annoying amount of time to type out the sentence. The spelling had changed for half the words, so that every time she typed in something, the computer gave her a list of alternate words to choose from. Now she realized she didn't know Joseph's last name, didn't even know if people had last names anymore. She went back to her entry, typing, *the daughter of the chairman of trade.*

She believed Elise about the story, and yet she didn't.

How could Echo be capable of having his own brother killed? People just didn't do that.

Perhaps Elise had made up the story. Perhaps it was Elise's way of getting them to confide in her and turn on Echo. If that had been the plan, it had worked perfectly.

Maybe Sheridan was trusting the wrong person.

Despite the lack of last names, the computer had no problem retrieving information about Joseph's and Allana's murders. Dozens of news links appeared on the screen.

Sheridan clicked on one and listened as a plaid-haired reporter rattled off the facts. "Tragedy strikes the chairman of trade's family as his daughter, Allana Arad, was killed outside the family's apartment."

The video changed from the newswoman to a view of a street corner where four Enforcers carried a limp young woman into a waiting car. Her hair was bright silver, but Sheridan couldn't see her features clearly. There was too much blood over her face, and the sight of it made Sheridan look away.

She typed in the word *end*, but the newscaster went on, telling how the chairman of trade demanded the government unplug Dakine power from the city.

She typed in the word *stop*, but before she pushed the Enter command, the newscaster moved on to cover Joseph Monterro's death. Sheridan looked back at the screen.

"The street cam captured the attack, another example of the growing problem the Dakine organization has become."

There, in perfect clarity on the screen, was Joseph. He had short blond hair and a small blue star on his cheek instead of a crescent moon, but besides those two details, he looked exactly like his brother. Echo walked next to him, shaking his head over something Joseph had said.

Echo really had been there when it happened. This fact made the event all the more horrible.

The computer video showed three cars simultaneously pull up beside the brothers. As the doors opened, the other people on the sidewalk scattered out of the way, darting down the street and into the doorways of nearby buildings. Somehow before the first weapon fired, the people on the street knew what was about to happen.

Joseph said something to Echo. Sheridan couldn't hear what, but as she watched his lips, she could think of only one phrase: *I love you.*

Could those have been the last words Joseph said to Echo? Did Joseph know what his brother had done? Was it a plea for Echo to call off the hit men?

Echo stood transfixed. Even from a distance, Sheridan could see the look in his eyes, the look of anger and despair, the look of an animal before it goes completely wild.

The reporter talked over the sound of the video, but Sheridan could tell what Echo said back. He shouted, "No!"

Joseph turned to run down the street. He'd gone only a few steps when men from the cars pointed black boxes at him. Flashes of light lit up the screen like tiny firecrackers; then Joseph fell to the walkway, red circles growing around him. The cars dispersed as quickly as they had gathered at the corner. None of the remaining bystanders, now peering out from the doorways, did anything to help. They simply watched from a distance—watched as Echo knelt beside his brother.

Echo took hold of Joseph, held him in his arms as though it didn't bother him to get blood on his hands.

The reporter was saying something about the debate in city council over signal-jamming detectors that could forewarn of

Dakine attacks. Sheridan didn't hear it.

She also didn't hear the footsteps behind her. A hand reached over her shoulder and switched off the computer. She jumped, startled, then turned and looked into Echo's face. He stood over her, rigid. "What are you doing?"

She pressed her back farther into her chair. "I just wanted to find out what happened to Joseph."

His expression vibrated pain and anger. Mostly pain. "Did watching that program feed fix your curiosity?"

All the anguish in Echo's eyes—it had to mean he was innocent, didn't it? Elise had said she was only guessing about his involvement. She might have guessed wrong.

Sheridan stood up. She wanted to hug Echo and squeeze her doubts away. Instead she put her hand on his arm. "I'm so sorry."

"I'll forget it. Just contract with me you won't do it again."

"I meant I was sorry about Joseph. I'm sorry he's gone."

"Oh." Echo let out a controlled breath. "I'm sorry too."

Sheridan ran her hand down his arm until her fingers touched his. "I know."

He didn't take hold of her hand. "You don't know. You couldn't begin to understand."

"I lost my family too."

His expression was distant, and she knew he was back on Plymouth Street. "You didn't watch them as they died."

She didn't want to ask the next question, and yet she had to. "Why did the Dakine kill Joseph?"

Echo sighed, and with that sigh, the anger in his eyes turned to resignation. "It's too complicated to explain."

She laced her fingers through his. "Try. I'll understand."

He took hold of her other hand. "Do you know why people never talk about the Dakine?"

"No."

"Because people who know too much about them are killed. Do you still want to know about them?"

She kept her eyes on his. "If it will help me understand you."

He gave her hand a squeeze. "You're a surprising strain. Did everyone in your century possess more courage than caution?"

"You don't want to tell me?"

"I don't want to talk about it anymore." He turned the full power of his blue-eyed gaze on her. "I can imagine better things to do while we're alone."

He took her chin, tilted her face up, then kissed her. She had told herself she wasn't going to kiss anyone until she knew them well enough to determine their natural hair color. Technically, she wasn't breaking that resolve, since she'd seen Joseph's blond hair in the newscast. And besides, she wanted to comfort Echo, to take away even a little bit of his pain. She slid her arms around him, felt his heart beating against hers.

He kissed her for another moment, then let her go.

He took a deep breath, reorienting himself, and stepped back over to the computer. "Where are Taylor and Elise?"

The question brought Sheridan sharply back to reality. She was supposed to be covering for Elise. "They went shopping for clothes. I didn't feel like going."

Echo's hands moved across the panels of the computer the same way Elise's had earlier. He was disarming the record function again. "Did you talk to Elise about her connections?"

Sheridan hadn't expected to answer this question. Jeth was supposed to have returned with Echo, which would have prevented this conversation from happening. She looked around the room. "Where's Jeth?"

"Getting authorization for more food credits for you and Taylor. Why didn't you answer my question about Elise?"

Because despite her attraction to Echo, she had no real assurance that she could trust him. Taylor and Elise didn't, and for their sakes she shouldn't tell him more than she had to.

"Taylor is going to talk to her while they're shopping."

He nodded casually, keeping his gaze on her eyes, and it seemed anything but casual. "Then why did Elise disarm the record function earlier?"

How did he know that? Could he tell just by looking at the computer? Sheridan's mouth went dry, but she tried not to show her discomfort. She refused to gulp. "Taylor asked her to. She doesn't like being recorded."

Echo's eyes narrowed. He was debating disbelief. "Jeth will wonder why it keeps malfunctioning."

"I'm sorry."

Echo stepped closer to Sheridan, took her hand again. "Today you were talking to Taylor in phrases we couldn't understand. What were you saying?"

"Nothing important."

His thumb caressed the back of her hand, making lazy circles. "You need to trust me. You don't understand the way things are now, all the dangers. I'm trying to help you." His eyes fixed on hers. "Do you believe me?"

"Yes." And in that moment she did.

A moment later her doubts returned.

He leaned down and kissed her again, more gently this time. Was it his way of eliciting an attachment from her, of getting her trust?

Despite her suspicions, she leaned into him until she was engulfed in his embrace. Well, who could blame her? Echo was gorgeous, and he'd said he wanted to specialize in her. He couldn't belong to the Dakine. He wouldn't have taken part in his brother's murder.

When Echo finally released her, she felt dizzy, torn in half. He took her hand and led her to a couch. "I forgot to tell you—I didn't have any problems deleting the memory wash order. As long as none of the scientists check to see how it went, you'll be safe."

She sat down next to him, nestled in the crook of his arm. "Are they likely to check?"

"Right now they're too busy going over data to see if and why the Time Strainer killed Tyler Sherwood. Once they fix that problem, they'll retrieve the next scientist on their list." Echo twined his fingers through the strands of hair that fell on her shoulder. "I'm glad you came through intact. Let's hope Elise can connect us with the DW, so you'll stay that way."

Sheridan shifted on the couch. What would she say if he asked, "What's taking them so long? Let's check on Elise's location." She needed to change the subject. In her hurry to do so, she said the first thing that came to mind. "Did they catch the people who shot Joseph?"

Echo stiffened. "No."

She didn't like making Echo uncomfortable but knew if she

didn't ask now, she'd never ask. "Isn't there some record of who uses the cars? I thought they didn't work unless you scanned your crystal in."

Echo's voice sounded calm, but his eyes were fierce. "The Dakine have ways of jamming their crystals' signals. And besides, even if people were traced to the crime location, it wouldn't mean a conviction. The Dakine are too powerful. People who interfere with them end up at funerals. Either their own or their families'."

Was that what had happened to Allana and Joseph? Had Echo interfered with the Dakine, so his girlfriend and brother paid the price?

"With the technology you have now, there must be a way to catch the Dakine."

Echo shook his head. "The government is slow to implement anything new, and the Dakine makes sure it has people who can manipulate technology as it comes."

Computigating. That was what Jeth had called Echo's skill. And that was what the Dakine needed to help run their organization.

As Sheridan sat leaning against Echo's side, his arm draped across her shoulder, she felt, with a leadlike sensation in her heart, that Elise's guess was the right one. Echo was part of the Dakine.

chapter chapter
17

A short while later, Jeth came back to the office. When he saw Sheridan and Echo sitting close together, a grin spread across his face. She wondered if this was because Jeth liked her, or whether he was just happy to have one more area to study—dating rituals of the early twenty-first century.

As he sat down, Elise and Taylor bustled into the room carrying neon-bright shopping bags.

"Guess what I got you?" Taylor said, setting her bags down on one of the coffee tables. She pulled out a metallic purple-and-red smock shirt with matching striped pants. It looked like an outfit that only someone in a circus would wear. "Isn't it cute?" Taylor chimed.

Taylor and her sick sense of humor. One day Sheridan would repay her for choosing that outfit.

"Yeah. Cute," Sheridan said.

"I found a few other things I thought you'd like, but I wasn't sure. Elise says we can go back tomorrow and do more shopping." Taylor sent an apologetic smile to Jeth. "You don't mind if we go out again, do you?"

"No. I'll go with you. It will be informative to see your reactions to things."

Taylor gave a half laugh. "You can't come with us. Men and women don't shop together unless they're married."

"Really?" Jeth cast a glance at Echo, perhaps to see if he knew about this taboo. "Not much was recorded about the shopping habits of the old twenties, but I don't remember reading anything that indicated it was segregated. . . ."

Taylor folded the purple-and-red outfit and handed it to Sheridan. "I'm surprised the practice hasn't lasted. I mean, I can't imagine trying on clothes or picking out items with just anyone. It's such an intimate process."

Jeth's eyebrows pinched together as he considered this. "But in the entertainment programs from your time . . . I'm sure I saw men and women in the same store together."

"They must have been married," Taylor said. "Or it was around Mardi Gras or Christmas. Then the rules didn't hold and everyone went out together. It was wild."

"How fascinating," Jeth said. "Tell me more about your shopping rituals."

It was Sheridan who ended up continuing the tale. Taylor asked Echo to help her learn more computer functions, and they retreated to the desk, while Sheridan answered questions about malls, grocery stores, and internet shopping. "My mom goes to garage sales nearly every weekend," Sheridan said, then stopped herself. "I mean, she went."

Funny how such trivial memories could slice through her, could bring back the loss. It felt like that world should still exist—like if she went to Tennessee, she could bring it all back. Her street, her house, the family portraits hanging on the wall.

Sheridan kept talking, answering Jeth and Elise's questions while Echo and Taylor sat close together, staring at the computer screen. Their hands moved across the control panels. Sometimes they whispered things to each other. Every once in a while Taylor smiled at him.

I'm not jealous, Sheridan told herself. *I'm not even sure I trust Echo.* Still, it stung to see him sitting as close to Taylor as he had been with her. She felt so replaceable.

And what kind of girl sat so close to the guy she'd seen kissing her twin sister?

These thoughts kept returning during her conversations on whether or not girls were allowed in auto parts stores (only before Father's Day) or men were allowed in grocery stores (yes, but they couldn't walk down the feminine hygiene aisle), and why girls had so many shoes. (It was an unwritten law. You had to have more shoes than would fit neatly into your closet.)

Finally Elise brought in dinner, and then afterward the wordsmiths helped Sheridan and Taylor dye their hair and faces. At first, Sheridan was surprised that the men stuck around for this job, but since hair and makeup were was no longer a girl thing, it made sense. Jeth and Echo were as expert at the practice as Elise.

Taylor chose white as her new hair color. She said she'd

always wondered what it would be like to be a platinum blonde. She also added six inches to her hair length. Not only could people change their hair follicles to produce different colors, they could brush on a synthetic goo that, when dry, was indistinguishable from the natural hair strand. Sheridan added two inches to her already long hair and wanted to dye it bright red. It was her own private joke—she really would be a redhead. Echo convinced her to dye it gold with a few red stripes. He said that pure red was no longer in style.

Since when did primary colors go out of style?

When it came to dying their faces, Taylor covered her cheeks and eyelids with blue-and-white swirls that looked like spinning wheels. Sheridan went with a flesh-tone face dye to erase her freckles; then Echo painted a succession of gold stars that dripped around one eyebrow and down onto her cheek. Elise applied lip and eyeliner dye, then transformed Sheridan's eyelids into two golden patches.

When her face was finished, Sheridan looked in a mirror. The hazel eyes that stared back at her were familiar, but nothing else was. She felt like a Las Vegas showgirl.

"You're beautiful," Echo said.

Did he mean it? Did he really think this sort of glitter was attractive? Perhaps it was his way of telling her he was still interested in her even though he'd spent half the day on the computer with Taylor.

Well, it wasn't going to work.

His voice turned silky. "Although you'd be beautiful no matter what sort of dyes you used."

It still wasn't working.

He tilted his head, appraising her, then grinned.

Okay, it was working just a little bit. But only for the moment. Once he stopped giving her that intimate smile, she would regain her senses. By bedtime, she would be completely over Echo.

chapterhapter
18

At bedtime, Sheridan was not completely over Echo. As she sank into the soft warmth of her gel bed, she told herself that he wasn't really that attractive, that there wasn't a sort of calm strength about him. He was a spinning womanizer.

Taylor went over to the computer in the corner of the room and turned off the record function. "Echo taught me a ton about programming and splicing," she said, and walked back to her bed. "He really is smart. You ought to see what he can do to get around encryption."

"How romantic."

"Romantic?" Taylor crawled into her bed. "Are you jealous because Echo spent the afternoon helping me on the computer?"

"Of course not. And he spent the afternoon *and* most of the evening helping you."

Taylor rolled her eyes. "You *are* jealous. I can't believe you, Sheridan. The guy is part of the Dakine. That's like having a thing for someone in the Mafia." She tilted her chin down. "If you're not careful, you'll end up doing something stupid to endanger us."

"Something stupid?" Sheridan turned over on her side to better see her sister. "You mean like pretending to be a man and publishing papers that have future scientists dredging the past to find you?"

Taylor flinched, then stuck her chin out defiantly. "I couldn't have known what people four centuries later were going to do. Besides, I had to create another persona. No one would have taken a fifteen-year-old girl seriously."

Sheridan propped herself up on her elbows. "Wait a second—Sherwood was my screen name when we were fifteen. Why did you use it as your last name?"

Taylor shrugged. "Sherwood Forest was a hidden place that kept Robin Hood safe. It just seemed fitting."

"Right. You go on and on about wanting your own identity, but you take my stuff easily enough."

Taylor ignored the accusation. "The Time Strainer apparently retrieves everyone with the DNA it's looking for. In our case, that meant both of us. I'm sorry you got dragged into this too."

Sheridan shifted her pillow. "So why did you use Tyler for your first name?"

Taylor turned on her back, one hand twisting through her newly whitened hair. "I didn't. They're pronouncing Taylor wrong."

"Well, they'll figure it out eventually, so we've got to leave soon. What plan did you and Elise come up with?"

Taylor continued to stare at the ceiling. The only sound in the room was an electrical hum from the computer. "With the passwords Echo hacked from the Scicenter today, he was able to remotely link into the Time Strainer research site. I found a lot of interesting data. I'm still absorbing it."

Sheridan watched her sister, waited. "Is it possible to get the Strainer to send us back to the past?"

"Not with their design, although theoretically time travel to the past is possible. I might be able to come up with a design that would work—but I still think it's too dangerous. I wouldn't want something like that to fall into the wrong hands." Taylor turned over on her side, and the gel bed conformed to her shape so she looked like a magician's assistant who'd been cut in two. "Speaking of theories, get this: they used my theories on the structure of matter to make the Time Strainer. Talk about your work coming back to bite you." Her lips drew together in determination. "Whatever else happens, I'm not helping them. I don't know why they thought I would. If anything, I'll think of a way to stop their Time Strainer so they can't kidnap anyone else. I just need to figure out how."

"You said you wanted to go shopping tomorrow. Didn't that mean we're escaping then?"

Taylor put her hands underneath her head and shut her eyes in thought. "The Time Strainer converts matter into energy and preserves it in the form of an energy flux wave. Energy flux waves are timeless—without the constraints of existing in a certain time period—so the scientists here bring that energy to their coordinates and reconvert it back to matter. . . ."

Sheridan tapped her fingers against the top of her mattress. "We need to think of something to tell Echo about leaving."

"The Time Strainer uses energy signals from DNA to find its victims. It searches with the same accuracy as the Find function of a computer."

"Did I mention Echo asked me if we had talked to Elise yet?"

"With Echo's help, I might be able to hack into the Time Strainer's mainframe and create a program to shut it down, but what's to stop them from building a new one? They might even be able to overcome the repulsive field from the dark energy next time."

"What?"

"Dark energy. Space is filled with low-grade energy created when virtual particles and their antimatter partners momentarily pop into and out of existence. It leaves a tiny field called vacuum energy, which produces a negative pressure, or repulsive field."

Sheridan turned onto her back. "You know, this made more sense when the Time Strainer was a freezer and I was an ear of corn."

Taylor's gaze flashed over to Sheridan, shocked, and then pleased. "A freezer, yes—you're brilliant." Taylor sat up, cross-legged, and held her hands in front of her. "I've been looking at it from the wrong end. That's why it didn't make sense. I was only looking at what the scientists were working on, but I should have paid attention to what they weren't working on."

Sheridan stared at the ceiling. "Are you ever going to explain this so it makes sense?"

"Think of the freezer in our house and pretend you found an ear of corn in it. The corn could have been from last year's crop, or a crop ten years ago—maybe even thirty years ago, but it couldn't have been from two hundred years ago. Why is that?"

"Because Mom would have noticed a two-hundred-year-old ear of corn in our freezer and thrown it away. And besides, they didn't have freezers back then."

"Right," Taylor said, gaining momentum. "To freeze something, you need a freezer, and to change something from matter into energy, you need a machine with that capability. Not now, but back then. Back in our time period. Then you send signals to it from this time period, telling it what to put in the freezer." Taylor placed one hand across her eyes and let out a groan. "The horrible part is that I know what machine they're using. I helped invent it."

Sheridan turned onto her side to better glare at Taylor. "You invented a time freezer?"

Taylor let out an offended huff. "It wasn't *supposed* to be a time freezer. I just wanted to prove you could transport matter from one location to another by changing it to an energy flux wave first."

Sheridan rubbed her forehead, trying to ward off the beginnings of a headache. "Couldn't you have done that without inventing a machine that zaps people into the future?"

"It's a quark-gluon plasma converter—a QGP." Her voice took on the patient tone she used for explaining science to Sheridan. "At high enough temperatures and densities, atoms come completely unglued from one another, forming a plasma of quarks and the energy that binds quarks together. At even higher energies, the plasma transmutes into an energy flux.

"The QGP was my doctoral experiment. Dr. Branscomb got the funding for it and was helping me keep it secret until we'd worked out the bugs." Taylor flung her hands upward. "It was only supposed to be for testing. What in the world did he do to it?"

She pushed herself off her bed and stomped back over to the computer, tossing her hair off her shoulder as though the new length annoyed her. She sat down with a thud and typed on the keyboard.

"What are you doing?" Sheridan called.

"I'm checking the history logs for information on Branscomb, to see if anyone ever recorded where he got his funding from." She stopped for a moment and muttered, "Everything before 2200 is encrypted, but if I could access . . . How did Echo get around that again . . . ?"

"Should we call Echo and ask for his help?"

"I'll figure it out. If Echo can do it, so can I. I'm not about to be shown up on a computer by some glorified English researcher."

"Wordsmith," Sheridan said, "and your disdain for people outside the science field is irritating."

Taylor didn't answer, and it was pointless to say anything else. Taylor wouldn't turn her mind to tomorrow until it was finished with the past. Sheridan lay back down on her bed and closed her eyes while she listened to the hum of the computer and the tap of Taylor's fingers against the keyboard.

Finally the tapping stopped. "He died."

"Well, obviously."

"No, Branscomb died three days after we left. His obit record says he died in an accidental lab fire." Taylor sat back in her chair, still staring at the screen. "Three days after we were taken."

An obit record? If Taylor could access those, that meant they might be able to find their family's records. She could learn how long each had lived, who their brothers had married, and how many children they'd had.

She opened her mouth to ask, then shut it. She didn't want to know. Not yet. Right now she wanted to remember them as she had left them. Young, happy, and only a little bit out of her reach. She wanted to believe that after she and Taylor left Traventon, Taylor would build a time machine that would take them back.

Taylor stared at the screen. "Something must have gone wrong with the QGP. If I had been there, Professor Branscomb might not have died." Then Taylor put her hand to her mouth, her finger crisscrossing against her lips. "Or maybe *I* would have died too. Maybe that's how I was *going* to die, and I should be grateful that I got time strained out of there."

"I don't understand," Sheridan said. "If the QGP was what turned us into energy waves, it had to be working *before* we were strained, didn't it? Why would it not be working three days later?"

"You're right. It had to be working." Taylor turned back to the computer, and her fingers tapped against the keyboard once again. After a few minutes, she said, "Listen to this: Dr. Don Reilly, Professor Branscomb's partner, gave a eulogy at the university. 'Dr. Branscomb's sacrifice in the quest for knowledge will not be in vain. I will continue my work and my experiments on the quark-gluon plasma converter in the hope that I can unlock the secrets of mass and energy we have so long sought after.'"

Taylor sat back in her chair openmouthed. "*His* work? I can't believe this. I never even spoke to the guy, and he took credit for my ideas. He stole my QGP."

"And may have killed your professor." As soon as Sheridan said it, she dismissed the idea. She had read too many spy thrillers. Professors didn't go around killing one another. She waited for Taylor to refute the notion, but Taylor didn't.

Which told Sheridan that there was money to be made with the QGP.

"How did he even know about it?" Taylor asked. "It was a secret."

"Dr. Branscomb must have told him."

"Branscomb was the one who insisted I keep everything a secret."

"Of course he did. He wanted to make sure he could take credit for your idea. What was the patent worth?"

Taylor's eyes narrowed at something on the screen, and Sheridan got up and went over to see what it was. A grainy picture of Don Reilly stared back at her. He would have looked like any other balding middle-aged man, but his expression, even in picture form, had an air of self-importance about it. His lips were slightly pursed, disdainful of something—perhaps humanity in general. He had bushy, unkempt eyebrows and a long thin nose, but his most noticeable features were jowls that hung down, making his face blend into his neck.

"If Reilly did kill Branscomb," Taylor said, "he had to have known the QGP was working. But I wasn't done with the programming."

"So Branscomb sold you out and finished the machine on his own. Maybe he needed Reilly's help. Whatever happened, before he could steal the credit from you, Reilly stole it from him."

Taylor glowered at the screen. "The love of physics. That's what Branscomb always said motivated him. Right. I'm glad he's dead. He deserved it."

"You don't mean that."

Taylor shot Sheridan a look that indicated she did indeed mean it.

Sheridan decided to change the subject. "Do you think Reilly knew about you?"

Taylor leaned back in her chair. "I guess it doesn't matter. I disappeared three days before the accident. Must have been awfully convenient for him."

"But someone knew about your involvement. Scientists wouldn't be searching for you four hundred years later if you hadn't gotten credit somewhere along the line."

"They aren't searching for me—they're searching for Taylor Sherwood, the pen name I used on papers in science periodicals." Taylor leaned forward again, her hands busy on the control panels.

An obit picture of Reilly came up. It looked about the same as the last picture they'd seen, except that he was smiling. It didn't improve his looks that much.

"What do you know?" Taylor said. "Reilly had an early

demise too. He disappeared two months later."

"Disappeared?"

Taylor scanned the article. "He went to work and never came home again."

"You worked on the machine and disappeared, then he took credit for it and disappeared. Do you think the scientists used the Time Strainer on him?"

"I hope they did." Taylor scowled at his picture. "It would serve them both right. Reilly will realize he missed out on his ill-gotten gains, and the scientists here will have someone who probably never conceived an original idea in his entire life. A perfect match."

But not so perfect if he knew too much. "Taylor, did Branscomb know you'd published as Taylor Sherwood?"

Taylor exited out of the obit record. "Yes, but Branscomb wouldn't have told Reilly about me. Not when he didn't want to share the credit." She pushed away from the desk, stood up, paused, then sat back down on the chair. She put her hands on the desk, then two seconds later raked them through her hair. "Do I leave before the scientists find out who I am, or do I stay and figure out a way to keep them from taking anyone else?"

Sheridan didn't answer.

"If I stay," Taylor went on, "I put my life and my sister's life in danger. If I go, they'll keep using the Time Strainer to take anyone who'll give them an advantage in the present. Scientists, leaders, enemies. Who knows how much damage they'll do?" Taylor swiveled in her chair to face Sheridan. "But Elise said she could take us to meet her contact tomorrow—as soon as we can get away."

Sheridan still didn't say anything. The two options struggled against one another in her mind. Which was better?

Softly, Taylor said, "Maybe you should go with Elise and leave me here."

Sheridan shook her head. "How would you ever get out of the city? How would we find each other again?"

Taylor lifted her hands, then let them fall back into her lap. "All right, then tell me what to do. You decide if we stay or leave in the morning."

It wasn't usual for Taylor to hand over decisions to Sheridan, and she didn't know how to answer. "Why do you want me to decide?"

"Because," Taylor said, frustrated, "whatever I decide will affect you too. Besides, you're better with moral decisions. Right now, all I can think about is that if we delay going, I'll probably be caught and then my good intentions will be for nothing."

Sheridan let out a slow breath while she considered the matter. "I thought you said that if you destroyed the Time Strainer, the scientists would just build another one."

"Yes, but they can't build another QGP back in the past. And without a functioning QGP in the past, they won't be able to take people from the last four centuries, change them into energy waves, and reconfigure them inside the Time Strainer now."

Sheridan turned this over in her mind. "How can you destroy something in the past?"

"The Time Strainer sends signals back through time to the QGP telling it who to change into an energy flux wave, so if I was able to send an autodestruct command, I could effectively seal off the past."

"How long would that take? Days? Weeks?"

"Please." Taylor gave an insulted toss of her head. "I helped create the QGP. I could program a destruct command tonight. Getting into the Scicenter to a place where I can send it will be the hard part."

"Echo could get you in."

"We can't depend on him. He's Dakine."

Maybe, but even if Echo was Dakine, he had to understand the danger the Time Strainer posed to everyone—to the Dakine too. "He'll help you," Sheridan said.

Taylor wrinkled her nose in distaste. "I don't know . . ."

"You said it was my decision," Sheridan reminded her. "We can ask for Echo's help in the morning. It will only delay us a few hours."

Taylor sighed in resignation, then turned to the computer. "Fine, I'll get started on the destruct command."

Sheridan settled herself in bed and shut her eyes, listening to the rhythm of Taylor's fingers. In the darkness of her mind, she saw the picture of Reilly hovering in front of her. The man was probably a murderer and he might already be here.

chapter
19

When Sheridan awoke, Taylor wasn't in bed. She probably hadn't slept at all. As Sheridan dressed in the hideous purple-and-red-striped outfit, she could hear her sister and the others talking in the main office.

Jeth said, "The word *okay* was used so frequently in your time period; what did the initials stand for?"

"Oklahoma," Taylor answered.

There was a long pause; then Jeth said, "Why did Oklahoma mean something was all right?"

"Because Oklahomans were that way. I mean, none of the world's problems ever originated in Oklahoma."

If their dad was right, and liars went to hell, Taylor was going to be in *so* much trouble. The wordsmiths would probably start injecting the word Oklahoma into casual conversation now, like they were all part of the musical.

Sheridan brushed her hair, then walked out to the main office. Echo turned from the computer he'd been working on and smiled, letting his eyes linger on hers. It seemed like such a genuine smile, not one that could be full of dark secrets.

She sat next to Taylor on the floral couch and picked up a roll from a tray on the coffee table. "So are your ducks in a row after burning the midnight oil?"

Taylor had never liked nuts and was picking them off her roll. "I think I can make my little Frankenstein kick the bucket, but we're still between a rock and a hard place. We'll be walking a fine line, and we could find ourselves up the creek without a paddle. You sure you don't want to jet?"

Sheridan took a bite of her roll. It tasted like maple syrup. "I'm not letting you give me the brush-off."

Taylor flicked another nut onto her plate. "Fine. I'll try to nip this thing in the bud, lickety-split so we can split."

Sheridan glanced at Echo, then looked away when she saw he was watching her. "We need a helping hand."

Taylor nibbled a bite of roll. "Ten-four. We'll cut a deal with Romeo."

"Is everything okay with your breakfast?" Jeth called over. "Sometimes I can't understand your comments."

"Everything is wonderful," Taylor said. "Sheridan and I were talking about how good the food is here."

They both took large bites of their rolls to prove the point.

Jeth swiveled in his chair to better look at them. "I never realized how much slang people used in the old twenties. I'll have to catalog it. It would make a fascinating study, don't you think, Echo?"

"Fascinating." Echo didn't look fascinated. He looked suspicious.

Sheridan gave him a weak smile, then turned back to Taylor. "The clock is ticking. I'll stay here and shoot the breeze. You ask Echo to give you a hand."

"A hand?" Echo repeated. "What do you mean?"

Taylor took another bite of her roll. "I need to interview you privately. It's normally the father's job, but since our father isn't here, I'll have to do it."

Echo raised an eyebrow. "Interview me?"

"Yes." Taylor finished off her roll and brushed the crumbs from her hands. "Back in our day, when a guy started dating a girl, the father interviewed him. You know, asked him about his intentions and stuff. Well, after yesterday, it's only proper that I interview you."

Jeth brightened. "I'm familiar with that custom. I saw it referenced in a movie from the mid-twentieth century. It was still in practice at your time?"

"Oh yes," Taylor said. "And it has to be done privately. And it might take a while." She stood up and strolled over to Echo. "Are you ready?"

"Do I need to bring anything?"

"Just yourself."

He stood and walked out of the room with Taylor, and neither looked back at Sheridan.

If Echo really cared about her, wouldn't he at least have glanced back as he left? The thought prickled, and it bothered her that it was bothering her.

She had to stop thinking of Echo that way. Taylor was right. It was like having a thing for a guy in the Mafia. All that was important was that Taylor find a way to destroy the QGP before it took anyone else. Then they could find their way to someplace safe.

Sheridan finished her roll and settled in to answer Jeth's questions. As they talked, her gaze traveled around the room, landing on the cabinet with the etched-glass front.

She tried not to stare or show any reaction, but she noticed it immediately. The gun was gone.

chapter chapter
20

chapter

Echo walked into the hallway with Taylor, taking note of her agitation. The interview was apparently a stressful thing. He wondered why.

"This 'hand' request," he said, "it doesn't actually involve some sort of severed hand, does it?"

Taylor caught hold of Echo's arm and pulled him down the hallway. "Of course not, it's just a saying."

"What does it mean? And what did giving hands have to do with dating?"

"Nothing."

Which meant Taylor didn't want to tell him. He knew giving hands had *something* to do with romance. He had studied enough historical marriage documents to know the term *take her hand in marriage.*

Taylor kept pulling him along at a quick pace as though she knew where she was going—or perhaps this was part of the ritual. Perhaps you pulled a guy around before you spoke of relationships, which might explain the phrases *leading him on*, *leading him around by the nose*, and *pulling your leg*.

They stopped in front of the elevator. Taylor pushed the button, and the doors slid open. He held on to her arm so she couldn't go in. "Where exactly did you want to go for this interview?"

"The Scicenter."

He didn't move. "We're not allowed to walk into any building we want."

The elevator door slid shut. Taylor pushed the button to open it again. "I have a lot to explain and not much time. We can talk in the car on the way over. If you don't want to help me, you can turn the car around and bring me back here, all right?"

She stepped into the elevator, and he reluctantly followed. When the door slid shut, he pushed the button that would take them to the parking lot. "Start explaining."

She took a deep breath. Her voice was calm even though her fingers tapped against the elevator handrail nervously. "You know about history. You've studied it. You must understand how dangerous the Time Strainer is. All of history could be changed. When you strain people, you don't just take them out of the time line, you take their descendants and everything those people did. If you strain the wrong person, nations could be wiped out."

Echo leaned against the wall and watched the floor numbers flash by. "I realize the Time Strainer is dangerous. What does that have to do with Sheridan and me?"

Taylor's arm fell to her side, slapping against her leg. "Nothing. I'm not talking to you about Sheridan. That was an excuse she and I came up with so I could explain to you why you have to help me destroy the Time Strainer."

He laughed. He couldn't help himself even though it was clear from her expression that she was serious. She expected the two of them to go to the Scicenter, walk into the restricted room where the Time Strainer sat—and what? Kick the thing until it broke? "You're wasting your time by even suggesting such a thing. And don't lie to me again. I'm a historian. I want to hear the truth, not fabrications you've made up to—" He let out a sigh. "What else did you lie about? The schools?"

"No, I just lied this time because I need your help."

He rolled his eyes. "You said you wanted to study *literature* in school. I should have known that wasn't true. You expect me to believe colleges gave out degrees for reading novels?"

Taylor held her hands up in the air. "Okay, you're right. I studied math, physics, and computers. And if you can splice into a program that accesses the Time Strainer signals, I can keep it from working."

The elevator stopped, and the doors slid open on the parking lot level. Echo didn't step out. "I understand how you feel about the Time Strainer, but it took our scientists years to develop and build it. Just because I know how to computigate doesn't mean I could sit down and figure out a way to destroy it."

The doors remained open. The elevator sensors could tell they hadn't left. He reached for the button to take them back to the Wordlab, but Taylor grabbed his hand. "I can do it, Echo."

"You don't understand our technology."

"But I understand the technology from my day, and once I destroy that, the Time Strainer won't work anymore. There won't be any more energy streams for it to reconfigure into people." She still held on to his hand so he wouldn't push the elevator button. "I already know how to do it," she said. "Just help me gain access to the right computers."

Her gaze didn't waver from his eyes. She was serious. She thought she could do it.

"You don't realize the difficulty of what you're suggesting. How could you . . . ?" And then he understood. In that one moment he saw Taylor differently. His hand dropped to his side, the dread of the situation outweighing the excitement. "You're Tyler Sherwood, aren't you?"

She gazed out at the parking lot and didn't answer.

He swore, then rubbed at his forehead. "Are you sure you can stop the Time Strainer?"

She nodded.

He walked out of the elevator, and Taylor followed. Sneaking into the Scicenter with the scientist the government was searching for was both dangerous and stupid. But he had no choice now. Taylor was right. A functioning Time Strainer was even more dangerous.

chapter 21

Echo watched Taylor's hands fluttering over the keyboard. He could tell her lack of familiarity with the board frustrated her, that she wanted to go faster than she did; and as it was, the numbers on the computer screen appeared in rapid course.

Sensatogy was the word people used to describe those who could computigate—who could understand, no, *see* math and programming as though it was as easy as writing words.

Years ago he'd heard his teachers use the word *sensatogy* describing him. They said he ought to work in the city's programming department. He hadn't wanted to work for the government, though. Too many rules, too many authority figures to please. Besides, he'd heard programmers were pressured to join the Dakine. It was better for him to work for Jeth. Much more comfortable. Safer.

Funny how your fears had a way of finding you no matter what you did.

A memory ran through his mind: he and his brother playing light ball in a VR center. It was almost their sixteenth birthday, and the deadline for submitting career applications was nearing. All that week, their class had listened to teachers lecture about the responsibilities of being an adult. "Don't pick a career that you want," the students were told again and again. "Pick a career that the city *needs*." Loyalty to the city produced self-respect. Self-respect produced happiness. And didn't they want to be happy?

Echo had not only ignored that particular advice, he had turned the whole "self-respect equaled happiness" saying into a joke. He'd spliced into the city's datalinks and posted a listing: *Self-respect for sale. Bargain priced.* He'd put the school director's comlink number as the contact information. The day after that, Echo had posted an ad in the personals: *Desperate woman looking for man with self-respect. Rank not an issue.* That one had their science teacher's comlink info. She had always been a pain. Then the next day there had been the fake news story: *Enforcers uncover criminal group selling covert self-respect. Saddened citizens proclaim, "But where will we buy affordable self-respect now?"*

Echo didn't get caught. He was skilled enough at splicing that it couldn't be traced. Still, everyone at school knew who had done it, and his rank that week soared.

"Which means the teachers were right," Echo had said as he aimed the ball at a moving yellow light on the wall. "Self-respect does produce happiness." He shot and hit a light, making it disappear. "I'm going to love programming."

Joseph caught the ball on the bounce-back and dribbled to the opposite wall. He hadn't hit as many of his lights, and the green ones were multiplying. "We can't be programmers. Too much stress. They all die early."

Echo jogged up to him, positioning himself to catch the bounce-back. "But programmers live better. Think of our ranks."

Joseph shot at a green light zipping across the wall. He missed, and it split in two. "Who cares about ranks?"

Echo recovered the ball. "Girls. Friends. Apartment managers. Employers. Strangers . . ." He jogged to the opposite wall, fending off Joseph's attempts to steal the ball. "Did I already say girls? *Pues*, it's worth saying twice."

"So we'll work for Dad and find a way to splice into the rank program. Then you can change your number to whatever you want. I think one hundred fifty-two would fit you."

"And that wouldn't be dangerous—cutting into the city's most guarded program." Echo threw the ball, and a yellow light blinked out.

He leaped for the bounce-back, but Joseph reached it first. "What's life without a challenge?"

Joseph jogged down the court, and Echo followed, grinning. "I've thought of my next news story: *Enforcers uncover criminal group selling covert challenges. Saddened citizens proclaim, 'Where will we buy affordable challenges now?'*"

Joseph dribbled the ball, hardly paying attention to the green lights. "Dad would be easy to work for. It will be fun. Besides, if you don't agree, you know I'm going to pretend to be you and put in your application for the Wordlab anyway." Joseph bounced the ball back and forth between his hands, presenting both sides of the argument. "Fun. Stressful. Fun. Stressful."

"Fun," Echo said, and swiped the ball away from him. He ran down the court laughing.

The two of them were so used to working together, to being together, they hadn't even considered choosing different careers. Maybe if they'd had different jobs . . . But it was no use going over it endlessly in his mind.

He brought himself back to the present, concentrated on the sensor clip he had taken off his belt. The screen read zero. Good. There was still no one within thirty feet of them. Occasionally he got a reading in the beyond-thirty-feet category, but that was just people passing by in the main hallway.

If someone came down the corridor that led to this room, Echo still didn't know what he'd do. He couldn't come up with a good excuse as to why Taylor and he were even in the Scicenter, let alone sitting in front of a computer in a restricted area.

Echo gave his sensor one last check, then looked back at the computer screen, following the symbols as they appeared. His job had been to splice into the Time Strainer's main command program, a task that was harder and had taken longer than he'd imagined. The scientists had done a good job protecting this programming, layering encryptions with a maze of wrong turns and warning bells. If Echo hadn't been able to see the program as a whole, to see the symbols as though they were a giant picture, he wouldn't have been able to navigate his way through it.

Now he waited silently for Taylor to finish typing in her command. She was using the same frequency that the Time

Strainer used to contact the QGP. Instead of requesting it to find and turn someone into energy, the signal would instruct the QGP to turn its own casing from matter into energy. The blast would destroy the QGP, and fortunately, there was no way to send anyone back in time to fix it.

Echo glanced down at the sensor. Still zero. He was glad he had it with him. He'd built it three years ago on a whim. Admittedly, it was a dangerous whim since such sensors were illegal, but the project had tempted him with its ease. Everyone wore tracking crystals. How hard could it be to create the software that would tell him when someone approached?

He'd kept it hidden in a drawer, forgotten, until the Dakine killed his brother. Then he'd added a new feature to it: a signal-jamming detector. If the sensor ever lost all signals, it would vibrate to let him know Dakine assassins were near.

Echo wore it clipped onto the inside of his belt next to two other illegal devices, which he'd spent the last month building: a lock disabler and a laser disrupter.

Echo hadn't needed the lock disabler to sneak into the Scicenter. He and Taylor had coincided their entrance with the morning shift change and they'd simply strode inside, past the front station with the crowd of incoming workers. The hallways had been so full that no one paid any attention to them as they branched off and went into the restricted area. And once they were there, no one had been around to see Echo use his lock disabler on the door.

Leaving would be harder.

They couldn't stay here till the next shift change. That was seven hours away. They would have to find a time when the hallways were empty. True, the building's surveillance cameras would record that they'd been here. Eventually the scientists would figure out what had happened, but by then Echo would be out of the city.

Echo fingered the clip that kept the disrupter hooked inside his belt. It wasn't a perfect invention. He could use the device only once. The disrupter put out such a strong electromagnetic pulse that it not only froze nearby laser boxes, it destroyed itself in the process. He had engineered it in case he needed to escape from Dakine assassins. He hadn't ever imagined he might have to use it in the Scicenter.

Echo watched Taylor's symbols marching across the screen and tried to quell his impatience. "You created a recursive loop there," he whispered, and pointed to the screen.

"I know. I have to give the security codes something to do while I access the database."

"Oh." He nodded. "I'm impressed."

"Don't be. I was up all night figuring this out, and I'm still not positive it will work."

As if all night was a long time to come up with this type of program.

Taylor pushed the Send command, then sat back and watched the screen. Her eyes darted across the rows of numbers that returned. "It didn't work. The signal bounced back as inaccessible."

"Check your input for a mistake."

Her foot jiggled against the floor in frustration. "There isn't a mistake. It's . . ." She sat forward in her seat, and her fingers flew over the panels again. "It's something that someone else did to it. So I can't turn off the QGP right after I left, but I bet I can turn it off after he left, and I happen to know the date that was."

Echo had no idea what she was talking about but didn't want to distract her by asking for explanations.

Taylor completed typing a sequence of commands, then copied and attached her earlier equations to it. "Let's try it now."

She hit the Send command, then clenched the armrests of her chair. This time when the numbers returned, they marched across the screen declaring the job was done.

"Bingo," she whispered.

Another new word. One that meant success.

Echo helped her with the shutdown functions, then turned his attention to his sensor. No one occupied the hallway in front of their room, but several people walked nearby in the next corridor. He and Taylor would have to wait until it was empty. Once they were in the main corridor, they'd hope for a clear path, or at least an empty room to dash into until they had another clear path.

It wasn't the best plan; and as he sat here watching his sensor, he could think of more and more problems with it. Still, what choice did they have?

chapter~~hapter~~
22

Sheridan sat on the floral couch and discussed the role of women in society.

"High heels weren't some sort of punishment inflicted by men on the female gender. Women chose to wear them because they thought high heels made them look elegant. No, really. They even paid a lot of money for them. Well, I don't know why anyone thought pointy toes looked elegant. They just did."

In between her explanations, she wondered how long it took to send a signal to the QGP. Any moment now Jeth was going to ask Sheridan exactly what a father's interview entailed, and then she'd have to make up some hugely inaccurate story like the gender-segregated-shopping thing yesterday.

No wonder Echo hadn't believed her about talking animals. It was so easy to lie about the past when it suited your purpose.

Elise sat across from Sheridan on the plaid couch, silent, arms folded. She was probably worried that Taylor was telling Echo about her Doctor Worshipping friends, afraid that by the end of the day the Enforcers would drop by to pay her a visit. Sheridan had no way to reassure Elise or explain anything.

Sheridan was in the middle of talking about why girls wore jeans with pockets, shirts with pockets, coats with pockets, and then carried everything they needed in purses, when Jeth's comlink beeped.

At first Sheridan was relieved. It had to be Echo and Taylor. They were calling to let everyone know where they were.

The wall lit up, and Helix appeared on the screen. Without issuing any sort of greeting, he barked out, "Where are the time riders?" His gaze landed on Sheridan and his brows furrowed. "Is that one of them?"

Helix didn't recognize her with her hair and face dyed. She hoped, wildly, that Jeth would deny it.

Instead Jeth stood up and nodded politely. "This is Sheridan. Taylor is out with Echo. Do you want me to beep him?"

Helix kept his eyes on Sheridan, a penetrating stare that made her insides shiver. "I'll talk to him myself. My men will come over to get that one."

Jeth remained calm. "What's the problem?"

"The problem is that not one of those scientists can read data. They're a bunch of vikers, and unless you want to be equated with their incompetence, you'll keep that girl tight. They're property of the Scicenter. You've no reason to let them wander the city."

A cold shower of dread drenched Sheridan. Helix knew.

The scientists had finally figured out that the Time Strainer hadn't malfunctioned but had just brought them twins. And one of them was Tyler Sherwood.

Taylor was in danger, and there wasn't a thing Sheridan could do to warn her.

The screen went blank, and Elise muttered in her modern accent, "Yesterday they wanted them memory washed, and today they're too valuable to wander in the city."

"*Pues*," Jeth said, "that's the government. They never know what they want, and it's always your fault."

Sheridan realized she should say something. She should pretend she hadn't understood the call. "Did Helix find out I didn't have the memory wash?"

Jeth shook his head. "The appointment time hasn't come yet. They couldn't already know we deleted it." He relaxed his shoulders. "That's probably it. They decided not to do the memory wash and want to be sure the Enforcers don't take you. I knew they'd be reasonable about it."

Elise's face was still drawn with worry. Apparently she didn't share Jeth's confidence in the government's reasonableness.

Jeth unclipped his comlink and pushed a button. "We'll coordinate with Echo."

Sheridan stood up, urgency twisting inside her stomach. Her only hope was that Elise would be able to help somehow. Sheridan walked over, sat beside her, and whispered, "You can't let Helix take us."

Elise forced a smile. "They probably just want to run more tests."

Jeth strode over to the computer. "Why would Echo turn

off his comlink?" He gave a small laugh as he slipped his own comlink back onto his belt. "You'll have to tell me exactly what happens during these father's interviews. It must be highly interesting." Jeth fingered several panels on the computer, then froze. The smile dropped from his face, as did much of his coloring. "*Sangre*, this is a problem. . . ."

"What?" Elise asked.

"Echo's tracking crystal," Jeth said. "It says he's at the cemetery."

"The cemetery?" Sheridan repeated. Unless Jeth was about to explain that there were now sophisticated computers at cemeteries, something was very wrong.

Elise said, "Echo's crystal always says he's at the cemetery when he doesn't want anyone to know where he is. He must think no one will bother him if he's visiting his brother's grave."

Jeth took out his comlink again, pushing a button repeatedly. It beeped, but no one answered. "Helix won't care about disturbing him. He'll send Enforcers to the cemetery." Lines of worry gathered around Jeth's eyes. "I told Echo not to tamper with his tracking signal. It's illegal." He pushed the button harder, pacing now. "He needs to go to the cemetery or transmit his true signal. They'll think he's Dakine if he doesn't."

Sheridan nearly asked why, and then remembered. The Dakine had ways of keeping their crystals from being tracked.

Of course the government would think Echo was Dakine if they knew he could change his transmissions. Why hadn't Jeth come to the same conclusion?

But then, perhaps he knew and didn't care.

Could that be possible after his other son was killed by the Dakine?

Jeth strode to the door, still pushing his comlink button. "I'll search the building. If he comes back, tell him the situation."

Jeth didn't wait for an answer before he left.

chapter
23

Echo checked his sensor. The hallway still wasn't empty. Why were so many people walking the corridors? He sighed and watched Taylor twist strands of her long white hair around one finger. A nervous habit. Funny how people had the same nervous habits four hundred years ago. He wondered if they bit their nails back then too.

Then he chided himself for wondering. When had being a historian overtaken his life? Here he was with a fugitive from the government, pondering his safety, waiting for the right moment to escape, and he was still analyzing data.

Echo—the old Echo—would have at least made good use of the time by flirting. But then, the old Echo was dead, and there was only so much he could do to resurrect the persona.

Besides, he didn't want to land in another romantic tripod.

And Taylor reminded him of Allana: bold, flippant, and self-assured to the point of arrogance. Allana had ruined him for that sort of girl.

Sheridan, however—with her soulful eyes and earnest sincerity—she had a warmth to her like you felt before you drifted off to sleep. When you could finally relax. It was ironic that he'd met her now, a girl who intrigued him on so many levels, right when he hardly had a say as to what he did or who he was.

"The hall still isn't clear?" Taylor asked. "How long will we have to wait?"

"There's no way to tell."

She let out an exasperated huff, stood up, and walked restlessly around the room. "When do you think the scientists will figure out what we've done?"

"Hopefully not until we're away from Traventon." He stared at the clip as though this would help give him the reading he wanted. "What have you set up with Elise?"

Taylor looked at the door and not at him. "Nothing yet. Well, I mean, Elise wants to help, but she's not sure how. She's going to make some inquiries to see if she can connect with someone who knows someone who is a Doctor Worshipper. She said it might take a while."

Echo frowned. Elise wouldn't have to make inquiries. She knew people who were DW. She probably was a Worshipper herself. Which meant that either Taylor or Elise was lying. Probably Taylor. He wondered why.

The lights on Echo's sensor glowed, showing an increase in activity. More people were walking in the main corridor.

Some of them were moving quickly. Maybe they were late for a meeting.

"We've been gone too long," Echo said. "I'd better tell Jeth we went somewhere."

Echo turned on his comlink and saw a list of his missed calls, most of them with urgent notices. Jeth had also left him several messages. Instead of listening to them, Echo called his father.

Jeth answered immediately, his voice strained with anxiety. "Where are you? I've been beeping you every minute for the last fifteen minutes. Helix is looking for you. He said he was going to track your crystal."

Echo couldn't speak for a moment. It had already happened. By now, Helix was on his way to the cemetery. There was no way to fix it. Echo shut his eyes wearily. "What does Helix want with me?"

"It's not you he wants, it's Taylor. They've decided the girls are Scicenter property, and they're not allowed to wander in the city."

Sangre. That was life for you. Echo was about to be caught, and it wasn't even *him* the government was looking for.

Jeth said, "Just bring Taylor back here. I'll beep Helix, tell him you're at the Histocenter, and then we'll claim his tracking computer malfunctioned."

"He won't believe that."

"He might if you have Taylor with you."

Echo checked the sensor again. More signals. More people in the main corridor. It was only a matter of time before some of them came down the hallway to this room. He turned away from Taylor to give himself some privacy. "Listen, I want to tell you something. I love you. Joseph did too. Maybe neither of us said it enough, but we both felt it."

Jeth's voice came over the comlink, shaky. "You'll be fine. Just bring Taylor back, and everything will be fine."

"I love you, Dad." Echo shut off his comlink but didn't clip it back onto his belt. With the right equipment, comlinks could be traced too. When Helix didn't find Echo at the cemetery, he'd run a comlink trace. Echo couldn't be anywhere near his comlink when that happened. And yet he couldn't leave it here in the Scicenter either. That would be as good as telling the government what he'd done.

Reluctantly, Echo replaced the comlink on his belt. He'd have to destroy it once he got out of the Scicenter.

If he made it out of the Scicenter.

chapter 24

As soon as Jeth left the Wordlab to search for Echo, Sheridan turned to Elise. "We've got to leave. Right now. Before they come for me."

Elise held up one hand to indicate silence, then walked over to the computer to turn off the record function. It seemed to take forever this time, and Sheridan felt the anxiety running through her like an electric current.

At last Elise said, "I can't take you anywhere. They'd track me and find both of us."

Sheridan paced back and forth between the couches. "If you can't leave, at least show me where to go. Give me a map and tell me who to contact. They can't track me."

Elise shook her head. Lavender-and-pink hair swished angrily across her shoulders. "I told Taylor that Echo couldn't know anything about my friends or leaving. Absolutely nothing. And now she's out with him. Maybe she's trying to lead him to the friend I introduced her to yesterday." Elise folded her arms tightly across her chest. "She won't be able to. I took precautions, but *sangre*, I thought I could trust the two of you."

"You *can* trust us. Taylor won't tell Echo anything. She knows he's Dakine."

Elise's arms remained folded. "Then why are they together? Don't give me that excuse about an interview. Echo could have told Taylor his intentions for you with one word: none. And why did Echo mask his signal and turn off his comlink?"

The door to the wordsmiths' room was still closed. That didn't mean the Enforcers weren't already in the building, though. It didn't mean they weren't walking down the hallway. "I can explain, but we need to leave first." Sheridan took a step toward the door, then a step back to Elise. "We have to find Taylor and warn her."

"If either of us leaves this room, I'll face a questioning."

Sheridan had no choice. She had to tell Elise. "Taylor and Echo went to splice into the Time Strainer's mainframe computer. Taylor thinks she knows how to shut it down."

Elise let out a grunt and tilted her chin down in disbelief. "Why would Taylor know how to shut down such a complicated machine?"

"Because she built the other end of it—the part that works back in our time."

Sheridan couldn't hear the breath that Elise drew in, but somehow she still felt it. Elise was holding that breath like she

184

was a tightrope walker keeping her balance. "What do you mean?" she asked.

The record function on the computer was off; still Sheridan only mouthed the words, "She's Tyler Sherwood."

Elise shut her eyes and let out a shaky breath. *"Sangre."*

"Now will you help us?"

Elise turned back to the computer. Sheridan walked toward her. "What are you doing?"

"Silence," Elise hissed. She put her hand on a panel and said, "Jeth, Sheridan locked herself in the back room. I can't get in. I'm afraid she went out the window. I'm going to look for her. I'll be back as soon as I find her."

Elise removed her hand from the panel, pushed a few more buttons, then motioned for Sheridan to follow. Once they were in the back room, Elise tapped a button by the door to lock it. Next she opened the box-seat underneath the window. "Fire escape," Elise whispered, and pulled a tangle of white crisscrossed ropes that made up a flimsy ladder. Giant suction cups were attached at one end of the rope.

Sheridan stared at them. Really, with all the technology the future had, people couldn't come up with a better fire escape ladder than this? And suction cups—wasn't that about as safe in an emergency as, say, Velcro?

Elise attached the suction cups to the wall and lowered the ladder out the window. Without another word, she took hold of the ladder and heaved herself through the opening.

Sheridan watched the suction cups, ready to grab them if they slipped. They didn't, and when she looked out the window, Elise was several rungs down. She motioned for Sheridan to follow.

Sheridan gingerly straddled the windowsill and took hold of the rope. *Don't look down,* she told herself. She'd heard that advice somewhere. *Don't look down and don't think about how high up you are.* She swung her second leg out, feeling for the flimsy rope beneath her. Hard to do without looking down. She finally felt the rope underneath her foot and took a wobbly step onto the next rung.

As far as that *Don't think about how high up you are* piece of advice—yeah, that was pretty much impossible. What else could a person think about while clinging to a rope seven stories up? Dinner? Basketball? She was going to die, and not for some meaningful reason—it was going to be death by suction cup malfunction.

Her thoughts were interrupted by voices. Men's voices coming from the outer room of the Wordlab.

Sheridan took two hurried steps down the ladder, and then it slipped.

At first she thought the whole thing had fallen out of the window. She gripped the rope anyway, and stifled the scream erupting from her mouth. Even now, when there wasn't a point to her silence, she didn't want the Enforcers to know where she was. She couldn't stand the thought of them peering out the window and watching her fall to her death. In another minute, she was going to look really gruesome.

It was a prideful thought, and her father had always said that pride went before a fall. Apparently it came afterward too.

A moment later, Sheridan realized she wasn't falling. The rungs were sliding downward, fast-paced, but the top of the ladder was still attached up at the window. This wasn't a ladder at all; it was some sort of makeshift elevator.

Sheridan leaned her forehead against a rung, let out several trembling breaths, and took back everything she'd thought about ladders of the future. They were wonderful. She and Elise never would have been able to climb down in time to get away from the Enforcers. Now they had a chance.

The rungs jerked to a stop. They had reached the ground. Well, almost the ground. The ladder didn't actually reach all of the way, and she was dangling six feet in the air.

Elise dropped to the sidewalk, then waved to Sheridan. "Hurry!"

She jumped. Her feet hit the concrete, and she pitched forward. She steadied herself, then dashed after Elise into the parking garage.

Elise ran to the closest car, opened a door, and gestured for Sheridan to get in. Once she had, Elise said, "I'm sending you to Salima Street. You actually want to go to Los Angeles Avenue, but since the government will trace the car, I don't dare send you there. Once the car stops at Salima, walk two miles north until you reach Los Angeles Park."

Sheridan sat on the edge of the seat. "We need to go to the Scicenter. Taylor and Echo don't know Helix is looking for them."

"If I have time before the Enforcers find me, I'll beep one of my contacts to meet you at the park. Someone will approach you and ask if your name is Hermana. That's your contact."

"But Taylor—"

"If Taylor told Echo who she was—and she must have to get his help—she's already with the Dakine. Just be glad you weren't with her."

Elise reached into the car and pressed her hand to the control panel. "Salima Street." She stepped back as the door slid shut and the car hummed to life.

"Wait!" Sheridan pressed her hands against the window to catch Elise's attention. "I can't leave Taylor. I've got to help her."

Elise never turned back to look at the car. She jogged out of the parking garage, her lavender-and-pink hair swishing around her shoulders until she went out of sight.

Sheridan hadn't said good-bye to Taylor, and as she watched the fading parking garage, she realized she hadn't said good-bye to Elise either. And now she was alone.

chapter

25

Echo watched the dots travel across his sensor. It was horrible luck to be trapped in the Scicenter now. The scientists would be the first people notified of Taylor's absence. They were probably organizing search schematics right now. That made it harder to sneak out unnoticed.

He glanced at Taylor, at her long white hair and the blue makeup swirls on her face. The scientists might not recognize her. She looked so much like an average citizen now, and not like the colorless time rider the scientists had seen before.

And it was possible that not all the scientists knew of Taylor's disappearance. Perhaps the people they passed in the hallway wouldn't be suspicious.

Echo checked the dots on the sensor one last time before he clipped it back onto his belt. "How well do you run?" he asked Taylor.

"What?"

"I know most people from the old twenties were weak and unexercised, but can you run long enough to make it out of the building?"

"Yes," she said tightly, "I can make it out of the building and a good mile down the street before I have to rest. Honestly, where do you get your information?"

Echo ignored her question. "Don't run down the street. When we get out of the building, we'll head to the first car we see. They won't be able to track me, and with any luck we'll lose them in traffic."

Echo walked to the door, then paused before opening it. "You remember which way the front entrance is?"

"Yes, and my weak and unexercised body will beat yours out of the building."

"We'll try to make it the elevator without anyone noticing us. If someone looks like they're about to stop us, then we'll have to sprint down the stairs. They're through the door to the right of the elevator. We'll go down four flights. Any farther than that and you'll end up in one of the underground levels. Understand?"

She nodded, and before he could think about it any longer, before he could think about all the reasons this wasn't likely to work, he opened the door, and they slunk out of the room.

They made it to the first turn of the hallway without being seen. This was vital. It was one thing to be caught in the Scicenter without proper clearance. It would be unthinkable to be caught coming out of a restricted area. He let out a breath of relief as they turned into the main corridor.

Several people were walking in different directions. None seemed to pay any attention to them—yet. Echo could see the outline of the elevator down the hallway, a tiny metal rectangle set against white walls. He forced himself to keep his pace casual, to not draw attention to himself by a hurried gait.

A few heads turned as he walked by. That didn't mean they suspected anything. It was normal for people to glance at each other as they passed.

Taylor picked up her pace a bit, pulling slightly in front of him. *Not yet*, he wanted to tell her, *don't give them reason to notice you*, but he didn't dare speak.

More heads turned. A couple of men who had been talking in the hallway stopped and began walking after Echo. That might be coincidence.

Echo lengthened his stride. They were almost to the elevator. Another few seconds and they'd be there.

"You there," the man behind Echo said.

Echo pretended he hadn't heard.

"You," the man said in a louder tone. "Aren't you a wordsmith?"

Echo paused. Could he talk his way out of this situation, or was it better to take his chances running?

Taylor didn't give him the choice.

She took off in a sprint, reaching the door to the stairs and pushing the open button almost before Echo realized she'd gone. He turned and followed after her without another look at the men.

The stairwell was dimly lit. Echo's feet clanged heavily against the steps as he ran. Taylor took them three at a time, and Echo matched her pace, hoping he wouldn't fall. He couldn't remember the last time he'd used stairs, let alone run down them.

Other footsteps sounded behind them, so many that the pounding noise vibrated through the stairwell. Echo didn't look behind him. He didn't dare take his eyes off the steps. It was all he could do to unclip the laser disrupter from his belt. He'd have only one chance to use it.

They passed the door for the third floor, then the second. One more flight to go.

Echo couldn't tell if any of the men chasing them were Enforcers or just scientists. No one had fired at them, but that might be because they couldn't get a clear shot among the twists of the staircase. Once he and Taylor ran out into the hallway, there wouldn't be anything to prevent laser boxes from cutting them down. And if any of the men had called ahead to the security station—and why wouldn't they have?—the exits would be well guarded.

Echo ran his thumb along the side of his laser disrupter, feeling for the switch. He would have to time things exactly right so that all the Enforcers were within the disrupter's range. If even one of them was out of range, he and Taylor would be shot and captured.

Taylor reached the first-level door, hit the control button, and was through it before it slid halfway open. He followed after her, searching the hallway as he emerged into it. The elevator door began to slide open as he ran past, and he saw men poised to pour out of it. He sped forward, faster now that he was on level ground.

His thumb hesitated on the disrupter switch. The building

entrance was still a couple minutes away, and several Enforcers were heading toward it in front of him.

Even if he disabled every single laser box, he wouldn't be able to get through so many men. Could he at least hold them off so Taylor could escape? He had youth on his side, and the strength of having had a twin brother who enjoyed wrestling for entertainment. But he couldn't win against so many. Besides, Taylor couldn't survive in the city by herself. She couldn't even access a car for an escape route. If they fought, they'd both be dragged to detention rooms. And his sentence would be even worse for inventing and using the disrupter.

Echo slipped the device back into his belt, picked up his speed, and with one last burst of energy lunged into Taylor, bringing her to the ground.

She twisted, trying to free herself, then saw it was Echo who'd tackled her.

She hit him on the shoulder hard. *"What are you doing?"*

He shifted his weight, pinning her arms down. "You've got to go back to the office!" he shouted, using his modern speech. "Stop fighting!"

She didn't stop fighting. She flailed and kicked, repeating every old-twenties swearword he'd heard of and some he hadn't. Still, he kept her pressed to the ground while Enforcers surrounded them. Echo glared up at the men and the weapons pointed in his direction.

"Put your boxes away!" he yelled. "If you damage her, Helix will see you in the shredder."

"Maybe," one of the men said, "but he won't mind if we use them on you."

"Me? I had her under control—I was bringing her to Helix like he ordered—until some of the scientists decided to scare her. Now look at her. Helix wants to talk to her, and she's writhing around on the floor. Put away your weapons before you give her seizures."

Slowly, the Enforcers put their weapons back on their belts, but none of the men moved away.

Echo took hold of Taylor's hands and tried to keep her from biting him. "Calm down," he said, using the old-twenties accent so she'd understand. "I'll do what I can to help you. Do you understand?"

"I understand perfectly," she spat out between breaths. "You're a slimy, two-faced rat!"

Two-faced rat? He'd never heard of those. Must have been an animal mutation from all the pesticides in her time period.

"It won't do any good to keep fighting," he said.

Taylor's eyes burned like recharge coils, but she stopped struggling. She lay on the floor limply, breathing hard.

One of the Enforcers had been talking on a comlink. He turned it off and glared down at Echo. "That was Helix. He's on his way from the cemetery and said to put the girl in a detention room until he can get here. He also said your signal is still at the cemetery, and he wants to know what you're doing at the Scicenter."

Echo shrugged as though it were a simple matter. "His tracker must be frozen on my last location. When my father told me that Helix wanted Taylor, naturally I left the cemetery and came here to find her. Everything would have been *bien* if your men hadn't decided to play Dakine assassin and scare her brainless."

The man's eyes narrowed. He didn't quite believe the story, but he didn't contradict it. He just waved his hand at a couple of the men in the circle. "Take her to room twelve."

Echo moved aside and let them grab Taylor. One man took her arms, the other her feet, and they carried her down the hall like a trash receptacle. She tried to kick her captors, and Echo hoped she succeeded, but he didn't look into her face. He didn't want to see the accusation in her eyes.

Instead he stood up, brushing at the wrinkles in his clothes. "If you don't need me for any immediate translations, I'll go back to the Histocenter to help bring Sheridan over. I assume Helix wants her too?"

The man in charge tucked his comlink neatly into his belt. "Helix wants her. She isn't at the Histocenter, though. She and one of your wordsmiths vanished from the building after Helix's first call. We've got a track on them, so we'll have them here soon." His words were almost an accusation, a threat that the wordsmiths had better not interfere anymore. Echo straightened, refusing to show signs of intimidation. Intimidation implied guilt.

He lifted a hand in feigned frustration. "*You scared off the other one too?* Don't you understand the delicacy of the twenty-first-century mind? These girls came from a violent time. Any hint of danger is likely to set them off like cosmic rays!" Echo clenched his jaw to force a flush of angry color into his face. "I'll speak to Helix about your incompetence. Beep me as soon as he comes. Right now I'm going to find Jeth, and we'll put together a formal report about this."

Echo turned and walked to the entrance, muttering insults

about the science profession. And they let him go. He walked right out of the Scicenter without another question.

Once outside, he signaled for a car, then found the nearest trash incinerator and dropped his comlink inside it. When the car arrived, he climbed in and sat exhausted against its seat. He couldn't return to the Histocenter. It had only been luck that those men had let him go. They'd been so relieved to catch Taylor and so flustered by his accusations that they hadn't processed the matter clearly in their minds.

The story about Helix's tracker being frozen, *pues*, it was only going to take one check to realize that was fiction. Helix would know Echo was hiding something. Worst of all, when the scientists tried to use the Time Strainer again, Helix would figure out what Echo had done.

Would it be just a memory wash or death they ordered for him?

He could hide out among the crowds of Traventon for a while, but eventually the government would devise a way to track his crystal.

He thought of Taylor, kicking her way to the detention center, and Sheridan—out somewhere—with Enforcers closing in on her.

There was only one place he could go to for help now. He set the car's coordinates for Caesar's apartment and shut his eyes as the car hummed toward its destination.

chapter
26

Sheridan sat stiffly in the car, watching the Histocenter through the back window. Four Enforcers rushed out the building's door, each going a different direction, searching for her on the grounds.

She shrank down in the seat, even though she knew no one could see through the car's tinted windows. The melodic voice on the car's radio said, "A loyal citizen is a content citizen. We handle the complex, so your life can be simple. Simply fun. Simply easy. Simply a rank above the rest."

Sheridan kept watching the window. She didn't know whether the men could track the car since Elise had used her crystal to activate it, or whether they could only track Elise's present location. Sheridan waited, half holding her breath to see if any other cars emerged from the parking garage to chase her. None did.

She didn't relax. Too many fears rushed through her mind, tumbling her thoughts like fallen leaves in the wind. What would the Enforcers do when they found Elise?

Worse, what would they do to Taylor?

Sheridan gulped, struggling against the feeling of helplessness that engulfed her. From the moment she had woken up in Traventon, she had always depended on the fact that Taylor could get them to safety. Now Sheridan was alone and Taylor was— But that was the horrible part: she didn't know what had happened to Taylor. Maybe she would never know.

Sheridan shook her head, pushing away these dark thoughts. She didn't want to believe that Echo had turned Taylor over to the Dakine. Echo had masked his signal because he was breaking into the Scicenter, and he hadn't answered his comlink for the same reason. It didn't mean he had kidnapped Taylor.

The voice on the radio cooed out, "The government takes care of you. Take care of the government. Report any disloyal behavior you see to the Enforcement Department."

Sheridan noticed her hands were shaking. She sat on them to stop the trembling, and then found herself rocking back and forth on her seat. How could she help Taylor when she didn't even know where she was?

Think, Sheridan told herself. Taylor always said a person could find a solution to any problem if they just thought about it hard enough. Well, now Sheridan had plenty of problems; she needed some solutions.

Think of something.

Think of something.

Think of something.

Her mind whirled, and she couldn't stop it for long enough to think of possibilities, let alone solutions. She didn't even know where she was going or if anyone would be there to help her.

The car stopped. Was she at Salima Street already? She glanced at the control panel. The light that represented her car wasn't even halfway to the starred destination. The car hadn't lost power. The radio was still going on about the virtues of the government.

She peered out the window. Other cars were stopped too. Was it some sort of energy-grid malfunction? Maybe she would have to get out of the car and walk. She studied the lighted map on the dashboard, trying to memorize the directions to Los Angeles Park. If only she had something to write with.

Out of the corner of her eye, she noticed movement on the street. She looked up to see several Enforcers skimming around other stopped cars, rushing toward hers. Sheridan pressed her hands against the car door. "Open," she said. "Open right now." When it didn't, she hit it with her fist, then turned to the control panel and pushed everything that looked like a button and several things that didn't. "Let me out of here!"

The Enforcers were in front of her now, descending on the car like spiders ready to wrap their prey.

She searched the interior of the car for something to use as a weapon. Anything. There was nothing.

The doors slid open. She didn't see the faces of the men, only their hands. They reached into the car pointing laser boxes.

She heard a ripping sound, saw flashes, then her body

tightened as every muscle contracted. She couldn't breathe. Her lungs refused to move. The last thing she heard was the soothing voice on the car radio. "Happiness can't be purchased. Happiness can only be given to you by the city."

chapterhapter
27

Slowly, Sheridan's thoughts began to assemble themselves. Her fingers throbbed. Her limbs felt unnaturally heavy. Numb. She tried to move her hands and found them cuffed behind her back. She tested her legs. They were restrained too. She blinked, struggling to make sense of what was happening.

Two men were carrying her into the Scicenter. She wanted to move, to say something, but the numbness that had overtaken her body hadn't completely left her brain. Were they going to do a memory wash on her now?

She didn't want to forget her life, or Taylor, or Echo—although she wasn't sure what she wanted to remember the most about him: that he had kissed her, or that he was Dakine.

Why couldn't she think straight?

That had been her problem in the car. She couldn't think

her way out of her problems. Taylor would be so disappointed.

Sheridan lifted her head, and one of the men said, "She's awake."

She turned her head to see her captor—an orange-faced man wearing a black Enforcer's helmet. He looked back at her with stark contempt, so she turned her head away from him. It was getting easier to move. Her muscles were slowly warming and losing their stiffness.

The first man shifted his hands to get a better grip on her. "You gave us quite a time, little runner. We had to go through a kilo of tracking to find your car."

He turned his attention to the other Enforcer. "We should ask Helix to authorize a priority crystal implant on them both. We can't have them evaporating into air again."

The orange-faced man shook his head. "Helix wants them in detention until he's through with them. No chance they'll turn into vikers there."

Vikers? Through with them? What was Helix planning? She almost asked, then, with a jolt of returning clarity, remembered she wasn't supposed to be able to communicate with people from the future. She didn't want to let them know she understood them.

The men stopped in front of a metal door and set her on her feet. A detention cell, she supposed. The orange-faced man bent down and removed the bands that restrained her legs but left her arms shackled. She lost her balance, took a wobbling step, and straightened up. It felt like she was stepping on pins.

One of the Enforcers pushed the door button. Even before it had completely slid open, Sheridan recognized Taylor's voice.

It was raspy and hoarse, probably from yelling. Maybe from screaming. "I don't know anything about it," she said wearily. "I'm not who you're looking for."

The room looked like some sort of office. Computers, desks, and chairs lined the walls. Taylor was strapped into a chair in the middle of the room. A man with green hair and matching green lips leaned over her, menacingly. His face contorted into a sneer, and he slapped Taylor across the face. It must not have been the first time. Her cheeks were covered in bright red patches, and a trail of blood leaked from a corner of her mouth.

The man raised his hand again, and Sheridan lunged toward him. "Stop it!" She meant to kick him; she still had use of her feet.

One of the Enforcers grabbed Sheridan's hair and yanked her backward. Pain shot through her head and she stumbled, nearly falling to the ground. The green-haired man smirked at Sheridan, then struck Taylor again. The smack reverberated through the room, as did Taylor's cry.

The green-haired man straightened, tugged his shirt back into place, and let his gaze run over Sheridan. When he spoke, his accent was different from the ones she'd heard in Traventon. A mix between the past and the future. "Perhaps your twin is the one we're searching for then. Should she take your place in this chair?"

Taylor's chin dropped against her chest. Her words slurred. "You made a mistake. Why can't you accept that?"

The man turned away from Taylor and walked toward Sheridan with slow steps. "Perhaps you're right. Neither one of you looks smart enough to wipe your own snot, let alone build a QGP."

Sheridan hadn't noticed how old he was before. The strength of his blows made him seem young, but as he came toward her, she saw wrinkles sagging across his face like crooked cornrows. His jowls sank into his neck.

He stood in front of Sheridan, his face nearly level with hers. That was odd. All the men she'd met in Traventon were much taller. The rank badge on his shirt read 43, which meant looks didn't play into rank nearly as much as power did.

A smile turned up his lips as though he was playing the host. "You came in here ready to take me on even though your hands are cuffed. Are you brave, or just stupid?"

Probably stupid. "Brave," she said.

He nodded. "Glad to hear you're not stupid, because if you've a gram of intelligence, you'll tell me everything I want to know immediately. Are you Tyler Sherwood?" His jowls moved up and down as he spoke. Something about them tapped at the corner of her memory, and a moment later she knew what.

He was older, decades older than the picture she'd seen, but it was the same man.

"You're Reilly," she said.

His green eyebrows rose in surprise. "You know who I am?"

"Yes. You're a thief and a murderer."

Taylor tilted her head back against her chair and let out a slow moan. Sheridan knew what Taylor was thinking as well as if she had said the words out loud. *Don't tell him you know who he is. To tell him is to admit you have a reason to know him, to admit you're connected with Tyler Sherwood. Think it through!*

But Sheridan *was* thinking it through. Reilly already knew one of them was Tyler Sherwood. If they kept denying the fact, it would lead to more beatings. Eventually, Taylor would give in and tell him the truth. If one of them had to admit to being Tyler Sherwood, it should be Sheridan. It had to be, because she couldn't possibly betray any scientific knowledge.

"A thief and a murderer?" Reilly's face swung in threateningly close to hers, so close she could smell the scent of coffee on his breath. "I was the greatest mind of the twenty-first century."

"Well, I'm not sure about your mind, but you're certainly the most lively four-hundred-year-old man I've ever seen."

"Brave and flippant. Dangerous characteristics for someone who's handcuffed." Reilly motioned to one of the men behind her, and Sheridan winced. He wanted someone to hold her so she couldn't run while he hit her.

Instead, the enforcer took off her handcuffs.

Sheridan brought her hands in front of her and rubbed her wrists, eyeing Reilly warily. "How did you get here?" she asked. "Did the Time Strainer bring you here?" And if so, what had happened to age him so dramatically—an accident? She was not quite so brave or so flippant as to ask him that.

His lips twitched in between a smile and a frown. "I brought myself here inadvertently." While he spoke, he turned and leaned against a desk, nearly sitting on it. "I made a careless error while I was putting the finishing touches on the quark-gluon plasma converter. I can admit that, you see, because part of being a great scientist is knowing when you've made an error and knowing how to correct it."

He seemed to expect some sort of response from Sheridan at this point, so she nodded.

"While I was experimenting with the plasma stream," he

went on, "I accidentally caught myself in it. Very tricky business that plasma stream. Without DNA specifications, the QGP has a hard time distinguishing one piece of matter from the next. If I had been working with a colleague, he could have reversed the accident and changed my state from energy back into matter. It would have been so simple, but I was working alone. That was the first lesson I learned. No matter how much you want the credit, never work alone. It's too risky."

"Dr. Branscomb might argue it's too risky to work with you," Sheridan said.

Reilly didn't flinch at her accusation. "I admit I killed him. I also admit it was a shortsighted thing to do." He smiled at her, deepening the wrinkles around his eyes. "You're surprised I've confessed my crime. That's the nice thing about living in the twenty-fifth century. No one cares about a murder that happened four hundred years ago."

Sheridan's gaze cut over to Taylor. Her eyes were still shut, but her hands were clenched into fists. Sheridan forced her attention back to Reilly. "I suppose they also don't care that you stole my QGP."

"You admit to being Tyler Sherwood then?"

Sheridan felt herself trembling and tried to hide it by standing straighter. "Would my admission be more convincing if you had to beat it out of me first?"

He appraised her, unimpressed. "Well, Tyler Sherwood, the science chairman put me in charge of a project to replicate the QGP. So much of their scientific knowledge was lost during the twenty-second and -third centuries. All those plagues and wars and whatnot. They've been rebuilding everything for the last hundred years, starting from scratch on a lot of things. Scientists like us, we're needed now. We're appreciated."

The twenty-fifth century was not a foreign place for him. He was talking about it casually. She looked at his face more closely. "How long have you been here?"

He ran a hand along the keyboard of one of the computers, stroking it as if it were a pet animal. "Back in the twenty-first century, when I was first testing the QGP and determining its parameters on living matter, I decided to transform a geranium for seventeen days—four hundred and eight hours. I had the QGP on a timer so that the energy flux would automatically reconfigure into matter. I wanted to see if the geranium would remain in its unchanged form or whether there would be a substantial energy loss during the transformation, which would affect its cell structure."

Sheridan gulped. Pretty soon he would be throwing out unintelligible phrases and schematics, gibberish that only scientists understood.

Reilly gave a shake of his head, which made his jowls jiggle. "I was caught in the plasma stream myself, and reconfigured not four hundred and eight hours later, but four hundred and eight *years* later." He smiled at her again, showing unnaturally white teeth. "Those are the types of glitches that just irk a scientist, aren't they?"

"You don't seem too bothered by it."

"Oh, I was at first. *Sangre*, I couldn't understand most of what anyone said for the first month I was here. I hated the tiny apartment they stuck me in and resented government officials always hovering around me—keeping me a secret. But I came to understand that they were guarding me from the Dakine."

He ran his fingers down the corners of his mouth while he spoke, caressing a beard he didn't have. "Once I convinced the science chairman that I could build QGPs here, everything changed. I've spent the last two decades working not only on that, but on building the Time Strainer. So I'm quite adjusted now. I even see the many benefits to living in the future." He swept his hand toward the computers. "The lab equipment is far superior to anything we ever had. I've been able to make my QGPs one-twentieth of the size yours was. And scientists here are well salaried." He pointed to the number on his badge. "Do you know what this means?" He didn't wait for her to answer. "It means I can have anything I want. Food, entertainment, drugs"—his eyes ran over Sheridan, lingering on her curves in a way that made her shudder—"company. The more important the project is, the better salaried the scientists are. You, my dear, will be well taken care of."

"What project will I be working on?"

"Didn't I make that clear?" He pulled out one of the chairs by his desk and gestured for her to sit down. Reluctantly she did.

After she was seated, he sat down in the chair next to hers. He seemed to have forgotten not only that there were two Enforcers in the room but that Taylor was sitting, bleeding, not far from them.

"I haven't been able to get my QGPs to work properly." Reilly's lips twitched in annoyance as he said this. "Right now I can't keep the energy flux stable enough for any practical use. I can't even get the plasma stream up to the efficiency that your

208

prototype had. Virtual particles keep creating a repulsive field, and every so often I get gauge bosons popping up, causing the protons to decay. That's why I needed to bring you here: to help me build QGPs."

It didn't make sense to Sheridan. If QGPs were just the freezers of time travel—changing people into energy waves that the Time Strainer could reconfigure again later—why build more?

"Aren't you worried about changing the past?" Sheridan asked. "Even small changes could have disastrous effects—"

He didn't let her finish. "This isn't about tinkering with the past. Let the historians worry about that. This is about now. Think of the power the QGP will generate."

The chair felt stiff and uncomfortable against Sheridan's back. "The power? I'm four hundred years into the future, and you're telling me the world still hasn't solved the energy crisis?"

Reilly laughed as though she'd been joking. "I was talking about the power of a strategic weapon. A person can't hide from the QGP. If you have his DNA signal, and he's within range— then zap. You can change him into an energy flux wave. With modification, QGPs could be used to take out large groups of people. Think of it. Wars could be won without any physical destruction."

The word *destruction* landed on her ears with a thud. She put a hand to her throat. "You want me to help you kill innocent people?"

Reilly hit one hand against the side of the desk with a loud slap. His eyes grew razor sharp. "That's just the point. The innocent people will be spared. It's a weapon that will kill only our enemies. You haven't been here long enough to learn about our society, but there are divisive groups here: the Dakine and the DW. They could be completely eliminated with the QGP."

A weapon. He wanted to use Taylor's machine as a weapon. No, not Taylor's machine. Sheridan couldn't allow herself to think that way or she'd slip up. It was her machine, and she was brave and smart, and she wasn't going to let some second-rate scientist intimidate her. "I've seen enough of this society to know how the government runs. I don't think I trust their judgment as to who the enemies are."

Reilly crossed his leg, another habit she hadn't seen in the twenty-fifth century. "You realize what will happen if you refuse to help? You'll be given a memory wash. It will take away your memories, but not your intelligence. When your memories are gone, you'll have to be taught math and physics all over again, but in the process you'll be indoctrinated to our ways. Then you'll help us, and you'll have no qualms about it. Why not save both of us the trouble? We will, as they used to say, make it worth your while."

Sheridan let herself glance at Taylor. Her head was still leaning back against the chair, eyes closed. Where the blue swirls didn't cover her face, red slap marks did.

"What will happen to my sister?"

"She'll stay at the Scicenter with you. If you get a memory wash, she gets one too. If you work with us, she'll be taken care of handsomely."

Could Sheridan propose a deal? She could promise to help Reilly as long as he let Taylor go.

Before she uttered the words, she stopped herself. That

sort of deal would only make Reilly suspicious. If she was really agreeing to help him, why would she want her sister to leave instead of sharing in the profits of her actions? Besides, even if Reilly agreed to free Taylor, Sheridan couldn't trust him to keep his word about it. How would she know if they actually let Taylor go free or just took her away somewhere?

Think, she told herself as harshly as Taylor had ever said the word. *Think your way through this.*

"You're considering my offer," Reilly said. "A wise decision. I trust you'll come to the right conclusion."

The only thing Sheridan could do was buy herself time. "I want to know exactly what I'm going to get. In writing. I want to know how much salary, how much equipment, and what living conditions the government is going to guarantee for the rest of my life."

"Easy enough to work out."

If it was easy, then she wasn't putting up a good fight. "And I don't want one of those crystals put in my wrist."

His eyes narrowed. "Why?"

"I don't like the idea of anyone tracking me."

"Everyone has a crystal. If you didn't have one, you wouldn't have a way to buy anything." He tapped the badge on his chest. "You wouldn't be able to display your rank."

He'd been here too long if he thought rank would sway her more than privacy.

"I won't have one. Tell the government, if they want my help, then no crystal."

Reilly shook his head, his jowls swaying like fish gills. "Being difficult won't serve you."

"Ideas are triggered by memories," she said. "Perhaps if you put me through a memory wash, I'll never be able to duplicate my success with the QGP. Perhaps great ideas only come to a person once in a lifetime. Think of that and talk to your government."

His lips pinched together. "Fine. I'll talk to them. In the meantime you and your sister will spend your time in detention cells—that's *prison* in our language. You'll have time to consider the reasonableness of your demands in there."

"Fine," she said. She had time. That was all she could ask for.

chapter
28

hapter

Sheridan sat alone on the floor of a dimly lit room no bigger than a closet. It was cold and smelled like garbage. She had hoped Taylor would be with her and they could devise some plan together, but the Enforcers had taken Taylor to a different room.

Minutes stretched into hours. She knew she couldn't keep up the pretense of being Taylor for long. Then what would happen to her and, more importantly, to Taylor?

Sheridan lay down, curled up for warmth, still thinking about every possible scenario, contingency, and option she might have. Most of the scenarios had bad endings. Memory wash or death.

Sometime before she fell asleep, she decided thinking was overrated.

She awoke when the door slid open. An Enforcer stood in the doorway motioning for her to come out. She got up, stiff and cold from the floor, and trudged to the door. She still had no idea what she was going to say to Reilly.

The Enforcer took hold of her arm and pulled her out of the room. Her feet were clumsy with sleep, but he propelled her down the hallway anyway, whispering, "*Rápido.*" They took an elevator to another floor, then went down a colorless hallway. Sheridan expected to be taken into a room with Reilly or Helix or at least some schematics of the QGP. Instead, the man took her to a back doorway and hurried her outside the building.

A car waited nearby, humming as it idled.

This didn't seem right. Where was Reilly sending her, and why hadn't anybody explained what was going on?

Her steps faltered, but the Enforcer yanked her along, half dragging her to the car. The door slid open and she saw Taylor lying limply against the seat. Her face was swollen so badly that the blue swirls now made lopsided ovals across her cheeks and her eyes seemed to have shrunk. Sheridan climbed in next to her sister and only then noticed Echo and Caesar sitting across from them.

The door slid closed, and the car moved forward. Sheridan's gaze ran over Taylor, checking for other injuries. "Are you all right?"

"Yes," Taylor said, slurring the word. "But what in the world were you thinking by telling Reilly that stuff?"

"I was thinking that I didn't want to see your face used as a punching bag anymore."

Caesar broke into their conversation, his metallic bronze eyebrows rising as he spoke. "Echo has a talent for finding beautiful girls. It's gripping to meet you."

Sheridan didn't answer. After all, Caesar didn't know she could understand him. She turned to Echo instead. "Are you translating for Helix again? Is that why you're here?"

"I'm rescuing you," he said. "That's why I'm here."

"Rescuing?" She turned in her seat, looking out the window to see if Enforcers were pursuing the car. She saw nothing except for the building growing more distant.

Echo gestured toward Caesar. "My friend has connections in the detention system. He was able to have you sneaked out."

Sheridan looked Caesar over more carefully. His chin jutted out confidently, all attitude and swagger. Although he smiled, there was something hard and calculating in his eyes that made Sheridan wary. Elise hadn't liked him. Was Caesar one of the bad friends who had led Echo to become entangled in the Dakine? She gulped and looked away. Caesar must be Dakine. Who else would have connections in the detention system?

Sheridan checked the control panel to see what street was starred. The entire panel was dark. "Where are you taking us?"

"To a place where you'll be safe," Echo said.

"Where? Out of the city?"

"Not out of the city. Just a safe place."

Taylor lifted her head from the seat so she was sitting more erect. "Safe until when? What's going to happen to us?"

Echo's blue eyes didn't waver, but his posture was tense, on edge. "You don't need to worry about that now."

Which only made Sheridan worry more. She looked from Taylor's sullen face to Echo's quiet one, and then at Caesar's grin. It slowly slid into a leer.

She turned back to Taylor. "Were you able to take care of . . ." She trailed off, not sure what Taylor had told Echo about the QGP or how far she'd gotten with her plan to destroy it.

Taylor understood what she was asking, though. "It worked," she said. "We unplugged the freezer."

That, at least, was a relief. "Good," Sheridan said. She wondered how many people they'd prevented from being shanghaied into the future. It seemed unfair that none of them would ever know the sacrifice Taylor had made for them.

Caesar leaned forward. "Tell Sheridan that I expect to be thanked for her rescue. In many ways."

"I wouldn't want to frighten her," Echo said.

Caesar laughed, a deep throaty laugh that filled the car. "I am rippingly frightening, aren't I? Tell her I think she's delicious."

Echo's jaw stiffened, but he turned from Caesar to Sheridan. "Caesar says he'd like to eat you. Are you interested?"

"Um, no."

Echo turned back to Caesar. "She's not interested."

Caesar's smile didn't falter. "Tell her I know how to create interest. Tell her I'll fly her places she can't go to in a VR center."

Echo turned to Sheridan. "Don't smile at Caesar. Just trust me about this. Now say something and shake your head."

Sheridan shook her head. "Thanks for the warning. I'm not smiling."

Echo shot Caesar an apologetic look. "She says thanks, but right now she's only interested in me."

"You?" Caesar sat back against his seat and humphed. "The girl has no *coraje*."

And whatever *coraje* was, she didn't want it.

Echo said, "Caesar hopes you'll be happy with his accommodations."

Happy? She was glad to be away from the Scicenter and Reilly, but how could she be happy if they'd been rescued by Dakine? It only meant that instead of being forced to work for the government, they would be forced to work for the Dakine. And if the Dakine knew about the QGP, well, there was no way Sheridan could help Taylor then. Echo already knew who she was.

No one spoke for a few minutes. Sheridan watched cars go by and wondered how strong Echo's affections for her were. When his loyalties to the Dakine came into conflict with his feelings for her, what would happen?

The newscast pictures of Allana and Joseph flashed through her mind, and she knew her answer. He wouldn't protect her.

Her mouth felt dry. "Do Jeth and Elise know where we are?"

"No," Echo said. "We can't tell anyone where you are or the government might find you. You've disappeared from the main life of the city. I'll take care of you now."

Her glance slid involuntarily over to Caesar. "You and your friends?"

"I need their help."

"In return for their help, what will we owe them?"

"We'll talk of that later."

So he wasn't going to tell her anything. Maybe he'd let Caesar give them those details along with his expectations of gratitude. Sheridan sat back against the seat, pressing her hands into fists, then forced herself to release her grip and relax. She turned to Taylor and said, "We've gone from the frying pan to the fire."

Taylor nodded and shut her eyes.

IT WAS PERHAPS an hour later that the car stopped. Sheridan couldn't be sure how far they'd traveled. After they'd driven a few miles, Caesar blindfolded Taylor and Sheridan to keep the route a secret. For all she knew, the car drove in circles half the time.

Caesar could have spared the dramatics. Sheridan probably wouldn't have been able to find her way around the city with a map, let alone give someone the location of the Dakine hideout. And even though Echo told them that the secrecy was for their protection, Sheridan didn't buy it. He was just making it harder for Taylor and her to escape.

Once they were sitting down inside the building, Echo took the blindfolds off. Sheridan squinted against the light and peered around the most elaborate room she'd seen in the future. Large swaths of velvety cloth hung from the ceiling to the floor, flowing around large pictures of the city landscape. The floor looked like one huge slab of beige marble but had a soft, cushioned feel to it. Golden-painted leaves trailed across the floor, walls, and ceiling. Forest-green gel chairs were positioned around the long glass table. Obviously the Dakine had the finances to afford luxury.

A young woman brought in plates of ham sandwiches and pasta salad. Sheridan eyed her sandwich carefully. It looked like ham and smelled like ham. For people who abhorred the thought of eating animal flesh, they certainly devoted a lot of time to duplicating the experience.

"It doesn't make sense," Sheridan told Taylor after her second bite. "They blame us for eating all the animals, then create food that tastes exactly like meat."

Taylor nibbled at her sandwich, not opening her injured mouth too far. "People don't make sense. Even back in our time, most people would have never butchered a cow or skinned a hog, but we thought nothing of picking up hamburger and hot dogs at the grocery store."

Echo put his sandwich back on his plate with a sigh. "You're talking about eating dead animals, aren't you?"

"Sorry," Sheridan said.

Taylor opened up her mouth to take a bite and winced.

Sheridan watched her. "I think you should have a doctor look at your mouth."

"Why bother?" Taylor said. "I'll probably have someone new punching me before nightfall."

Caesar set his fork on the table with a noisy clang. His mouth twitched at the corners. "She said the word *doctor*, didn't she? What is she saying?"

Echo put his sandwich down again. "It didn't mean the same thing back in the twenty-first century. Sheridan was only suggesting that Taylor have a med look at her mouth." Then to Sheridan, Echo said, "The word we use now is *med*. If you say *doctor*, people will think you're religious."

"I am religious."

His voice dropped lower, and she knew he was warning her. "Sheridan, have enough sense to value your life. If not for your sake, then for Taylor's. She needs you, you know."

Yes, Sheridan did know. She hadn't fully realized how much

Taylor needed her until she'd seen Reilly hitting her, but now Sheridan understood. Taylor had to be protected at all costs.

"Besides," Echo went on, "you don't worship the doctor. You worship . . ." He stopped, unsure.

"The Messiah," Sheridan finished.

Echo's brows drew together. "I don't know that word."

"It means 'the anointed one' in Hebrew," Taylor said.

"Anointed to do what?" Echo asked.

Sheridan let Taylor answer. Her mind had suddenly turned in another direction. It struck her how many different names religious people had for God. Christians used Heavenly Father, the Creator, the King of Kings and Lord of Lords, among others.

Judaism had so much reverence for the name of God that Jews didn't write it often, and when they did, they didn't spell it all the way out. When they spoke, they used words like Elohim or Adonai that meant "authority" and "master." Muslims used the name Allah, which literally meant "the one true God," but they had other names they used as well. When you added in Hinduism and other religions too, there must be hundreds of different names.

Or at least there had been. What terms would religious people use in the twenty-fifth century? Not the Good Shepherd, which was her father's favorite term. They didn't have shepherds—or, according to Echo, sheep. The reference wouldn't make sense. What metaphors would they use now?

Doctors healed people, saved them from death, brought forth life.

Could *doctor* be a word people used for God? Echo had

said the Worshippers wanted freedom of belief. Did that include religious belief?

She wanted to ask about it, but Taylor was explaining life after death to Echo and telling him how people would be held accountable for their deeds.

Echo finally shook his head. "You can't speak of your ideas to anyone here. If people understood you, *pues*, it's too close to the kinds of things the Doctor Worshippers say."

Sheridan felt hope flutter inside her, come alive again. She smiled. Religion wasn't gone. More than ever, she wanted to find the DW. "What else do you know about them?" she asked Echo. "I want to hear everything."

"No," Echo said firmly. "If I say more, my friend will get suspicious." Then to Caesar, Echo said, "They didn't have our Doctor cult in the twenty-first century. They're curious about it. I was explaining."

"They didn't have Doctor Worshippers in the old twenties?" Caesar snorted and finished off the last bite of his sandwich. "They tell everyone they've been on earth since the first sunrise. It's a double shame we can't use these girls to expose them, but then, our guests have more important things to do."

Echo didn't reply, just went back to his food.

Sheridan ate silently too, wondering what exactly the Dakine expected them to do.

chapter
29

After they finished eating, Caesar gave Taylor and Sheridan comlinks and then took them on a tour of the building. Echo went along, interpreting what Caesar said. Sheridan felt uneasy the entire time, as though she might be shown something terrible. Instead, they walked past meeting rooms and residents' rooms, and then to the compucenter. "This," Caesar said as they walked in, "is where you'll find Echo most of the time."

Echo didn't translate that part of Caesar's comment. Instead he went on repeating Caesar's instructions about what they could and couldn't touch, what rooms were off-limits, and how they needed to get supervision before accessing anything. Echo told them, sternly, that they couldn't ever leave the building by themselves. It wasn't safe.

"Don't clue them about the alarm system," Caesar told

Echo. "We'll test their intentions by letting them think they could leave if they wanted."

Echo said nothing, and Sheridan kept her face impassive, expressionless.

Caesar and Echo talked for a few minutes about something called the Prometheus project; then Echo took them down the hall to an office. "Lobo runs this building," Echo said. "He wants to talk to me and to meet you."

When they walked into the room, a man stood up from the desk. His silver hair shone like chrome, and Sheridan couldn't help but notice his rank number, 522. Lobo was someone important.

Echo stood stiffly, his nervousness shadowing him like a tangible presence. "Caesar said you wanted to meet the girls. This is Sheridan," he said, gesturing to her, "and that's Taylor."

Lobo sauntered around his desk, surveying them. "These are the time riders, the government's costly mistake?"

"Yes," Echo said.

"Do they have any skills?"

"They were students back in their time. Most of what they learned isn't useful to us."

Lobo ran his tongue across a row of straight, silver teeth. "They don't have tracking crystals. That could be useful to us. They'd make effective assassins—even if someone had a signal-jamming detector." He took slow steps around Sheridan and Taylor, still looking them over like they were cattle he was purchasing. "How long until they can understand our language?"

"Learning new languages takes months," Echo said.

"Sometimes years. But since the language we speak is based on theirs, it shouldn't be that long. I'd guess they'll be able to understand us within a few weeks. Maybe a month."

He certainly guessed wrong. Still, Sheridan kept her face blank.

"Help them," Lobo said. "They need to be upbooted as soon as possible."

Echo nodded. "Caesar wanted me to work on the Prometheus project, but your orders will come first."

Lobo waved a hand of dismissal at them. "Report back in a week and tell me if their language skills are ready."

Echo didn't move. "A week isn't long enough to relearn how to pronounce every word in a language."

Lobo was already returning to his desk. "I believe in your abilities, Echo. I always have. Besides, we can't delay the Prometheus project too long, can we?"

Echo nodded, then motioned to Sheridan and Taylor that it was time to leave.

As they were about to go through the door, Lobo called out, "And, Echo, you're done with your grieving time, aren't you?"

Echo stopped walking. His posture went rigid. Sheridan saw a flash of hatred in his eyes, but the next moment it was gone, evaporated like a drop of water on a hot stove. He turned back to face Lobo, and when Echo spoke, no emotion spilled out in his voice. "I'll never be through grieving for my brother."

Lobo sat down, unconcerned and unmoved. "We're all fond of our families; but when you joined us, we became the only family that mattered. You understood that."

"Yes, I understand."

"The need to protect ourselves takes priority. We let you have time by yourself because it wasn't your fault, but now, *pues*, we expect more from you."

Echo nodded. "I'll do my best with the time riders."

Lobo leaned back in his chair. "You have full responsibility for them. Don't disappoint me."

Even after they left the room, the suffocating feeling of tension remained hovering over them. Echo was clenching his jaw. No one spoke.

As they walked down the hallway, Echo took Sheridan's hand in his.

He has full responsibility for us, Sheridan thought, *and he's worried about it. He knows we'll try to escape, and he can't let us.*

Or maybe she was being overly suspicious of his motives, of him. He hadn't told the Dakine who Taylor was. On the other hand, the Dakine had murdered Echo's brother and girlfriend, and yet—unfathomably—he was still working for them.

Lobo had said it wasn't Echo's fault. Surely that meant Echo hadn't requested their assassinations in a jealous rage because Allana chose Joseph over him. But then, what *was* the reason Joseph and Allana died?

Echo took Sheridan and Taylor to a bedroom. It had half a dozen gel beds pushed up against two of the walls. Apparently they weren't sleeping alone, although no one else was in the room at the moment. Shelves, drawers, and vanities lined the other two walls, and computers sat on a multiseat desk in the middle of the room.

Echo pointed out the bathroom door, the closet where they'd find clothes, and a bowl on the desk full of multicolored balls that looked like huge marbles. "Candy," he said. "In case you want something sweet."

Echo didn't seem to be seeing anything he showed them. His eyes had a distracted look. Would he tell Taylor and her that these people were Dakine? Would he admit Lobo wanted to train them as assassins?

Echo walked to one of the computers. "Lobo wants me to teach you our way of speaking. Can you understand any of our language?"

"Not really," Taylor said.

Echo nodded. "I'll help you, but I have to leave right now, so I want you to listen to the conversations on the computer and repeat what you hear. You can do that while I'm gone, can't you?" He ran his hands across the keyboard, accessing a children's television program. It showed a little girl talking to animated dolls. They were, not surprisingly, discussing how much they loved the city. Echo straightened. "Get a feel for the way we say our vowels and consonants. Most *e*'s sound like long *a*'s now, and *i*'s sound like long *e*'s. If a word ends in a vowel or *n* or *s*, the next to last syllable is stressed. Otherwise it's the last syllable. *R*'s are trilled."

Taylor sat down at the desk obediently, watched the girl, and did a poor imitation of the sentence.

Echo gave her a forced smile. "Keep practicing. I'll be back as soon as I can."

Sheridan didn't move. "Where are you going?"

"The compucenter. I have some work to do."

So, despite the fact that Echo had just told Lobo that his top priority would be teaching her and Taylor, Caesar was right. Echo was going to spend his time in the compucenter.

Didn't Echo tell the truth to anyone?

Sheridan frowned and waited for him to leave.

Instead of walking out the door, Echo sighed and took her hand. He pulled her behind a freestanding full-length mirror so that they were blocked from Taylor's view.

"Don't wear that expression, Sheridan; I'll be back as soon as I can. Oh, and don't go out the doors. They're alarmed."

At least he had told her the truth about that. Still, Sheridan didn't change her expression. "We're prisoners here, then?"

"You just came from a detention room—you tell me, do you think this the same?"

"It might be. Who are these friends of yours, Echo?"

His gaze left her face and swept around the room. Looking for . . . what? "I can't talk about that now. I can't talk about a lot of things. You're going to have to trust me, all right?" He gave her hand a squeeze. "All right?"

Sheridan let out an exasperated breath. "Echo, I have been chased down by Enforcers, shot, and dragged to a room where I watched Taylor being beaten—knowing full well that I was going to be next. Then I was taken to a detention room, taken to your car, blindfolded, and brought to this place. I know nothing about these people except that they make you nervous, and at this point, I'm running low on trust."

"Running low?" he repeated.

"I want to know what's going on. Are these people Dakine?"

He stepped closer to her. "Don't say that word. You're not supposed to know what it means and you'll get us in trouble."

She inwardly groaned. He wasn't going to give her any answers.

"Listen to me, Sheridan." Echo put his hands on her shoulders and whispered, "Whatever happens to either of us, this is what you need to know. I care about you. I'm doing everything I can to help you, to help all of us. Do you believe me?"

She looked into his blue eyes and wished he hadn't asked this particular question. How could she believe him? And yet she wanted to, and for her own safety, for Taylor's, Sheridan couldn't say no.

"Yes," she said.

He bent down and dropped a soft kiss on her mouth. "I'll come back soon."

He gave her a smile as he left, a smile that seemed completely genuine and caring. It was amazing how he could smile like that and at the same time be Dakine. And it was amazing how she could know he was Dakine and still feel her heart beat faster because he smiled.

chapter
30

hapter

Sheridan watched Echo go, then walked over to the computer, noting as she did that the children's program was already gone from the screen. Taylor had switched it to the computer function. Her hands moved quickly across the keyboard, accessing what appeared to be a monitor full of numbers and squiggles.

Sheridan squinted at the screen. "What are you doing?"

Taylor didn't take her eyes from the monitor, just held up one hand to indicate she wanted silence. Finally she said, "If there's a recording function on this computer, it isn't turned on now. None of the sensors are intaking data. We can talk."

"Good." Sheridan slid into the chair next to Taylor. "So what do we do now?"

Taylor exited out of one page and brought up another. "We're going to get out of here as soon as I can figure out how to turn off the door alarms."

"What about Echo?"

"I guess he'll have to find some other girls to train as assassins."

Sheridan sighed, unable to abandon Echo quite as easily. "He says he's helping us."

"Yeah, he says a lot of things. Did I mention that he tackled me in the Scicenter, turned me over to the Enforcers, and then turned us both over to the Dakine?"

"He didn't have a lot of choices, did he?"

Taylor kept her eyes on the screen, skimming through rows of numbers and signs. "Look, I know the guy is hot, but despite that sterling quality, I don't trust him. So you can't tell him anything about our escape plans."

"Isn't it possible that he's trying to get away from the Dakine?"

Taylor grunted the way she always did when Sheridan failed to grasp the obvious. "Judging from our accommodations, I'd say no."

"Didn't you see the way he looked when Lobo mentioned Joseph's death? It was pure hatred."

"It may have been hatred for Joseph."

"I think Echo has made mistakes, but he's basically good—"

"Listen," Taylor said, turning in her chair toward Sheridan. "I let you make the last important decision. Instead of looking out for ourselves and escaping first thing this morning, I went to the Scicenter and destroyed my QGP.

"Around the time Reilly was pummeling my face, I started questioning the wisdom of that decision. So this time we're not taking the moral high ground. We're not trusting in the goodness of human nature or in your crime-lord boyfriend. We're leaving alone." Taylor turned back to the computer, typing quickly.

Sheridan watched her, noting her swollen face again. "You don't regret staying to destroy the QGP, do you? Think of the lives you saved."

Taylor kept typing. "Right now I'm too busy thinking of my own life."

Sheridan didn't say anything else. There was no arguing with Taylor when she was like this.

A grid came up on-screen. Taylor examined it. "We're in quadrant two-C in the refuse outtake district, smack-dab next to a city wall. They process garbage here." A jaded smile crossed her face. "I'm sure the location comes in handy when the Dakine are getting rid of their unwanted bodies."

"Does it say that on the computer, or are you just guessing?"

"I don't guess. I make educated deductions." Taylor brought up another screen and then another. Some had words on them, but most were numbers and squiggles. With each new page of data, her expression grew grimmer. "If I didn't already know Echo was involved with these people, I would now. These programs have his handiwork all over them."

"He wrote the Dakine computer programs?"

"He showed me the loopholes in the government's programs, but every one is plugged here. He knew how to use them, so he knew how to prevent them from being used." She applied more pressure to the keyboard than needed. "The alarms are controlled by the computer system, but I can't get past the security grid without an approved DNA scan. He's also blocked out the locks to the weapons room, the layout of the building, the personnel file—just about anything that might be useful to us. Oh look, the Dakine have their own set of cars, and I can't get to them either."

She flipped to another screen, a list of names and figures. "I should have known I'd find this. The Dakine keep track of everybody's rank. I bet if you pay them enough, they're willing to rearrange some number for you."

Taylor typed in Jeth's name, then found his picture among a list of similar names. His number was 4,583,776. "Ouch," she said. "That's gotta hurt." Next she typed Echo's name. His picture appeared with the number 98,704.

Taylor let out a low whistle. "That's nothing to be ashamed about. He's in the top one percent of the city."

The top one percent? The number made Sheridan pause. She would never be in the top one percent. Not in this time period or her old one. Echo probably knew that. Could he really be interested in her?

It bothered her that this thought had even crossed her mind. Rank didn't exist. Not really.

Taylor left the rankings and went to another site. Her fingers stopped their tapping. "Here's something interesting."

"What?"

"I guess they didn't feel the need to protect this information."

"What?" Sheridan asked again.

"There are doors leading out of Traventon in quadrant two-C; city workers use them to take unrecyclable garbage outside. Anyone who uses those doors has to have their signal approved and temporarily shielded by the government or they'll receive a deadly shock from the city's force field.

"The Dakine have a stealth program that cuts into the government's, so they can block their signals and use the doors." Taylor leaned back with a satisfied smile. "Of course, Echo has cleverly installed security devices around that program, so I can't access it."

"But you don't need to," Sheridan finished for her, "because we have no signals to block."

Taylor grinned, the tension draining from her shoulders. "If we can get out of this building, we can walk out of the city."

Sheridan reached for the candy bowl and popped a piece into her mouth. Chocolate. That hadn't changed in four centuries. She emptied half the bowl into the pockets in her dress, then handed the rest to Taylor. "We'll need something to eat while we're out there."

Taylor didn't take the candy. "If anyone catches us with food in our pockets, they'll know we're up to something."

"Or they'll think we're chocolate addicts. We did come from the twenty-first century."

Taylor closed out one screen and went to another. "If we can manage it, we'll take the candy right before we escape. But we'll need to do some foraging once we leave the city. Luckily, we're used to the outdoors."

Sheridan took another handful of candy. "We've never foraged in our lives."

"If it looks like nettles or poison ivy, we won't eat it." Taylor's concentration returned to the computer, her fingers already punching in a succession of numbers and letters. "I'll find a way around the alarms. I'm not about to be undone by that glorified English teacher."

Glorified English teacher. Honestly, did Taylor even remember that Sheridan had planned on being an English teacher? Sheridan popped another chocolate ball into her mouth. "You just can't bear to think that anyone is as smart as you."

"I can bear to think someone is as smart as me, just not Echo."

"Why not him?" Because he liked Sheridan instead of her? Did Taylor think that showed a glaring lack of intelligence?

"Because instead of doing something useful, the guy joined the Mafia and studied words for a living."

Sheridan leaned back in her chair. "Which bothers you more?"

Taylor shot Sheridan an exasperated look. "He should have been an engineer, a scientist, a researcher. He could have been someone great."

"And people who use and study words are never great?"

"They're great when you need a good book, but even you have to admit that none of the important advancements in society—the breakthroughs in science, technology, and medicine—were discovered by English majors."

And science, technology, and medicine were, of course, the only valid advancements society ever made. Sheridan usually would have let it drop. This time she didn't. "Words create thought. Thought changes society."

"Maybe, but words don't create automobiles, computer chips, or penicillin. If all the great minds had studied words, we'd have some really nice novels we could read by candlelight in our caves."

Sheridan pushed herself away from the desk. Taylor needed

to work on the computer, not debate the merits of the literary profession. Still, it irked her. Sheridan might not be able to understand computer functions on first sight or invent machines that changed matter into energy, but that didn't mean she wasn't smart in other areas.

As Taylor mumbled threats against the computer, Sheridan pulled the mirror around so that it blocked the view from the door. That way, if Echo came back soon, or if anyone else came into the room, they wouldn't see what Taylor was doing. Then, because Sheridan needed a plausible excuse for having moved the mirror, she took some of the jeweled things from the desk and clipped them into her hair. It looked ridiculous, but at least she could pretend she'd been preening in front of the mirror.

After a while, she peered around the mirror at Taylor. "Any luck?"

"He's blocked every way I can find around this encryption. It's not even a two-dimensional block, it's three-dimensional."

Whatever that meant.

Taylor pushed her chair away from the desk and ran both hands through her hair. "It's impossible to get around this."

"Then we'll find another way to accomplish the same thing. Can we trick someone into taking us outside?"

"I doubt it."

Sheridan returned her gaze to the mirror, to the reflection of the freckleless girl with golden eyes. "What happens when the alarm goes off?"

"A loud noise blares through the speakers, and all the doors in the building automatically lock."

Sheridan considered this. "Could you change it so that the

alarm still goes off but at such a high pitch that no one can hear it? And then the doors—"

"The sound level is unchangeable," Taylor said sourly. "It's part of the door, not part of the program."

"Could you make the alarms go off continually? If they malfunctioned, then the Dakine would have to turn them off."

The frustration slowly melted from Taylor's face. She looked up at the ceiling as though considering invisible equations written there. "That might work. As long as I hide the problem so they can't fix it easily . . ." She returned her attention to the computer and typed out a line of numbers and letters on the keyboard. "If I made it look like it was part of the original programming . . . next time it cycled through a reset . . ."

She didn't finish speaking; instead, she kept typing.

chapter

31

No one questioned Echo's presence in the compucenter. He checked in, sat down in front of a computer, and accessed the control panels in what he hoped was a natural manner.

That was the problem. He'd been tense for so long, he'd forgotten how to act natural. Had anyone here noticed him acting differently?

But then perhaps they expected it. After all, he'd just become a fugitive from the government, cut off from his father and everything in his old life. It would seem more unnatural if he acted like the old Echo—happy and carefree.

He brought up the Prometheus program on-screen and gave it an algorithm loop to run so that he could do his real work undetected.

Elise was still the only chance of a safe way out of Traventon.

He had to contact her. It was risky to send a message to her comlink, though. If Enforcers had her in custody, they would be monitoring her comlink for information. They could use it to set a trap for him.

But that was only if they had taken her into custody. Jeth and Elise couldn't be blamed for losing the time riders. The Dakine had taken them from the government's own detention rooms. Still, the wordsmiths might be in trouble for the things that had happened beforehand, when Echo went off with Taylor and Sheridan escaped from the Histocenter. Hopefully Jeth and Elise could make their innocence convincing, or at least slide the fault over to Echo. By now the government had certainly realized the contradictions in Echo's Scicenter story. They were looking for him. He was certain of it.

Would his father have the sense to blame Echo, or would he give way to parental loyalty and defend him? Echo could see Jeth standing in front of Helix, the anger on his face shining as brightly as the green circles he wore. "Of course Echo disappeared along with the time riders. The Dakine knew they'd need a translator to speak to the girls, so they kidnapped him too. How can you accuse him of crimes when you should be finding and freeing him? I'll contact the mayor himself about this!"

Yes, Jeth would probably defend Echo, the same way he'd defended him to anyone who implied that Echo had something to do with Joseph's death. Jeth would defend Echo even if he didn't believe in his innocence himself.

Sangre, Echo would miss his father. He hadn't realized how severely until this moment. The thought of never hearing Jeth's voice again—his continually cheerful voice—brought a sharp pain to the back of Echo's throat.

He swallowed hard, tapped his fingers against the keyboard, and ignored the pain the best he could.

If only he knew for certain his father was safe. And then Echo realized he could know. The Dakine computers had a spliced link into the government ones. He could check the detention log to see if Jeth or Elise were listed as prisoners.

Echo made the link quickly, half afraid someone at the compucenter would catch him but at the same time feeling justified in doing the search. Even if he hadn't been planning to send a message to Elise, he would still want to know what had happened to her and to Jeth. The compucenter leader could only be mad that Echo hadn't gotten proper clearance before he did it.

The list came up on the screen. Echo scanned it. With each unfamiliar name, his hope rose. Jeth and Elise weren't listed in the detention log, and a few minutes later he found they weren't scheduled for memory washes either. They were safe for now.

He would have liked to track Jeth's and Elise's crystals to find out where they were, but it was too dangerous. The government might trace the signal back to him.

Echo spent a few more minutes searching recent Scicenter interlogs looking for either Sheridan's or Taylor's name— anything that would give him an indication of how much the scientists knew about them. Did they know for certain that Taylor was really Tyler Sherwood, and if they did, were they foolish enough to state that fact in their logs? Both the government and the scientists must know that the Dakine kept track of their doings.

Echo found the classified Time Strainer file. He skirted around the encryption encoding it and skimmed through it. It listed medical statistics for Taylor and Sheridan, then gave a detailed record of the interviews the wordsmiths had helped with. Next came the mandate for Taylor and Sheridan's arrest. The charge: withholding information.

Someone had questioned the girls, and while he had found Taylor uncooperative, he indicated that Sheridan would be willing to negotiate.

Echo moved the cursor over the words again, searching for any missed links. It didn't make sense. Who had interrogated them? What had Sheridan been willing to negotiate about?

The last entry recorded that Taylor and Sheridan had been taken from the detention cell by Dakine operatives, and a citywide search was under way to find them along with the missing wordsmith, who was presumed either in Dakine custody or dead.

Pues, they certainly were getting closer to the truth. Luckily, there was no indication, at least from this log, that Jeth and Elise were in immediate danger of arrest.

Echo unlinked himself from the government mainframe and tried to decide what to put in his message to Elise. As he wrote it, questions nagged at the corner of his mind. How had someone communicated with Taylor and Sheridan during their interrogation? There was no mention of a wordsmith being present at that interview.

Echo coded his message as much as he could. He

addressed it to Candy Cane. That had been his nickname for Elise when she first started working in the Wordlab. At the time, her hair had been striped red and white. She would recognize the term, but no one else from this century would. He added a few other references to convince her that it was really from him.

He requested a meeting time, and in one final attempt to convince her of his genuineness, added, "When you meet us, bring Jeth with you."

Jeth wouldn't go. He wouldn't ever think of leaving the city. Still, Elise ought to know that Echo would never set a trap for her and tell her to bring Jeth. If she wasn't sure about anything else, she knew he loved his father.

Echo hit the Send button. It was done. Hopefully she would get it, hopefully he'd be able to get away from the Dakine when he needed to, and hopefully—*pues*, there were too many things to hope for.

After putting in an hour on the Prometheus project so that no one would be suspicious of the time he'd spent in front of the computer, Echo headed back to the girls' bedroom.

Taylor and Sheridan were probably tired of repeating phrases by now.

He was almost to their room when he realized that Taylor and Sheridan weren't repeating phrases. Most likely, as soon as he'd left, Taylor had tried to computigate through the computer files.

If he hadn't been so preoccupied with sending his message to Elise, he would have thought of this before. He shouldn't have left Taylor alone anywhere near a computer. Who knew what information she'd been accessing and what trouble she'd caused?

She might have alerted the Dakine about her abilities, and all for nothing. The computer system was secure. He'd seen to that. It was just one more monumental regret in his life.

chapter
hapter

32

Sheridan was standing in front of the mirror weaving a string of glowing white lights into her hair when Echo returned. She smiled at him in what she hoped was a pleasant and not guilty manner. "I got tired of imitating talking dolls and decided to do my hair."

Taylor still sat by the computer, obediently repeating dialogue from a show.

He sat down on the top of the desk and flipped off the computer. "Were you two practicing the whole time I was gone?"

"Well, I was," Taylor said. "Sheridan keeps getting distracted by her hair. Her *r*'s aren't nearly as trilling as mine."

"But now I look like I've got a halo," Sheridan added, admiring her reflection. "Something Taylor has certainly never experienced."

Echo kept his gaze fixed on Taylor. "I'm glad you didn't try to computigate. The systems on this computer are secure, and you'll only get into trouble if you tamper with anything."

Taylor gave him a wide-eyed look of innocence. "Oh, really?"

"Taylor." He said the word softly. "Don't do it."

She sighed as though giving in to his request. "I'll be an angel while I'm here. Even if I don't have a halo."

For the rest of the evening Sheridan and Taylor worked on pronunciation with Echo. He spent most of his time with Sheridan, although she wasn't sure whether this was because he liked her or because she just needed more work than Taylor.

He sat across from her on a couch, his knees touching hers. "If a *d* is between vowels, it's soft. Almost like your *th*. Watch my mouth. *Adult. Adding. Adopt.*"

She looked at his lips and could barely speak at all. It didn't help that she could see Taylor out of the corner of her eye making kissy faces. Taylor was supposed to be working on some phonetic alphabet charts that Echo had downloaded, but she was obviously listening to them instead.

Sheridan repeated the words, knowing she would probably forget to say the soft *d* the next time she used the words. Who thought about whether a *d* was between vowels while they were speaking? "How long did it take you to learn our accent?" she asked.

"Over a year. In your era, English didn't follow many pronunciation or spelling rules, so I had to memorize how to read and say each word individually. I still can't think about the words *psychology, rhythm,* or *hors d'oeuvres* without wanting to kick something."

Sheridan nodded. "I never saw the point of having an

apostrophe in the middle of *hors d'oeuvres*. That's just putting on airs."

"I would probably agree with you," Echo said, "if I had any idea what *putting on airs* meant."

She nudged his knee with hers. "You should agree with me anyway. It's good policy."

"Let's work on diphthongs again."

Sheridan didn't want to work on diphthongs. "Why did you decide to learn our accent?"

"The government ordered it about five years ago. They told Jeth to have the language ready to speak in six months. I guess it took them longer to finish the Time Strainer than they expected." Echo sent her a smile. "I would have worked harder on learning the accent if I had known part of the project involved talking to beautiful girls."

She smiled back at him and then felt guilty. It seemed wrong to smile at him when she and Taylor were planning on escaping from this place, from him.

Finally, it was time for bed. Echo had arranged for Sheridan and Taylor to be by themselves for a few nights. "Until you adjust to our society," he said as he left. "I know you had all sorts of sleep taboos."

And thank goodness for them. After he'd gone, Taylor went back to the computer and finished installing her alarm-program change.

Sheridan lay in her bed listening to Taylor's fingers tap on the keyboard. Tomorrow the alarm would go off. Tomorrow they would run away. Perhaps Sheridan would never see Echo again. The thought shouldn't bother her so much. He was Dakine. His friends wanted to train Taylor and her to be assassins. But when she thought of sneaking off, it still felt like a tear in her stomach.

Taylor turned off the light and went to bed. Sheridan lay there in the dark, unable to sleep. Thoughts tumbled around her mind like clothes in a dryer. Echo. Reilly. Caesar. QGPs. Time Strainers. Dakine.

"Taylor, as long as the government has both a QGP to turn you into an energy flux wave and a Time Strainer that can turn you back, they can strain you into the future, right?"

"Yes."

"Well, what's to stop them from straining us right now? They have our signals."

"Reilly said he couldn't get his QGPs to work."

"He said they didn't work properly. He never said they didn't work at all. What if he gets one functioning next month or next year . . . ?"

"Thanks," Taylor said. "Now I won't be able to get to sleep."

"Sorry. Think of horseback riding; that's what I do."

"With my luck, I'd get trampled."

Sheridan turned on her side. "Not if you're riding Breeze. She's too gentle." Sheridan imagined herself cantering along a trail, but this time instead of relaxing her, the memory made her feel sad. According to Echo, horses were extinct. Eventually her memories of horseback riding would fade, and then she'd have nothing left of Breeze.

In the morning, Echo beeped Taylor and Sheridan on their com-links to wake them up.

Taylor took the beeping box from the side of her bed and

chucked it across the room. "Stupid technology."

It didn't stop beeping.

Sheridan answered her comlink, happier than she should have been to hear Echo's voice. The sound of him was comforting, like a blanket you could wrap around yourself. And after today, she would probably never hear it again.

They had breakfast, then worked on reading and pronunciation. Then they had lunch and worked on reading and pronunciation. By dinnertime Sheridan's tongue hurt from trilling her *r*'s. At last, Echo turned off the phonetic alphabet charts, and they went to the cafeteria.

When they walked in, Caesar waved them over to the table where he sat with Echo. For the first time, Sheridan noticed the number on his badge: 651,205. She felt a sort of smug satisfaction that both Echo and Elise had better rankings. And then she felt bad that she'd even checked. Was ranking individuals so ingrained into human nature that you did it even when you didn't want to?

She turned her attention to her surroundings instead. Considering how big the building was, there weren't many people in the dining room. Only a few groups of people sat eating at the tables.

During a lull at dinner, Sheridan asked Echo about the lack of people.

"The size of the room is for meetings and darties," he said. "Most people don't live here. The building has equipment that jams crystals' signals, so while the government is looking for us, we'll stay here."

Caesar immediately asked Echo what Sheridan had asked,

and Echo repeated the conversation for him. Poor Echo. With all the translating he did at mealtimes, he hardly had a chance to eat.

Caesar cut into his potato, then waved a fork in Echo's direction. "Tell her we're having a darty here after dinner. She'll meet lots of people then."

Echo told her, and Sheridan noticed that Taylor's face lit up with relief before he'd even started his explanation. Bad timing on Taylor's part, but neither of the guys seemed to notice.

Taylor's relief was because the alarm program was almost to its next cycle, and it was imperative that Sheridan and Taylor be with people when it went off. That way everyone could see they hadn't set it off.

After the alarm stopped sounding, Sheridan and Taylor would know the doors were unlocked. Then it would just be a matter of timing. They had to find an opportunity to escape before the Dakine discovered and fixed the problem.

Taylor spooned the last of her soup into her mouth. The swelling on her face had faded into a general puffiness, but she still didn't look like herself, or like Sheridan. Purple-and-green bruises intermixed with her blue swirls. "Will there be dancing at the darty?" Taylor asked.

Echo nodded.

"How do people dance in the twenty-fifth century?"

Caesar fingered one of his metallic eyebrows while he listened to Taylor. "What did she ask?"

"How we dance," Echo answered.

Caesar stood up and held out his hand. "I'll show her."

Taylor hesitantly took his hand and walked with Caesar

to an empty space on the floor. He turned on music through one of the menu computers, and there between the tables he showed Taylor an assortment of dance moves—most of which looked like he was being electrocuted.

Taylor laughed and imitated his moves, which only encouraged him to show her more elaborate ones, some of which involved rolling on the floor.

And all this while, the people around the room ate, watched, and cheered them on. People here in the twenty-fifth century apparently had no sense of public embarrassment.

"What do you think of our dancing?" Echo asked.

"I wasn't sure if that was really dancing or whether Caesar was playing a practical joke on Taylor."

"Meaning you don't like it?"

Sheridan tilted her head as she watched. "Does everyone roll around on the floor? Don't people get stepped on?"

"You can teach me how you dance instead."

How sweet. He was offering to learn her dance steps. Of course, she didn't really have dance steps. At home she just danced like everyone else. How would she teach him that?

"Okay," she said.

He stood and held out his hand to her.

"You want to dance now?" she asked. "While the lights are on and everyone is watching?"

He cocked his head in question. "Was dancing secret in your time period?"

"No, it's just that . . ." It wasn't worth explaining. She took his hand and stood up. "Fine, let's dance. I'll teach you to slow-dance first." Slow-dancing would be less painful to teach. There was less to watch, less to do.

They walked to the same spot where Taylor and Caesar had been dancing before their rolling episode. Sheridan took Echo's hand and placed it on her hip. She put one hand on his shoulder, then held on to his remaining hand. "This is the basic slow-dance position. Now we sort of rock back and forth slowly and take small steps to the beat of the music."

He watched her feet and matched his rhythm to hers. "Okay, now what?"

"That's it. This is slow-dancing from the old twenties."

"You're joking."

"Well, there are other dances: the country swing, the waltz, that sort of thing, but most people didn't know how to do those. So this was the average slow dance."

He paused and looked at their feet. "No wonder you didn't want people watching. It was a silly dance."

"You're one to talk."

"One to talk? What does that mean?"

"It means rolling around on the floor looks even sillier."

"I wish I could understand your slang."

She was glad he couldn't.

Taylor and Caesar were now doing some strange step in which they half pulled each other up from the floor, and then fell back down like human jack-in-the-boxes.

Echo took his hand from Sheridan's hip and touched her hair, letting his fingers linger on a golden strand by her face. "At least you like our hair decorations. I was surprised last night when I came into the room and saw you'd put up your hair."

"Were you?" Not as surprised as he would have been if he'd

seen what Taylor was doing instead.

Almost as though he could read her mind, he said, "I meant what I said to Taylor earlier. It won't do her any good to splice into the computers here. When it's time to leave, I'll take you." He leaned very close to her, which wasn't hard since he was already close to begin with. "I sent a message to Elise that we wanted to meet with her."

Elise would never go for it. "What if that doesn't work?" Sheridan asked. "Then what will we do?"

"Let's plan on it working."

Sheridan slid her hand across Echo's shoulder until her fingertips touched his hair. It felt silky, soft. Somehow she had expected it to be rugged like him. "Could we find a way to leave the city on our own? I mean, the government wouldn't search for us outside, would they?"

"It's too dangerous."

"Dangerous how?"

"Storms, freezes, heat, dust—"

"Dust? What's dangerous about dust?"

"Shards, crevices, vikers—"

"What are vikers?"

"Just trust me, it's too dangerous. We'll depend on Elise."

Elise didn't trust him, and he knew it. So why come up with this story about meeting with her? Was he trying to convince Sheridan that he still wanted to help her escape so she wouldn't attempt to leave on her own? Did he think she was naive enough not to realize she was at a Dakine base, or that Echo himself was Dakine?

Dinner must have officially ended. The remaining eaters

stood up, and the tables sank into the floor. The room was suddenly one big dance area, and several people joined Taylor and Caesar in their wild gyrations.

Echo and Sheridan stayed off to the side, swaying gently to the music, while people streamed past them. He pulled her closer and gave her an easy smile. It was the first time she'd seen him completely relaxed since they'd come here.

"I can see some benefits of dancing this way." His hand moved upward along her back. "I can talk to you. It's soothing. And your hair smells good."

"Does it?"

He lowered his face until it rested against the top of her head. "It's been a long time since I smelled anyone's hair."

She nearly asked him who'd been the last recipient of his hair sniffing, but the answer came to her before she opened her mouth. It was Allana. Allana's long, silver hair. The hair Sheridan had seen splattered with blood on the news show.

More people came into the room. She only caught glimpses of Taylor—an arm waving here, a head shaking there; every once in a while her full body twirled into view, then disappeared behind the other dancers again. She might have changed partners. It was impossible to tell with everyone orbiting around in all directions.

Echo bent down to speak into her ear again. "I did some checking on the computer and looked into your government file. They said someone had interrogated you. Who was it?"

So the government had kept Reilly a secret. She wasn't about to enlighten the Dakine on that subject.

"Some man who questioned Taylor by hitting her repeatedly."

"Didn't he realize she couldn't understand him?"

"I guess he thought the more he hit her, the better she'd understand."

"That seems strange." Echo's brows furrowed together. "What did he want from you?"

Sheridan wondered if her file had said anything about the QGPs. If Reilly succeeded and made them into weapons, the government would use them to destroy their enemies, including the Dakine. If the Dakine found out about the QGPs and built some first, they would have absolute control over the city.

And here was Echo asking her what Reilly wanted.

She looked over his shoulder at the spinning dancers. "I couldn't really understand him."

"The file said you were willing to negotiate with him. What did it mean by that?"

She shrugged, keeping her eyes on the dancers. "I suppose it meant I didn't scream at everyone the way Taylor did. You know how she gets when she's upset."

"Oh," he said. It sounded like an I-don't-quite-believe-you type of oh.

Well, what did he expect? He was Dakine. He was probably only holding her so gently now and smelling her hair because he was using her.

Sheridan hated these thoughts. She hated trusting Echo one moment and the next moment suspecting him of everything. She tilted her head up to speak more directly into Echo's ear. "Do you remember before, when you told me that you couldn't explain everything, but you wanted me to trust you?"

He nodded.

"You don't have to explain everything, but I want to know one thing. Promise me you'll tell me the truth about this one thing."

In the bright light she could read his expression clearly—could see him emotionally drawing back, becoming cautious. "All right," he said.

"I won't judge you," she said. "I just want to know. Do you belong to that organization whose name I'm not supposed to say?"

She held her breath as she waited for his answer. *Tell me the truth, Echo. Be honest with me once so I know whether I can believe in you or not.*

He leaned forward until his lips were brushing against her ear. It probably looked like he was whispering adorations, but his voice was completely serious. "I'm not Dakine. If you don't believe me about anything else, believe that."

Sheridan looked out at the dance floor, at the wild, flailing colors. She felt stiff in his arms. Everything in the room seemed too bright, too harsh, too false.

He thought she was an idiot, and Taylor had been right about him all along.

Before either of them said anything else, a shrill alarm cut through the music, filling the room with its wail.

chapter
33

The shriek of the alarm cut through Echo. He scanned the room for Taylor. She wouldn't have tried to escape—not after he'd warned her the doors were alarmed.

The dancers were stopping, the human wave of motion calming. He searched for her white hair until he finally saw her standing beside Caesar.

"What's that noise?" Sheridan asked, looking around.

"The door alarm."

"Why is it going off?"

"Someone probably forgot it was on and tried to go out. They'll turn it off in a few seconds."

It did not turn off. The dancers stood on the floor waiting for the music to resume, but the only noise that came from the speakers was the overpowering pitch of the alarm.

What was taking them so long?

Several people left the room, probably to fix the problem. Someone had the sense to reduce the speaker output, so the noise only came out as a buzzing moan.

Caesar and Taylor walked over. He had one hand on Taylor's back, buried in her long white hair. "Echo, I need some translating. Tell Taylor she sweets like a riot."

Echo glanced at Taylor. "Caesar says you dance well."

"Thanks," Taylor said breathlessly. "Now I know how you guys keep in shape. By the way, what's that awful noise?"

"Someone's set off the door alarm." To Caesar, Echo said, "Taylor says you make interesting shapes."

"Tell her I want to show her more than dancing." Caesar gave Taylor a significant raise of his eyebrows. "She'll be surprised at the things we can do now."

Echo turned his attention back to Taylor. "Caesar likes you, but he'd fail a father's interview. Do you understand what I'm saying?"

"Yeah." Taylor moved away from Caesar's grasp and walked over to Sheridan.

Echo shook his head at Caesar. "She isn't interested."

"What? Did they have special rituals? I'll spritz for a history lesson then." Caesar stepped toward Taylor, as though about to grab hold of her.

Echo stepped in his way. "Find something else to do. These girls are my responsibility."

Caesar's eyes narrowed. "You just want them both for yourself. *Sangre* then. They won't always be your responsibility."

Caesar stalked off without another word. He went back to

the main crowd, put his arm around a girl, and squeezed her shoulders.

The shadler.

Before Echo could say anything else, someone tapped him on the shoulder.

Echo turned and saw—what was his name? The man was one of the superiors, and now Echo would have to hide the fact that he couldn't remember his name.

"Something's wrong with the alarms," the man said. "They won't reset. We've checked the locking system, so it has to be the program. Lobo wants you to look at it."

Echo gave a curt nod. "*Bien.* I'll take the girls back to their room and then go to the compucenter."

"Be *rápido*," the man said.

What *was* his name? After Echo finished checking the alarm program, he would have to report back to the man. Echo couldn't very well do that without his name.

Echo took hold of Sheridan's hand, and gestured for Taylor to follow them to the door. Someone had brought in a portable music player, and the dancing started up again.

As they walked to the girls' bedroom, Taylor asked questions about darties. How long did they last? Did everyone go to them? Echo answered her distractedly.

The man's name started with an R. Remond? Ronis? Robert? If only the personnel files weren't so hard to access; then he could scan through them until he found the name. That was the problem with the Dakine. They expected you to remember too much.

When the group reached the bedroom, Echo said, "Work

on your pronunciation until I come back."

Taylor fingered some of the chocolate candy. "We'll keep ourselves busy pronouncing."

He turned to leave, then paused. Something about Sheridan's expression drew his gaze back to her. She stood staring at him, her eyes shining sorrowfully.

"What's wrong?" he asked.

She smiled, but even that was tinged with sadness. "Nothing. The alarm hurts my ears."

"I'll fix it soon."

"I hope so." She paused as though she meant to say more, but then decided against it. She simply smiled again. "Bye, Echo."

THE MAN whose name Echo couldn't remember was waiting for him in the compucenter. In some ways that made things easier. Echo wouldn't have to send him a report. Then again, something might come up in conversation that would let the man know Echo had forgotten his name—a bad thing to do to one of your superiors.

Echo sat down in front of the computer and accessed the alarm program, tapping one finger against the control panel impatiently while the security program identified his DNA and unlocked the encryption.

The man strolled over and sat down on the table next to the computer. "How long will this take?"

"That depends on what the problem is."

"What do you think it is?"

"I won't know until I look at the program." *Or until I*

258

develop psychic powers. Really, what did the man want? He was obviously one of those impatient leaders. Someone whose name people didn't generally forget.

Ronaldo? Reese? Regent?

It was bad enough that Echo had to deal with Lobo, the man who could apologize for having his brother killed in one sentence and call himself family in the next. If Lobo found out about Taylor—or rather, *when* he found out about Taylor— he'd make the government detention officials seem like well-mannered gentlemen.

Echo didn't want to think about the Dakine methods for getting information. And he'd have to see it all, because Lobo would want him there to translate his demands. Lobo wouldn't make the government's mistake of asking questions the girls couldn't—

Then, like a small current wave inside him, Echo realized that Sheridan and Taylor could understand. They'd been listening to the new accent ever since they got here, and somehow they'd managed to decipher it. That was why the government hadn't called in a wordsmith to translate for them. The government had discovered what he'd been too oblivious to notice.

What had they heard? What had he himself said when he was with them?

"What's wrong?" the man asked. "You're scowling."

Echo's attention snapped back to the screen in front of him. "I'm still not sure what the problem is. It may be more difficult to find than I'd expected."

The man grunted, crossing his arms in disapproval. "Discontinue the alarm function then. We can't have that thing shrieking at us all night, and we can't stay locked inside the building. It's already making Lobo nervous. He thinks the government found us and sabotaged the program so they could trap us here."

"They can't splice into the program," Echo said. "It's too well encrypted." Still, as his fingers glided over the control panel, he worried Lobo was right. The government would do everything it could to get Tyler Sherwood back. Perhaps they were better equipped than he'd thought.

He finished the disarm command, and the system disconnected. He let out a relieved sigh. No one had tampered with the program after all. His security encryption, the one he'd created with his brother, was still unbreakable. He wasn't sure whether to feel proud of that fact or not.

"Much better," the man said. "That sound could pierce metal."

Echo didn't reply, just kept scanning figures on the computer.

Normal. Normal. Normal. Everything seemed to be working exactly as it should.

He scrolled through the screen, all the time aware that the man with the forgotten name was near. After ten minutes the man stood up from the table, stretched, and found something to look at on a different terminal.

Normal. Normal. Normal.

After another five minutes the man called over, "Did you fix the problem yet?"

"I haven't found the problem yet."

"You haven't found it? *Sangre*, how hard can it be? The

alarm wouldn't shut off. *That* was the problem."

How helpful. Next he'd be staring over Echo's shoulder asking what each subroutine function did. "According to the computer, everything is working within the right parameters. I can't fix anything until I find something wrong. Are you sure it wasn't the alarm sensors that malfunctioned?"

The man threw one hand up in the air with disgust. "Computigators. You always blame someone else when your program fails. The sensor engineers say it's the program, now you say it's the sensors."

"It may be something subtle the sensor engineer didn't catch on the first scan. I'm assuming they only did preliminary testing before they decided the program was at fault?"

The man gave another grunt and walked to the door. "I'll go talk to them and have them run another test. You keep checking the program."

As if Echo had been planning to take a nap. He still couldn't think of the man's name, but could think of some descriptive adjectives.

Normal. Normal. Normal. Of course everything was normal. This program had been cycling for months. If a problem existed, it generally showed up right away. So something had changed, only nothing could have changed because the program was security encrypted. Only those people given access by Dakine authority could change it.

One of them must have done something. Only he wasn't sure any of them had the ability to code the alarm to freeze, let alone do it in a way Echo couldn't detect. Besides, why would one of them have frozen the alarm?

Who would be helped by a frozen alarm?

Taylor.

Then he saw it—in his mind, and on the screen. There wasn't a program change but an addendum, a message sent to the program making it so sensitive, it activated when dust particles crossed its path.

He reached for his comlink, buzzing Sheridan first and then Taylor. He knew, even as he pushed the buttons, that they wouldn't answer. They'd probably left their comlinks sitting in their room.

They were gone. They'd fled as soon as he'd unlocked the doors.

Of all the stupid, reckless ploys—not only would they get themselves killed, they had conveniently ordered the same fate for him. If the Dakine realized he'd let them escape, if the government caught him . . .

Echo gripped his comlink. Where had they gone? Why hadn't they told him?

Or perhaps they had. Perhaps all those questions Sheridan had asked about the outside meant they were headed that way.

No, they wouldn't be *that* idiotic. Not when he'd warned them about the weather and the vikers.

Echo made himself think calmly. They would try to find Elise—only they didn't know where she was and couldn't use a car anyway. They'd be walking down one of the streets not far from here. He would take a car and search every street until he found them. Was it better to let the Dakine know what had happened or disappear on his own to look for them?

Echo's comlink went off the next moment, but it wasn't

Sheridan or Taylor. "This is Renold," the man's voice said. Renold. That was the name. *Pues*, it didn't matter now anyway. "The sensor engineer says in order to run another diagnostic, he needs the alarm turned back on."

This was not the time for another lockdown. "It will take a few minutes before I can cycle the program back to functioning. Which door are you testing the sensors at?"

"The main entrance."

Good. Echo would make sure he didn't use that door. "Give me a few minutes to have it working."

"Fine," Renold said.

Echo put his comlink down on the desk. He was cutting himself off for good, from everyone and everything. Still, he had no choice. He had to find Sheridan and Taylor, and no one could find him first.

chapter 34
hapter

Sheridan and Taylor stood in front of a door big enough to drive a truck through. And judging by the rails on the ground, that was what it was used for. An orange glow stretched across the entrance, letting out an angry electric hum. Sheridan couldn't see anything through it.

Taylor peered at the orange light that rippled in front of them. "That's the force field that zaps anyone who doesn't have their crystal blocked."

"But it won't hurt us," Sheridan said.

"That's the theory anyway."

Sheridan shot Taylor a sharp look.

Taylor didn't move. "Anything is just a hypothesis until it's tested."

"All right," Sheridan said, "I'm testing it." She took a deep breath and walked through.

A buzzing noise filled her ears, and the orange light washed against her. Then she was on the other side. She turned to tell Taylor it was safe, and found Taylor right behind her.

"We made it out," Taylor said.

"But where are we now?" Sheridan answered.

She had expected to see wilderness. Instead she saw another city. Or more accurately, the remains of a city. Broken gray slabs of concrete jutted upward, and bits of unidentifiable trash lay everywhere. Rebar stuck from the ruins like thin fingers reaching out of the ground. In the distance, skeletons of buildings stood against the horizon, blackened shells that hadn't tumbled to the ground yet.

Sheridan saw splotches of green—grass and weeds growing among the debris. A few spindly-looking bushes perched on top of the wreckage, testifying that the destruction wasn't a recent event.

Taylor peered around. "It can't all be like this."

"Let's hope not."

The rail ran toward the rubble and curved out of sight behind a pile of concrete. It must lead to wherever Traventon dumped its garbage. Sheridan and Taylor walked along the city wall away from the door so that truckers wouldn't see them.

As they went, their feet kicked up small clouds of gray dust. Cement dust, or perhaps ash.

"We want to go east," Taylor said. "To be sure of our route, we should wait until we see what direction the sun is going. From the look of it, we're about an hour away from either sunrise or sunset."

Sheridan glanced at the sun. It hung above the horizon in the cloudless sky. It felt strange not knowing whether it was morning or evening.

They kept walking along the city's edge, the hum of the wall keeping them company. Minutes went by. Taylor kept checking the angle of the sun. "I think the sun is getting higher. Which is good news, because it means we're going in the right direction and we'll have hours of sunlight. It is getting higher, right?"

They walked for a few more minutes. It did seem to be getting higher, or at least it wasn't getting any lower.

Off to their right, a jumble of broken cement slabs stood twice as tall as they did. Sheridan surveyed it grimly. "I doubt we'll have much luck foraging and gathering around—" She stopped speaking. Something had ducked behind a pile of rubble.

"What was that?" Taylor asked.

Sheridan squinted at the rubble. "I don't know."

They picked up their pace, still scanning the wreckage. A long shadow moved, then disappeared behind a twisted concrete slab.

Something was here, watching them. Sheridan heard a noise behind her and spun around. "Taylor," she breathed out.

Figures were emerging from the ruins—half a dozen men. They wore tattered clothing wrapped around their bodies like layers of bandages. Gray dust covered them from head to toe, so that only their eyes stood out, cold and fierce against their gray, bearded faces.

Sheridan immediately noticed one other feature about the men. They were each missing their right hand. Where it should have been, they only had a stump. Despite this deformity, the men seemed more than able to take care of themselves. Each carried a piece of sharpened metal and waved it ominously. A few paced slowly toward the city wall, and Sheridan thought they were heading to the entrance. But then they stopped, and Sheridan understood. They had gone that way only to keep Taylor and her from running back into Traventon.

"What do you want?" Sheridan called to them, forgetting that her speech was foreign.

They seemed not to notice or care that she'd said anything. They took slow steps forward, jabbing their metal sticks and growling like wild animals.

"We're friendly," Taylor said, and she nearly had the accent right, at least close enough that they should have understood her. If they did, they didn't care.

Sheridan took a step backward, searching the ground, looking for anything she could use as a weapon. If she bent down, would they lunge at her? Her hand brushed against her pocket. The candy. It wasn't large or sharp, but the surprise of having something flung at them might cause the men to back up long enough for her to grab one of the smaller cement pieces lying around.

She took a handful of candy and hurled it in their direction. Several hit the men, bouncing off their chests. They didn't back up. Instead they dived to the ground—not in fright, but to grab the candy.

They scuffled in the dirt, sending up a new gray cloud, writhing and pulling at each other like animals.

Taylor yelled, "Run!" and took off along the edge of the city. They didn't dare run into the wreckage. It was unfamiliar to them, but certainly not to these men. Sheridan followed after Taylor, adrenaline pushing her legs forward with more speed than she expected.

Seconds later, the men streamed after them, screaming out something Sheridan couldn't understand. Perhaps it wasn't words at all, but just the sound of savagery.

Sheridan gulped in deep breaths, trying not to choke on the dust. The men were gaining on her. She wore a long skirt, which wasn't helping matters. It fought against her strides. The men's footsteps were too close. In another moment, someone would grab her. She reached into her pocket, took out the rest of the candy, and tossed it behind her.

The footsteps stopped, but before she could feel relieved, she spotted more men flowing out of the rubble ahead of them. They were blocking the pathway, trapping Sheridan and Taylor between them and the other group.

Sheridan stopped and spun around. The men who'd chased them this direction still knelt, scrabbling in the dirt for the candy. Since they only had one hand each, they'd left their weapons on the ground.

"Run to the door," Sheridan shouted. She didn't wait to see if Taylor followed. She dashed toward the kneeling men, darting away from their grasp the best she could. One man reached up and clutched hold of her skirt, jerking her backward. She turned, kicked at his face, and was free.

The scuffle had allowed Taylor to pass her, and Sheridan was glad to know her sister was safe. As they ran, Taylor pulled farther ahead. Sheridan's skirt slowed her. She pulled it upward to free her legs, but then couldn't pump her arms.

The men were getting closer. Their shrieklike laughter was almost upon her. They enjoyed this. The chase was sport for them.

The door to the city—where was it? Certainly she should be able to see the rails by now. She tried to make herself go faster but didn't pick up any speed. Her lungs felt like they were on fire, and the men were still gaining ground. She and Taylor could fight off a few of them. There were so many, though, and she was so tired.

Taylor looked over her shoulder. Fear flared across her face. Taylor emptied her pockets of their load of candy to buy them more time. Some of the men must have stopped to gather the candy, but not all of them. Sheridan still heard footsteps behind her. The calls came again, gaining in volume. They were hunting her down like a pack of wolves on a deer.

They would kill her. And she wasn't even sure why.

Up ahead, sunlight glinted off the rails that snaked away from the city door. She could see them now.

One of the men grabbed her hair and yanked her backward. She fell to the ground with a tumbling thud, skidding through the gray dust.

She clawed at her captor's arm but couldn't dislodge his grasp. The other men circled around her, darting at her with weapons drawn, like they were performing some morbid dance. She kicked out at them, twisting to keep them at bay.

Someone screamed, and it took several seconds to realize that it was her own voice. She was screaming and couldn't stop.

More men came, circled her, all of them shrieking, and still her scream was the loudest.

chapterchapter
35

Sheridan didn't hear the shot. She wouldn't have known that it had happened if several of the men hadn't fallen to the ground, some of them on top of her. She pushed them off, still screaming but now taking gasping breaths between her cries.

Another shot came, a ripping sound like when the Enforcers had shot her in the car. The men who didn't fall to the ground ran and scattered, disappearing behind the piles of rubble. All around her, Sheridan could smell the scent of burning flesh. Blood seeped into the dust where the men had fallen, turning it dark, almost black. She rolled over, trying to get away from the bodies and the expressions of death on their brutal gray faces.

Sheridan expected to see Enforcers, was even afraid they might shoot her next. Instead, she saw a guy with broad shoulders and a blue crescent moon. He was striding toward her.

"Echo," she called out. She couldn't catch her breath to say more, couldn't say how happy she was to see him.

His laser box was still outstretched, and when he reached her, he seemed as out of breath as she was. "Did they stab you?"

Spots of blood flecked her dress, but it wasn't hers. "No, I'm fine."

He took hold of her hand and pulled her, to her feet. "Surprising, since suicide seems to be your latest plan." It was then Sheridan noticed how his eyes smoldered with anger.

Taylor reached Sheridan and threw her arms around her. "I was so afraid," she said through labored pants. "I thought they were going to kill you. And I couldn't find a weapon."

Echo scanned the rubble, still looking for attackers. His voice was as sharp as the broken concrete around them. "You shouldn't have come out here. I told you it wasn't safe."

Taylor released Sheridan. Her face was red and damp with sweat. "You never told us the outside was populated by one-armed thugs."

"Vikers." Echo said. "They're criminals who fled the city to avoid death sentences."

Sheridan realized how they'd done it. "They chopped off their own hands to get rid of their tracking crystals, didn't they?"

He didn't answer her question. When he'd finished checking the area, he turned back to her. "Do you know how much danger I've put myself in for you? And this is the wage you pay me: you run away. Why?" He'd spoken in the modern accent, not the old one.

Taylor and Sheridan both stared silently at him.

"Stop pretending," he told them. "I know you can

understand. You deceived me about it just like you deceived me about everything else."

There was no point denying it. Sheridan said, "Sorry. We figured help from the Dakine was dangerous help."

His eyes narrowed. "And you're sure I'm Dakine?"

Sheridan and Taylor glanced at each other. Neither spoke.

"I told you I wasn't," he said. "I promised you it was the truth—but you didn't believe me. Just like you didn't believe me about the vikers." He took the sensor box from his belt and checked its reading.

"Echo," Sheridan said, "you told me Dakine hit men could block their tracking crystals, and when you were out with Taylor, you blocked yours. You must have blocked it again to leave the city."

He looked at the sensor and not at her. "I nearly didn't leave, you know. I was going to search for you on the streets. I kept telling myself you wouldn't be stupid enough to walk out of Traventon." He jabbed the sensor back into his belt. "If I had decided to check outside a minute later—if I hadn't had a weapon with me—the vikers would be dragging your body back to their camp right now. I just saved your life, and you stand here and tell me I'm Dakine."

Sheridan couldn't speak. All her previous accusations about him sat silently on her tongue.

Taylor put her hands on her hips and stared back at Echo. Apparently her accusations didn't have any qualms about gratitude. "I thought only Enforcers and Dakine had access to weapons."

"I'm not Dakine." Echo walked over to one of the dead

men, flipped him over, and took his knife.

"We heard Lobo talking about Joseph's death," Taylor went on. "You told us the Dakine killed him."

Echo walked to where a second man lay and retrieved his knife as well. "You don't know what you heard, and you only think you understand."

Taylor cocked her head. "You honestly expect us to believe we weren't at a Dakine base?"

Echo walked back over to them, handing each of them a knife. "I don't care what you believe anymore. Think whatever you want, but from now on you will follow my orders. Exactly. No questions, no lies. Let's go." He turned and set off along the city wall, away from the door they'd come through.

Sheridan followed after Echo. Taylor did as well, although more grudgingly.

Echo's stride was fast paced, determined. "You might have ruined the one chance we had to leave Traventon."

"We've already left," Taylor said. "We just need to find somewhere safe to go."

Echo waved a hand at the piles of wreckage. "Well, this isn't it. We have no shelter, no food; and don't think my laser box will be enough to protect us. If you stay in one spot too long, the vikers hurl concrete at you." His eyes skimmed along the top of the rubble as he spoke. "The DW have a system for getting people out of the city and through the wilderness safely. Elise sent me a message saying she'd meet us in front of the Fairmore swimming center in two hours. We'll probably miss her."

Taylor glanced back at the door they'd come through. "Then why are we going this way?"

"That door is too close to the Dakine base. They'll be looking for us now."

Sheridan and Taylor exchanged an exasperated look. Echo admitted that they'd just left a Dakine base, and then was angry at them for thinking he was Dakine.

"Stay close to me," he said. "We'll come to another entrance in a few miles."

For several minutes no one spoke. If anger had been visible, though, it would have been flowing off Echo's shoulders in waves. He never checked behind him to see if they were keeping up.

Sheridan watched him and wondered why he'd saved their lives. Was it a sense of friendship, responsibility, or something else—perhaps because Taylor was a valuable commodity?

She had to stop thinking that way. He'd helped them in every situation. He'd kept Taylor's identity from Lobo. He was leading them away from the Dakine base instead of taking them back. She could trust him, should have trusted him all along.

With this realization she felt miserable. If they missed their meeting with Elise, how would she ever make it up to him?

The minutes went by, and went by, and went by. Finally Sheridan took a few running steps so that she could walk by Echo's side. She glanced at his profile. His features stood out, harsh and determined against the background wreckage of the city.

"So, what happened to those buildings?"

"War."

"Oh."

More walking. More silence.

"Echo, I'm sorry I didn't trust you."

275

He didn't answer.

"Thank you for saving my life."

He still didn't answer.

"If we're captured by the government, and they give me a memory wash, I hope you'll visit me. Although, if you do, don't tell me everything I did wrong. It would depress me to know about it."

"If we're captured by the government, I won't be able to tell you anything because my memory will be erased too."

If only mistakes could be erased as easily. If only she could erase time and start this day over at a better point. "Well, on the bright side, if our memories are gone, at least you won't be able to blame me for everything."

He didn't comment.

She pushed herself to keep up with his pace. Bits of rubble spit from underneath her shoes. "Echo, if you were in my place, and the evidence pointed to the fact that I was Dakine, would you trust me?"

A flash of pain crossed his eyes. She thought he wouldn't answer, that it was hopeless, then he spoke. "It's been hard for me to trust people since my brother's death. I've analyzed and scrutinized everyone's motives. Are they with the Dakine? Are they watching me? Will I be safe tomorrow?"

His gaze slid over to her. "That was the nice thing about being with you. You had no connections to anyone. You hadn't already judged me, my past, and who I should have been. I thought you saw me as I really am." He looked away from her, staring at the broken pieces of civilization again. "It's never that easy, though, is it? People see our mistakes like they were posted on our rank badges."

"I'm sorry," she said.

"The thing I liked about you," he went on as though she hadn't spoken, "was that you weren't afraid of being you. You never hid your beliefs—well, except for your beliefs about me. When you acted like you cared about me, that was a lie, wasn't it?"

"No." She had tried not to care about him but had never managed it. Even now while he was angry, she wanted to reach over and take his hand.

"You thought I was Dakine and still cared for me?"

"I thought you were a reformed Dakine. I wasn't sure, though—you wouldn't admit to anything. If it was only a question of my life, then perhaps I would have stayed, but how could I leave Taylor at a Dakine base? I couldn't endanger her life just because I thought you'd changed—at least I hoped you'd changed. Have you changed?"

"I'm not Dakine."

She let out a sigh. He was determined to be angry with her.

They kept walking. The sun moved higher in the sky, but she had no idea how much time had passed. The dust on the ground thinned, then disappeared, replaced by rubble that slid beneath their feet. It made speed impossible.

Echo had said the next entrance was a few miles away. Did that mean three or ten?

Suddenly Echo stopped. "What's that?"

Sheridan gripped her knife and looked left and right, expecting to see more vikers. Or Enforcers. Or Dakine. Then she noticed Echo was looking upward. She followed his gaze and a saw solitary dark figure gliding overhead, wings outstretched, lazily looking down at them. A hawk possibly, or maybe a vulture.

"That, Echo, is a bird."

"A bird?" he repeated in disbelief.

"Yes," Taylor said, joining them. "Why don't you talk to it, and see if it answers."

Echo, still unmoving, watched the bird, then called, "Hello!"

When the bird didn't answer, he added, "We want to talk to you!"

The bird continued to circle, then glided off in the opposite direction. Taylor laughed, shook her head, and walked on ahead of them.

Echo turned to Sheridan. "Why did it leave?"

"Because it's a bird, and it doesn't understand you." She started walking again, slower paced now. "You see, I didn't lie to you about everything. Oh, and in case you're worried, I have absolutely no desire to eat that thing."

He stared up at the sky for a moment longer, then caught up with her. As he walked, he scanned the gray wreckage beside them. "Do you think there are other animals around?"

"The bird has to be eating something. Although if it's a vulture, we may have supplied it with dinner."

"What do you mean?"

"Vultures eat dead animals that are lying around. In this case, those friendly vikers who tried to kill me."

Echo looked over his shoulder, checking behind them. "You're making that up."

"Nope," Sheridan said, with more enthusiasm than the

subject probably warranted. "Lots of animals ate people. Lions, sharks, wild dogs—pretty much any carnivore that was big enough. Oh, and the mosquitoes were terrible. I bet those are still around too."

"Mosquitoes ate people?"

"Well, they tried." She made a couple of mincing steps over a particularly jagged patch of rocks. "Mostly mosquitoes just sucked a bit of blood and gave you itchy welts. Piranhas, however, were these little fish that could skeletonize a person."

Echo's jaw went slack.

She wasn't sure if he was amazed or horrified. "We can talk about something else." She tilted her head, trying to gauge his thoughts from his expression. "Unless you want to hear about killer bees."

"Total," Echo said.

"Total?" Sheridan repeated.

"Wasn't that a saying from your time?"

Sheridan shook her head. "It was a breakfast cereal, and something you did to a car." Tiny pieces of broken glass were mixed into the rocks, which made the ground in front of them glitter. "You probably mean *totally*," Sheridan added. "Which is only something you said if you also used the word *dude* frequently."

"Dude," Echo said, trying out the word.

She shook her head. "Don't start saying *dude*. It wouldn't become you."

"Become me what?" Echo asked. "What would I become?"

Sheridan smiled at him. "Don't become anything. I like you as you are."

"Do you?" he said, and there was a smattering of anger back in his expression.

"Yes, I do." She reached out and took his hand. She almost expected him to pull it away, but he didn't. "I'm sorry I didn't trust you before, Echo."

He squeezed her hand and smiled back. "From now on we'll trust each other, right?"

"Totally," she said.

chapter

hapter

36

By the time the next entrance came in sight, Sheridan's spirits had risen. Her feet, however, ached and the soles of her shoes were in tatters. Gray dust covered the bottom of her skirt. She wiped off as much as she could. Taylor and Echo did the same, but mostly managed to smudge the dust around.

Then Echo stood in front of the door. "If we're lucky, we won't find any refuse handlers on the other side." He fiddled with his laser box. "I'm lowering the voltage to stun level. Wait for me to come back and tell you the way is safe."

Sheridan looked at him questioningly. "If you could have stunned the vikers who attacked me, why did you kill them?"

"Because they wouldn't have run away if they'd seen my box was on stun. They know I can't stun them all, so they would have attacked and killed me."

"Oh," Sheridan said with a sickening jolt. He was right, of course. She wasn't used to dealing with people who killed each other, wasn't used to thinking that way. She needed to get wise fast.

Echo took a deep breath. "I'll be right back," he said, then ran through the door, weapon outstretched.

Sheridan and Taylor waited. Seconds went by. Sheridan didn't hear any sounds of laser fire. That at least was a good sign. Then she realized the electric hum would have covered the sound. Maybe Echo had been shot as soon as he went inside.

She was beginning to feel panicky about this possibility when Echo stepped back through the doorway. "Come," he said.

Sheridan and Taylor left their knives on the ground. Knives would draw attention inside the city walls, and that was the last thing they wanted.

Echo disappeared through the orange light again, and Taylor and Sheridan followed. Sheridan nearly stepped on a sprawled man who lay on the ground in a colorful heap of metallic clothing. Echo took her arm and pulled her past him. "The Dakine were waiting for us. They must have suspected you went outside."

It was only when Echo said the word *they* that Sheridan saw the second man. He lay farther off, his arms and legs stretched out like he was making a snow angel.

Echo motioned them on. "Hurry before any others come." He took off at a slow run, and Sheridan and Taylor followed him, weaving between building-high refuse tanks. Every step brought sharp pain to Sheridan's feet. Her legs ached. She pushed them forward, forcing them to keep going.

In the distance, a few people worked by various tanks, but no one paid attention to them. Once they reached a main street, Echo slowed to a walk. A couple of cars were parked in front of a cylindrical building not far away. The group headed toward the nearest one.

As Echo caught his breath, he said, "I should warn you that the government may have figured out how to track my crystal. If they come after me and we're together, you'll be caught too."

Taylor gazed around nervously. "I thought you said the Dakine had ways to block their signal."

"They do," he answered, "but mine isn't a Dakine block. I'm hoping the government won't realize that and won't even try to trace me, but, *pues*, you can only count on the government's incompetence to bring you so much luck."

Echo didn't have a Dakine block. The knowledge lifted Sheridan with hope. Perhaps there were explanations for the other things too. Although the fact that Echo had taken them to a Dakine base was a bit harder to explain away. Still, she had decided to trust him. "We need to stick together," she said. "We'll just do the best we can."

The three climbed into the car, each collapsing onto a seat. Sheridan's feet throbbed to the rhythm of her heartbeat. Echo held his crystal to the car's control panel and said, "Fairmore swimming center."

The panel lit up, showing the digital clock. It had been two and a half hours.

Echo let out a groan and rested his head in his hands. "It will take another twenty minutes to get to Fairmore. We're too late."

"Won't Elise wait for us?" Sheridan asked.

"Not this long. She'll worry it's a trap."

"We have to try at least," Taylor said.

Sheridan kicked off one shoe and examined her foot. Flecks of blood dotted the underside. "Could you track Elise's crystal and see where she is?"

Echo lifted his head and shook it. Gray smudges marked where his hands had touched his face. "I can't go to a location where there's that sort of computer. We have to stay out in the open with the crowds. That's the only way we'll be safe."

"Maybe she'll wait for us," Sheridan said again, and then no one spoke for the rest of the trip. Echo laid his head back against the seat and shut his eyes. Sheridan put her shoe on. She and Taylor tried to wipe the dust off their clothes again but mostly just created a small dust cloud in the car.

Finally they pulled up to the Fairmore swimming center. A structure with slides that swirled and looped stood perched over the large pool. It looked like a gigantic plastic crab.

While the car slowed to a stop, Echo scrutinized the people mingling in front of the building. "She was supposed to be out front. I don't see her."

Taylor and Sheridan joined in the search, looking for Elise's striped hair among the bystanders. Men, women, children. People standing, sitting, talking. No Elise.

"She's not here," Echo said, then put his wrist to the control panel. "Drive west."

The car pulled forward and continued down the street. No one spoke. Sheridan's throat felt tight, like she'd swallowed too much of the gray dust and now it was choking her.

Echo leaned back in his seat. "Sheridan, when Elise helped you escape from the Wordlab, where did she tell you to go?"

"Los Angeles Park. She said to wait for someone to call me Hermana."

Echo pressed his crystal to the control panel. "Los Angeles Park."

"No one will be expecting us there now," Taylor said. "What good will it do to go there?"

Echo shrugged tiredly. "We have to hope that since Elise didn't find us at the swimming center, she'll check the park. We have to hope for a lot of things."

Sheridan kept her gaze on the window, willing the car to go faster and knowing it wouldn't. The buildings and walkways slid by in a leisurely procession. The lilting voice of the government commercials went on about the benefits of the immortality tax. *A small price now, so you can enjoy eternity later.* Finally the car reached Los Angeles Park.

Sheridan had expected to see grass and trees. It was just more concrete. Admittedly, there were spinning swings, a jungle gym with slides, and something that looked like a wavy merry-go-round, but no green. On one side of the park several children skated in a multilevel concrete pit. Brightly colored sparks shot out of their skates, and the skaters seemed to hover in the air for an unnaturally long time. Gel benches were scattered over the park, and adults sat and talked to one another while they watched the children. That hadn't changed over the centuries.

Echo, Taylor, and Sheridan climbed out of the car and slowly walked around the park. Sheridan searched every face she saw. The only person who returned her gaze was a teenage guy who was walking by with skates. He looked her over, saw she wasn't wearing a rank badge, and kept walking. He apparently wasn't interested in anyone who was so low ranking she wasn't wearing a badge.

After they'd made a circle around the park, Echo led them to a bench in the middle. Sheridan sank down into it gratefully. Her feet hurt more now than while she'd walked over the rocks.

"Recognize anyone?" Echo asked Taylor.

She shook her head.

The group fell silent again. They waited. Once in a while a car pulled up to the park. Every time one stopped, Sheridan's breath stopped with it. She hoped to see Elise, and was afraid it would be Enforcers. But it was never either. It was just more people coming to the park.

She scanned the area so frequently, it imprinted in her mind. The curve of the street, the edge of the skating pit, the neon street sign that read LOS ANGELES on the top portion and PARADISE BLVD on the bottom. A circular building stood beyond the park like a giant soap bubble that had landed on the ground and would momentarily pop.

Finally Echo ran one hand across his face, covering up the blue moon on his cheek. "I don't think anyone will come."

Taylor kept her voice low. "Then what are our options?"

"You met one of the DW," he said to Taylor. "You must have some idea, some clue about where Elise took you."

"I was blindfolded on the way there, and the room we went to was completely bare." Taylor chewed on her lip, thinking. "She let it slip that it wasn't in the fashion district."

Echo shook his head. "That's not enough. There has to be some detail you're forgetting. A smell, a sound. We have no idea where to go, and every organization in this city is searching for us. Think."

Taylor drew in a shaky breath. "I am thinking."

"Think harder."

It was probably the first time someone had ever told Taylor to think harder. All her math, science, and computer knowledge couldn't help them now. What could?

Sheridan looked out over the park again, her gaze resting on the street signs. LOS ANGELES. No Hollywood stars here. No angels, either.

Her eyes shifted to the other sign, PARADISE.

And then an idea came to Sheridan—not just an idea, a whole story, an understanding of how things must have been.

"Words always leave a trail," she whispered.

Echo turned to her. "You've remembered something Elise said?"

"No, but I think I may have found a trail."

He leaned closer. "What do you mean?"

She couldn't explain it, didn't want to, for fear it would sound foolish, so she stood up instead. "I want to see if you're right about word trails."

Taylor looked at Sheridan blankly, then turned back to Echo. "I think she's having a nervous breakdown."

"I am not." Sheridan motioned for them to join her. "I'm just thinking—but not in math or science or computer thought. I'm thinking in English, history, and religion thought. Come on—we'll need a car."

Echo and Taylor slowly got to their feet.

"Where are we going?" Echo asked.

"I'm not sure," Sheridan said. "Maybe in circles. It might be a coincidence, but it might be a trail, and we've got nothing else we can do, do we?"

Echo sighed, then set out toward a row of cars by the edge of the park. "No, unfortunately we don't."

Once they were seated in the car, Echo put his crystal on the control panel. "All right, where are we going?"

Sheridan leaned toward the panel. "I need to see the map. What connects with Los Angeles and Paradise?"

Echo pushed a button that illuminated the street map and sat back so Sheridan could see it.

"I think I have a trail," she said, examining the streets. "But I don't know where we are on it. Did Elise give us a location at the end or at the beginning? I guess it's possible that she gave us the middle of the trail, and then we'd have to try both ends, assuming of course that there really is a trail and I can find it. It's been four hundred years. Who knows how much has changed."

Echo tilted his head toward Taylor. "How long does a nervous breakdown usually last?"

"I'm not having a breakdown," Sheridan said, and ran her finger along the lines of the map, tracing the streets.

Echo turned to Taylor but gestured at Sheridan. "What is she doing?"

"Don't look at me," Taylor said. "It was your father who told her that words leave a trail. You can apparently think in this mysterious English thought she's talking about. I think in hard science thought."

Sheridan straightened up. "Let's hope it's the beginning of the trail. If it's the end of the trail, then all that's left for us to do is

sit on a park bench, and we've already done that. So here. . . . ."
She drew her finger from Los Angeles across Paradise down
several miles to Isaiah Street. She tapped the screen. "We want
to go this way."

Echo pushed his crystal into the panel. "Isaiah Street."

"We don't want to stop there," Sheridan said. "From Isaiah
we'll go to . . ." She followed the street on the map with her
finger again, silently repeating the names of the intersecting
streets as she went. "Sacramento. We'll turn on Sacramento
Street. I'm not sure yet if we want to go right or left. . . ."

Taylor scooted closer to the map. "Are you looking for
Californian names? Spanish words?"

"No," Sheridan said, still tracing Sacramento to the right.
"Religious ones."

"Sacramento," Taylor repeated. "Sacrament. And Los
Angeles means 'the Angels.'" She turned the words over slowly
in her mouth. "Angels, Paradise, Isaiah, Sacrament."

"What do they mean?" Echo asked.

Taylor didn't answer him. "It might be coincidence," she
told Sheridan.

Then Sheridan saw the next street: Prodigal. It wasn't
coincidence, couldn't be. Not with that many linking streets.
"We turn left and go to Prodigal Boulevard and then . . ."

But she couldn't find a street connected to Prodigal that
had any sort of religious meaning. She ran her fingers over
the left side again, repeating each name for some clue she'd
missed. "Bartlett Road, Market Lane, Wall Street"—she wasn't
sure whether to be glad or not that that name had survived four
centuries—"State Street, Hancock . . ."

"That's the banking district," Echo said.

Well, Sheridan supposed that's where you would put a Wall Street. She kept going through the names. "Goldman Ave, Profit Way, Mercedes Drive"—that was sort of a pun—"Green Street, Fleet Street." Nothing, nothing, nothing.

Then she realized she'd gone past it twice. The only reason she hadn't found it before was because the spelling had changed. Prophet Way. "We'll turn right on Sacramento until we get to Profit."

"What do you think these names mean?" Echo asked again.

Sheridan momentarily stopped searching Profit. "You told us that religion was banned ninety years ago. All the people who remember life before the ban have died. These terms don't mean anything to the population today, but the religious knew them, and they left a trail."

Echo glanced at the map, unconvinced. "Do you also remember that the religious left during the ban? They built their own city. No one was here to leave a trail." The car slowed. They'd come to Isaiah. Echo put his hand on the control panel, said, "Profit Way," and then leaned back in his seat. "So if the religious moved from the city, who left a trail?"

"They didn't *all* leave," Sheridan said, her eyes and finger still on the map. "You said the ones who left had food to sustain them while they built their new city. Not all the religious had enough food, and maybe some weren't convinced they needed to leave yet. So they stayed and renounced their religion, but they didn't forget it. They taught it to their children along with the symbols and phrases that went with their beliefs. It's not the only time in history religions have had to go underground."

Echo's brows drew together. "But why put religious words on the street signs?"

Sheridan went back to the map. "I think as time went by and things got worse in the city, religious people planned in secret how to leave. They left a trail so that others who still held their beliefs would recognize the words and come find them. Look"— she pointed to another street that led off Isaiah—"Menorah. That's a Jewish term. And this one here—I thought it was Salem at first, but I bet it's not. It's Salaam. That's a greeting meaning 'peace' among Muslims. Who knows how many more names there are that we just won't recognize because we don't know those religions well enough. They all left trails for their followers."

Taylor had traced her finger along Profit Way while Sheridan was talking. "Here's the next turn. Maria Ave. Or Ave Maria if you're musical."

Sheridan smiled at her. "And I thought you never paid attention to the church choir."

Echo stared at them skeptically. "We'll find a contact at the end of this trail?"

"I hope so," Sheridan said.

The car slowed again and Echo put his crystal to the control panel. "Maria Avenue." The car hummed back to its normal speed. "Where do we go after that?"

Taylor traced the street going left. Sheridan traced it going right.

"I don't see anything," Taylor said.

Sheridan's finger reached the end of the short street. "This end runs into a shopping plaza. I don't see anything either."

"We're probably just not catching it." Taylor kept checking

the map. "Who knows how many religious terms they came up with since we've been gone. Look on the surrounding streets and see if we can pick up the trail again."

Sheridan searched the names of the nearby streets. Nothing rang a bell. Minutes went by. She examined larger and larger areas.

"We're almost to Maria Avenue," Echo said. "Which way should I turn?"

Sheridan peered from one window to the next. "We'll have to go both ways and see if we can recognize anything. For all we know, this may be the end of the trail."

Taylor turned her attention back to the map. "Try right first. It's shorter."

As Echo gave the car the direction, she added, "We're searching for a religious symbol on something—an angel, a cross, scriptures. Maybe light."

"Light?" Echo said. "Light is everywhere. How am I supposed to look for light?"

The car turned. Sheridan eyed the passing buildings, trying to find a clue among their shrubless walkways and rows of windows. She read the shopping plaza sign, turned her attention to the buildings on the other side of the street, then stopped. Her gaze snapped back to the sign.

Taylor leaned toward the window to get a better view of the top of a building. "I don't see anything. Maybe it's on the other end of the street."

"No," Sheridan said. "It's up ahead."

chapter
37

Taylor stared down the street. "What do you see?"

Sheridan gestured to a curved bridge that acted as a walkway over the shopping plaza. A large sign hung there:

Recreacion Senter
traverton plaza
2nd entrans

Taylor's face remained blank. She simply said, "Wow."

"I know," Sheridan agreed. "It's clever, isn't it?"

Taylor blinked her eyes in frustration. "No, I was saying 'Wow' as in: Wow, I must have really missed a lot of Dad's sermons, because I don't remember any stories from the Bible with a bear in them."

"It's a code, Taylor. Read the first letter of every line."

Taylor silently did and gasped.

Echo did the same but only looked perplexed. "RT Two. What does that mean?"

Sheridan read it for him. "The *R*—'our.' And do you see how the *t* looks like a cross? The number two, and then the bear. 'Our cross to bear.' It's a religious phrase. Our contact will be somewhere inside there."

They had almost reached the parking structure.

Taylor scanned the area and bit her lip. "What if it's just a fluke? We might be grasping at straws."

Echo let out a sigh of exasperation. "We're supposed to look for straws now?"

"No," Sheridan said, "we're looking for . . . Well, I'm not sure what, but hopefully we'll know it when we see it."

The car stopped. "Here goes nothing," Taylor said.

Echo was the first to climb out. "Would you two stop talking in slang? I have no idea what you mean."

Taylor climbed out of the car and smirked at Sheridan. "Yeah, cut it out."

Echo shook his head as Sheridan emerged from the car. "Light, straws, and now scissors?"

Sheridan took his hand and gave it a squeeze. "Don't worry. Taylor and I will find the symbol. All those years of being preacher's kids are about to pay off."

The three walked slowly from the parking structure into the plaza. A sunken fountain splashed upward in the middle of the open area, surrounded by bleacher-type benches that led up to the ground level. Several statues were clustered in the area; past them, walkways led to dozens of stores and restaurants around the perimeter of the plaza.

Sheridan strolled up to the nearest statue. Could one of these hold some clue? One looked like a jumble of *Y*'s, another resembled a rabbit with two tails and three ears, but that could have just been Sheridan's viewpoint. Why would anyone make a huge statue of a mutant rabbit? Another looked like a stack of ten-foot milk jugs, and the last, well, Sheridan wasn't sure, but she got the feeling it was something obscene.

"What are the statues supposed to be?" Sheridan whispered to Echo.

"They're art. You're supposed to decide for yourself what they are."

"A waste of space," Taylor said.

Sheridan tilted her head to get a different angle. "An indication that sculpting skills have decreased over the last four centuries."

Echo rolled his eyes. "Are you two even trying to find a symbol?"

They left the statues and wandered around the plaza, weaving in and out of the crowd of peacock-colored shoppers. Time after time, people they passed would gaze at them, smile, then glance at their shirts to check their rank. As soon as the strangers saw they weren't wearing badges, they looked away and moved on, no longer interested.

Well, this was one time Sheridan didn't mind being snubbed. The fewer people who paid attention to them, the better.

As they walked, Echo told them what each building was. "Clothes store, hair-decorating salon, jewelry shop, furniture store, Mexican foodmart, Italian foodmart, VR center . . ." He spoke in his regular accent so as not to draw notice to himself. When Sheridan and Taylor spoke, they kept their voices low. They could understand the accent but not duplicate it.

They strolled past a variety of restaurants: pasta, Thai food, seafood. The smells wafted out into the plaza. It had been hours since they'd eaten, and all the walking had made Sheridan hungry.

When they'd made it around the plaza, Echo stopped. "Did you see anything familiar?"

Sheridan shook her head. Taylor did as well.

Echo rubbed his brow, disappointed. "Let's go around again. Maybe you missed something."

Sheridan's feet ached, but what else could they do? They walked more slowly this time, looking closely at shop displays for something that might be a clue. Sheridan saw lion figurines in one store. C. S. Lewis had used a lion as a Christian symbol, but then again, half a dozen sports teams had used lions too. The railing on one building had ends that looked like shepherds' crooks. A clothing store had a selection of white dresses, which could symbolize purity, or marriage, or that it was spring.

How would they ever find a contact? It was worse than looking for a needle in a haystack. At least you could tell the difference between hay and needles.

After they'd completed their second trip around, Echo led them over to a bench. "Did you see anything from any religion?"

"The farthest VR center has five pillars," Taylor said. "There were five pillars in the Muslim religion. One of the paintings in the art store showed a woman with three eyes. That could symbolize the Hindu inner eye. Or it could be a Picasso reproduction. Or just more of your funky twenty-fifth-century art. I couldn't really tell."

Sheridan rubbed her calves. "A vague knowledge of other religions isn't going to help us. Even if the other religions' trails did lead here, we've got to sound like we know what we're talking about. We can't fake being Hindu."

Irritation made Taylor's voice crisp. "Well, we've got to do something. Everybody is looking for us."

Echo held out a hand to keep them from fighting. "We're tired and hungry. We should get something to eat and then keep looking." He turned and surveyed the nearest restaurants. "I can only use one food credit at a time. I'll have to go in alone and bring something out for us to share."

"All right," Taylor said, slouching against the back of the gel bench. "Get the biggest meal you can. I'm starving."

"What do you want to eat?" Echo asked. "There's a Japanese foodmart, a pasta place, Mexican food, another Mexican food-mart, a seafood restaurant, or a pizza bar."

"Mexican," Taylor said. "It's the most filling."

Sheridan didn't answer. Her gaze was riveted to the res-taurant directly across the plaza. She grabbed Taylor's arm, almost jumping off the bench with excitement. "Fish!"

"All right," Taylor said, "if your heart is set on seafood, Echo can go there instead."

Sheridan pulled Taylor to her feet. "No, the Christian fish symbol. I bet there's one in the restaurant. It's our contact point. I know it is."

"Fish?" Echo repeated as though he hadn't heard right.

"Christ told his apostles he would make them fishers of men," Sheridan said, and set off toward the restaurant.

The other two followed after her. Echo caught up to her side. "Didn't fishermen eat what they caught? How is being a fisher of men a good thing?"

"It's symbolic," Sheridan said. "Christ is called the alpha and omega, the beginning and the end. So the picture of the fish looks like the ancient Greek letter alpha—open tailed."

"What's an open tail?" Echo asked.

Taylor drew the picture in the air with her finger. "It sort of looks like a pregnant X."

"Back in the early years of the church," Sheridan said, more to herself than the others, "when Christians were persecuted, they had a secret way of identifying themselves to strangers who they suspected might be fellow believers. They would draw a line on the ground—the upper curve of the fish. If the stranger was a Christian, he would draw the lower curve, finishing the picture. Just two curved strokes. Quick to draw, quick to erase."

Echo gaped in disbelief. "Wait—are you saying we have to go around the restaurant drawing half a fish?"

"It will be a complete fish," Taylor said. "Not enough people would know about the secret curved sign. I didn't."

"You didn't?" Sheridan asked, and felt an odd sense of satisfaction at knowing something her sister didn't.

They were close enough to the seafood restaurant to see a plaque over the door. It read FISHERMAN'S FEAST. A simple fish shape with an open tail sat at the end of the words.

"That's it," Sheridan said, stepping toward the building.

298

Taylor took hold of her arm and pulled her back. "What if you're not right? We can't go in there, order something, and then say, 'Oh, I'm sorry, I don't have any food credits because I have no crystal. But do you happen to know a way out of this city?' They'll report us to the government. We'll be arrested."

"I'll go in alone," Echo said.

Sheridan shook her head. "You won't know what to say. It has to be all of us."

No one answered. Sheridan said, "They won't report us once they know what we want."

Echo ran his hand through his hair, blending gray dust into the blue. "You'll have to pretend you're feeling sick—that's why you don't want anything to eat. You're there keeping me company, but don't speak while the waiter is around. I'll order, and I'll have to eat the meal myself. It would look strange if you didn't order anything, then shared my food."

"Great," Taylor said. "Not only will we probably be arrested, I'll get to see and smell food and won't be able to eat any of it. Order something really unappetizing so I won't feel as bad. Does any of that bioamino protein come in squid flavor?"

Sheridan tugged on Echo's hand. "No, listen to me. Tell the waitress you want the bread of life so you'll never hunger again. When she asks you what you want to drink, tell her you want living water. Remember to use the words *bread of life* and *living water.*"

"Manna," Taylor added. "Ask if they serve it."

"You think those are the contact phrases?" Echo asked.

"No," Sheridan said, "but they'll recognize those phrases. Language may change, but scripture doesn't. And if we're wrong about the restaurant, the waitress will just think you're one of those odd, difficult customers."

Echo let out a slow breath. "I want the bread of life and living water?"

"Yes," Sheridan said.

Echo recited the phrases under his breath while they walked to the restaurant. He paused when they got to the front door. "What if the waitress asks me questions I don't know?"

"We'll whisper the answers to you," Sheridan said.

Echo sighed, resigned. "That won't seem suspicious."

"We don't have anywhere else to try for contacts," Sheridan said.

Echo opened the door, and the three walked in.

They sat in a booth in the corner. Sheridan had forgotten that you ordered your meal through the computer, and the waiter came to the table only to bring you your food. For a moment she panicked. Their requests for bread and water were going to go unsaid—but Echo pushed a button on the bottom of the computer she hadn't noticed before. It read Recommendations.

A waiter immediately appeared on the computer screen. He was young, perhaps a teenager, with white clouds on his face. He peered over them as though looking over a storm. "What can I recommend for you?" he asked.

Echo ran his fingers across the table, fiddling with his silverware. "I'd like the bread of life."

The waiter leaned closer to the screen. "The what?"

Echo's words came out stiffly. "The bread of life."

The waiter pursed his lips and considered Echo. "The only bread we serve is for the fish sandwiches, and we cook it so the yeast is dead. Would you like to order a fish sandwich?"

Echo shifted in his chair. "Do you have any manna?"

The waiter smiled, but it was more a smile of agitation than pleasure. "We're a seafood restaurant. The items we serve are listed on the menu."

Echo glanced at Sheridan, and she fluttered a hand of encouragement at him. He turned to the computer again. "I'll have a fish sandwich, and to drink, I want living water."

The waiter raised an eyebrow, his smile still intact. "Our water is filtered. If there were any bacteria living in it, you'd have to go to the Medcenter after your meal. You wouldn't want that, would you?"

Echo tapped one hand against the table and glanced at Sheridan again. *Well,* his expression seemed to say, *what do I do now?*

She shrugged dejectedly back at him. It wasn't going the way she'd expected. All her hopes of freedom—now they seemed for nothing. The waiter had no idea what Echo was talking about.

The waiter's gaze moved to Taylor and Sheridan. "What about the ladies with you; do they need any recommendations?"

"No, they won't be eating right now. They feel sick."

It was true.

The waiter gave the group one last insincere smile and turned away. Before the computer screen changed back into a menu, he mumbled to someone offscreen, "How come I always get the memory-washed customers?"

Echo nodded and let out a long sigh. "He thought I was crazy."

Sheridan slouched in her seat. "Maybe we should have used different phrases."

Taylor propped her elbow on the table and put her chin into her hand. "Yeah, let's make Echo call the waiter back and ask him if he'd put a candle under a bushel."

"I'm not calling the waiter back," Echo said. "They would think I'd had a neural failure and call the meds."

The noises of the restaurant seemed artificial, too loud, too happy, too confining. "I was so sure it would work," Sheridan said.

"Maybe we got the contact place wrong," Taylor said. "Maybe we can think of something else." She turned to Echo. "When the food gets here, let's take it outside to eat. They may think it's strange, but we've set a precedent for strange behavior, so it won't matter."

Echo didn't answer. Instead his gaze shot to the aisle by their table. Sheridan turned to see what he was looking at. A waiter was approaching them, and not the teenager from the computer screen. This waiter was tall, at least six feet seven, with hulking broad shoulders and arms that looked like they could snap chairs in two. Braids of black hair hung down past his shoulders. He wore no colors on his face, and somehow it seemed even more menacing to be able to see his features clearly.

It's the bouncer, Sheridan thought. *We've acted too strangely and now we'll be thrown out of the restaurant.*

When the man reached their table, he smiled at them calmly. "I heard you had some special menu requests. I thought you'd like to see the chef. Perhaps he can help you."

Echo's gaze ricocheted between Taylor and Sheridan, but neither of them answered. They just rose from their chairs. He joined them. "Yes, we'd like that."

"Come with me." The waiter turned and walked back the way he'd come. They followed him down the aisle, through a door, and along a hallway with more doors. He opened a side door and a light automatically came on, showing a staircase. With each step down the stairs, Sheridan's optimism grew. They weren't going to a kitchen. He was taking them somewhere else, somewhere secret. He stopped at the bottom of the stairs, then pulled a calculator-looking box from his shirt pocket. He held the device up first to Taylor, then to Sheridan.

"Scanners are illegal," Echo told him.

The man held the device up to Echo. "So are weapons, but my scanner tells me you have one." He held out a hand to Echo. "Before I take you any farther, you'll need to give me your laser box."

Echo's jaw clenched. He pulled the black box from his belt and slapped it into the waiter's hand.

The waiter checked his scanner and held out his hand again. "And whatever other electronics you have."

Echo took his sensor box and his lock disabler from his belt and gave those to the waiter too.

The waiter slipped them into his pocket, then checked his scanner again. "*Pues*, you've got as many gadgets as an Enforcer." He motioned with his fingers to Echo. "Give me the last one."

Echo grimaced. It was clear he didn't want to turn over this last device. Slowly, he unclipped a silver box from inside his belt and handed it to the waiter.

The man turned it over in the palm of his hand. "What is this? A tracker?"

"A project I'm working on."

The waiter grunted and slipped it into his pocket with the rest of the things. He eyed Echo suspiciously, then gestured for the group to follow him down the hallway.

He stopped at what appeared to be a normal stretch of wall, took a small disk from his belt, and inserted it into a nearly invisible slit in the top of the molding. Immediately the outline of a door appeared amid the wall markings. It slid open, and the waiter moved aside so they could go in.

A desk stood at one end of the room and chairs sat at the other. Abstract paintings hung on two of the walls, and low cupboards topped with counters lined the other two. The waiter motioned for them to have a seat. He went and sat on top of the desk with his arms folded. "*Pues*, tell me who the three of you are."

Before Echo could answer, Sheridan leaned over and whispered what to say.

Echo hesitated, as though he hated saying these things that made no sense, but he repeated her answer anyway. "We're people searching for a Good Samaritan."

The waiter's eyes narrowed. He looked from Echo to Sheridan. "How come you don't answer for yourself?"

"She has a sore throat," Echo said.

Sheridan smiled, which was probably not the best indication that she was ill. She couldn't help herself, though. She wanted to go hug the stern look from the waiter's face. He could help them.

The waiter's eyes remained narrow. "Who sent you here?"

Echo opened his mouth, and Sheridan thought he was going to say Elise's name, but his gaze went to something behind the waiter. Echo folded his arms. "You told us we were going to see the chef—your boss. If we answer questions for anyone, I want to answer to the person in charge."

The waiter briefly glanced behind him, checking to see what Echo was looking at. "You're afraid to answer to me?"

"I'll answer for your boss."

The waiter slid off the desk and sauntered over to Echo. His eyes were cold with barely masked anger. "*Bien.* I'll tell my boss you want to talk, but you'll have to wait. He's busy running the foodmart." The waiter strode to the door, put his disk into the wall again, and went out. His footsteps thudded down the hallway away from them.

Echo leaned back in his chair and let his head fall against the cushion. "I don't have my laser box, my lock disabler, or my disrupter, and now we're locked in."

"Why didn't you answer his questions?" Sheridan asked. "Why antagonize him by insisting on seeing his boss?"

Echo turned to her, and she could see the exhaustion in his eyes. "Because these people aren't Doctor Worshippers; they're Dakine."

chapterhapter
38

The room felt hot, small, and suffocating, yet the room hadn't changed. It was only Sheridan's dread wrapping around her in an oppressive blanket. "You're wrong. How could they be Dakine when we used Christian symbols to find them?"

Echo reached out and put his hand over hers, a gesture of sympathy. "Maybe there was a trail here once. Maybe this used to be a contact place, but if it was, it's been taken over by Dakine."

Taylor turned to face him, mouth open in disbelief. "How would you know that?"

He gestured at the paintings. "Christians aren't the only ones who have symbols. Dakine have them too. They're in the artwork."

Sheridan's gaze swung to the first painting, and then the

second. It was abstract art; basically it looked like someone had emptied a bag of shapes and squiggles onto the canvas. "Where?" she asked.

"The one behind the desk has their most important symbol in it." Echo stood up and began checking the cabinets. They were locked. "Only sworn Dakine members know it. It's a way they identify each other."

Sheridan stared at the painting. Which of the squiggles was the Dakine symbol? She supposed it didn't matter. Tears stung at the back of her eyes, and then just as quickly were replaced by anger. Anger at the Dakine. Anger that she'd worked so hard to find a way out of the city and had only gotten them captured again. Anger at Echo for all of his secrets. "I thought you weren't a member of the Dakine. How do you know their symbols?"

Echo tried the last cabinet. It was locked too. "That isn't important right now. We need a strategy." He looked across the room, thinking. "There are several different organizations within the Dakine. This one might not realize that others are looking for us. If we pretend to be Dakine and say we're searching for contact places in order to trap the DW, they might let us go."

"How did you know the Dakine symbol?" Sheridan stood, facing him square on. "Are you Dakine or not?"

Taylor folded her arms. "We're just taking your word for it that there's a symbol there. How do we know these people aren't really DW, and now that you know how to find them, you want to leave to go report it to the Dakine?"

Echo held up one hand as though trying to make his logic appear in visible form. "If I thought these people could get us out of the city, I'd be the first one to strap provisions on my back, but the DW wouldn't have two pictures with Dakine symbols in them. These people aren't who we thought they were." Echo walked over to Sheridan and put both hands on her shoulders. Gently, he said, "I'll talk to the boss. It's our only chance to get out of the building."

And then what? More running, more fear, more of Echo's half answers?

Taylor looked to Sheridan, waiting for her input. Did they trust Echo now or not?

Sheridan turned back to Echo, searching his blue eyes as if she could see past them into his soul. "Why do you want to leave the city?"

He dropped his hands away from her shoulders in frustration. "Ever since you arrived, you've told me how horrible Traventon is, and now you're asking why I want to leave?"

Sheridan lifted her chin. "If you want us to trust you, it's time to tell us the truth. All of it. Are you trying to leave the Dakine? Is that why you need to leave the city?"

"Something close to that."

"Because they killed Joseph and Allana?" she asked.

His eyes flashed. "Because they killed my brother."

He hadn't cared about Allana—no, it was worse than that, Sheridan realized. Echo blamed Allana for Joseph's death. "Why did the Dakine kill Joseph?" she asked.

The muscles on Echo's jaw pulsated, and every part of him looked stiff and pained. He didn't answer.

"Was it something Allana did?" Sheridan prodded.

Echo looked away from her, his expression still tight.

"It's hard for me to talk about it. There are things you don't understand, things about my past."

Sheridan put her hand on his arm. Her anger had been replaced by concern. "Then tell it to us like a story, like it's just the story of two brothers you know—Echo and Joseph."

He gave a half smile then, the kind that isn't really a smile but an acknowledgment of the bitterness of life. "If I tell you, will you trust me enough to do what I say?"

"I hope so."

"All right," he said, "I'll tell you the story of Echo and Joseph." His gaze traveled past the desk to the painting on the wall, but he didn't seem to be seeing it. It wasn't a confession he was offering, or even an explanation. It was an accusation against fate. "People don't understand how close brothers are, because hardly anyone has them anymore. No one has a twin brother. It was just Echo and Joseph in the whole city.

"There are two sets of identical twin sisters living in Traventon, both of them very old. One of the sets visited the boys when they were seven. Back then, the boys were too young to know what questions they should have asked. They hadn't thought much about the tracking crystals at that point. But then, the sisters' crystals might not have worked the same, and sometimes asking the wrong questions brings more trouble."

Taylor turned in her seat to better see Echo. "What didn't you ask them?"

Echo waved off her question. "I'm sorry. I'm telling my story out of order. I'll go back to the beginning. Only sometimes I don't know where the beginning is or when things changed. But in the beginning, Joseph and Echo had no secrets between them. They could work together to create or destroy a program like they had one mind. Sometimes they used to switch places to see if anyone noticed. Every once in a while their caretakers would catch them at it, but more often the caretakers would accuse them of switching places when they hadn't. No one could really tell because they were so good at being each other."

Echo began pacing, his hands thrust into his pockets. "The problem was that things changed for Echo, and Joseph couldn't see it. Echo wanted to be more than a wordsmith. He wanted prestige, rank. Once the Dakine found out about his computigating skills, they offered him a membership and promised him a rank that would always be under a hundred thousand.

"I suppose the Dakine would have gone after Joseph too, but they didn't need to. Joseph shared everything he knew about computigating with Echo, helped him with any problems."

Echo let out an angry grumble from the back of his throat, almost a growl. "Allana dated both of the brothers. She was beautiful, influential, and used to having everything she wanted. Why she wanted both of them, I still don't know. Perhaps it was the novelty. Perhaps she wanted to see if she was powerful enough to destroy a bond that nature had created. Maybe she just couldn't decide. Whatever the reason, there began to be . . ." He paused, searching for the right twenty-first-century word.

"Friction?" Sheridan supplied.

"Yes. Echo shouldn't have been jealous. He had enough charm to spin with anyone he wanted. But you see, Joseph was the one the caretakers always favored. He was the son who Jeth talked to the most, so it was important to Echo that he be the one the girls liked best."

Echo shook his head, his eyes so cold they seemed brittle. "Allana was good at playing the brothers on different sides. She knew how to push them apart from each other and pull them toward her. It was entertainment to her—manipulating other people's lives."

Echo reached the wall of the room and paced back the other way, unable to stand still. "One day Allana chose between the brothers, and she chose Joseph. The problem was that Joseph was still too loyal to Echo. He didn't want to hurt his brother. Joseph knew Allana meant too much to Echo, so he told her no."

Echo's voice was calm, barely raised, but there was a churning intensity in his eyes. "Allana told Joseph that he didn't really know Echo, and Joseph laughed because he knew his brother better than anyone. He could *be* Echo when he wanted. The more Allana tried to convince Joseph, the more he laughed. And then she told him that Echo was part of the Dakine.

"She knew because she had recruited him.

"Of course, Joseph didn't believe her. He went straight to Echo and confronted him." Echo paused for a moment. "No, that isn't right. Joseph did believe her. He went to Echo not to confirm the story, but to yell at him. He kept saying, 'How could you be so stupid? How could you align yourself with the Dakine? Don't you know what you've done?'"

The pain on Echo's face grew as he spoke. Sheridan walked to him, wishing she could take the hurt from him, and feeling helpless because she couldn't. "I'm sure Joseph didn't mean it."

"Oh, Joseph meant it." Echo turned away from her. "Echo didn't defend himself. He couldn't admit that what Allana said was true, or reveal his membership to anyone who wasn't in the organization. It's against Dakine rules.

"So when Echo went to the Dakine base that night, he was furious at Allana. Furious because she'd chosen Joseph, and furious she'd told Joseph about him. To reveal your own membership is forbidden; to reveal someone else's, to put them in danger that way, is to break the first Dakine law.

"I've thought about it over and over again, and I'm still not sure why Echo told his superiors what Allana had done. If only he had put away his anger and pride, if only he'd considered the consequences of what he was doing—but he never realized how dangerous the Dakine were. He only thought of punishing Allana, not about endangering her or his brother."

Echo grimaced and rubbed absently at the crescent moon on his face. "I guess that's a fault both the brothers had: acting in anger. If only Joseph hadn't confronted Echo that way, yelling about his stupidity. So many ifs. So many trips in the wrong direction."

Echo's jaw tightened. It hurt him to say the next words. "That night Lobo decided the punishment. Allana was to be executed for revealing a Dakine membership, and Joseph was to die for hearing it.

"Echo never imagined such a harsh sentence—not for Allana, and certainly not for Joseph—but once a sentence is given, nothing can reverse it. With tracking crystals, you can't hide from the assassins. Only those in the government who warrant bodyguards are safe from the Dakine. For anyone else with a death decree, it's just a question of when the assassins will find you vulnerable. All Echo could do was beg for time to say good-bye to his brother. They granted him that, because as you heard Lobo say, the Dakine are fond of their families. So Echo went to see Joseph."

Echo's voice grew heavy and uneven, and then he stopped talking altogether.

The tears Sheridan had pushed away earlier spilled onto her cheeks. "You don't have to say any more."

Echo shook his head with resignation. "I have to finish it. I can't let you think that Echo didn't care about his brother." His gaze slid away from Sheridan, shifting back into his memories. "Echo told Joseph he wanted to switch places with him for the evening. Joseph didn't know what Echo had planned, but he went along with it because he felt bad about their fight. It wasn't until after they had reversed their hair and face colors that Echo told Joseph the switch needed to be permanent. He told Joseph what he'd done, and what the Dakine had ordered."

Echo's voice dropped until it was hardly more than a whisper. "Joseph didn't want to let his brother die in his place. There was nothing he could do, though. Echo stood there writing down every Dakine fact he could think of—locations, passwords, symbols, everything he'd computigated for the organization—all to help Joseph play the part of Echo. Joseph kept refusing, but Echo told him he wasn't about to let Joseph pay for his stupidity. Echo wouldn't live with that debt in his heart. Either they would both die, or only Echo would die, and Joseph needed to think about Jeth."

He let out a shuddering breath, as though the story had exhausted him. "So I thought about Jeth, and I let my brother die in my place. And I'm still not sure I did the right thing."

Sheridan put her hand to her lips. "You're Joseph."

"I am, and I'm not. I died with my brother on that day. I can't ever be who I was before."

Sheridan leaned over and put her arms around him, holding him tightly. Joseph. He was Joseph, and he'd carried the staggering weight of his brother's death. She wanted to speak but found her voice was caught behind a tight ball of sorrow in her throat. Such things shouldn't happen. They just shouldn't.

Joseph put his arms loosely around her and rested his cheek against her head. "Now do you trust me? Now do you understand why I have to get out of the city before the Dakine discover what's happened?"

"Yes."

"But the tracking crystals," Taylor said, still sitting on her chair. "Why doesn't your crystal reveal who you really are?"

Joseph lifted his head, keeping his arms around Sheridan. "The crystals work with a person's DNA. Identical twins have the same DNA. Supposedly the scientists did something to the crystals to make them work for twins, but whoever was in charge of that project must have decided it would be easier to fix the data than the problem. I'm sure he got paid the same, and what few twins there are in the city never brought the matter to the government's attention. Echo and I learned early that if our caretakers were trying to track one of us, the tracker picked up whichever one of us was closer. After Echo died, I made sure I was closest to the records building, so it was my crystal that the government turned off and not his."

"Which is why when someone tracks you, you show up at the cemetery," Sheridan said. "Echo's crystal is the one that's still on."

Joseph nodded. "I answered my comlink as much as possible so that no one needed to track me. I spliced into the life bank and the car systems' computer logs to make them keep my account open. Sooner or later someone would have noticed that a dead person was eating three meals a day. I was planning to leave the city before I was caught. Although now . . ." He didn't finish the sentence, but his meaning was there anyway. *Now that everyone is looking for us, now that we're locked in a Dakine room, now that things are hopeless, it doesn't matter.*

chapter 39

Joseph turned away from Sheridan's embrace and walked across the room. He suddenly wished he hadn't told the truth. As long as he had pretended to be Echo, it was almost as if Echo hadn't really died. Now that he had admitted to being Joseph, in one short moment Echo had disappeared entirely. No, not disappeared. The memory of that day stayed with Joseph. Always. Like a data loop in his mind. A horrible memory, and yet somehow the most vivid one of Echo that Joseph could recall. Horrible and comforting. He clung to it.

Joseph tried to clear his mind from the past and concentrate on this room, on this problem. He glanced back at the painting behind the desk. The Dakine symbol stuck out like a giant snake wrapping itself around the rest of the lines in the picture.

How often had he seen that symbol before he switched

places and not realized what it was? Now he saw it everywhere. In stores. In offices. On the clothing people wore.

He pulled his gaze back to Sheridan. She would be the hardest to convince. "We need a plan. When the boss comes, I'll pretend to be angry with him. I'll claim his organization hasn't properly revealed itself to mine. We've spent weeks closing in on the DW, and all of that could have been avoided if they'd followed the correct protocol. They'll ask us to swear an oath that we're Dakine and not DW. I'll need to teach it to you—"

"No," Sheridan said flatly. "I won't pretend to be Dakine. I can't deny my beliefs in the hope that it will buy me another chance at freedom."

I won't pretend to be Dakine. Funny, he'd said those same words once. And then he'd seen reason. She would too. "Sheridan, the Dakine don't let people out of their bases who aren't Dakine. They'll kill us all."

Her shoulders sagged. "You can pretend to be Dakine if you want. I'll be the prisoner you captured while setting your trap."

"Sheridan, no." There was a sharpness to his voice he hadn't intended. "No," he said again.

"Haven't you ever believed in something?" She sat down tiredly in the chair next to Taylor's. "You said that when your brother died, a part of you died too. If I denied my beliefs, a part of me would die."

Joseph sent Taylor a pleading look. "Convince her to be reasonable. She'll listen to you."

Taylor looked up at the ceiling, considering the matter. "Have you ever thought about all the people throughout history who died for their beliefs? After the Reformation, life for Protestants in some parts of Europe became so difficult that it was safer to get into boats and sail across the ocean to America than it was to stay in Europe. And the Jews during the Holocaust, the early Christians . . . so many more in so many countries. How did they do it? How were they that strong?"

Taylor's gaze turned to Joseph, still deep in thought. "With every decision we make, we're telling the world what we believe. Honesty or expediency? Work or play? Help a friend or help ourselves?" A hint of a smile crossed her lips, a plea for Joseph to understand. "I've already lost everything else. When it comes down to it, I don't want to lose my character too. I won't deny my beliefs either."

Incredulous, Joseph stared at Taylor. Now, when he needed her to be logical, she'd become philosophical about human nature? Joseph threw up his hands in frustration. "For people who came from such a violent time, you don't have a very well developed fear of death."

"There are worse things than dying," Sheridan said.

"Not many," Joseph said.

Taylor shot a look at the door. "Being forced to make weapons for the government or the Dakine—that would be worse."

Sheridan stood and crossed the room to Joseph. She took one of his hands in hers and caressed his fingers softly. "You can do whatever you want. We won't blame you."

He resisted the urge to grit his teeth. "I can do whatever I want? I can watch the execution, you mean. I've already done that once, and I don't need a repeat here. You said if I told you the truth, you'd follow my instructions."

Sheridan's fingers were warm against his skin. "I can't."

He pulled his hand away from her and let out a low groan. "The last time I cared about a girl, my brother was killed. Now I take a spin with you, and we'll probably all die. If I do come out of this, I'm completely giving up dating."

She took a step toward him, reached for his hand again, but he turned away.

He expected her to become angry, to defend her position; instead her voice was as gentle as a lullaby. "I'm sorry."

Her decision was final then. She was already planning her death, just like Echo had done. Joseph hadn't been able to save his brother, and now as he stood here waiting for fate to reenter the room, he desperately tried to think of a way to save Sheridan and Taylor.

Before he could even begin dredging up ideas for a plan, the door slid open, and two men walked in.

chapter
40

Joseph surveyed the men quickly, assessing them in case he had to fight. The waiter with dark braids was followed by an older man. His gray hair was tied behind his head the way restaurant workers usually wore their hair, and his face looked worn, but there was an energy, a sense of power about him, that made him seem too vital to be very aged.

The waiter nodded in Joseph's direction. "These are the customers I told you about."

The boss sauntered toward them, scrutinizing each one of them so carefully, Joseph was sure his first question would be about the gray dirt on their shoes. Taylor and Sheridan both waited, statue still. Taylor, he noticed, was trembling, and trying to hide it by crossing her arms tightly across her chest.

"Who sent you here?" the boss asked.

"We came on our own," Joseph said.

"Your requests for dinner were peculiar."

"We're peculiar people," Joseph said. The answer earned him a raised eyebrow from the boss, though Joseph wasn't sure why.

The boss walked around Joseph, eyeing the back of him. "Were you planning on meeting anyone for dinner?"

"No, and we want to leave now."

The waiter crossed his arms, flexing massive muscles as he did. "Tell my boss who you planned to meet for dinner."

Joseph could see no way out of the question. Sheridan and Taylor wouldn't take the Dakine oath, but he could still save himself. He ought to save himself. Still he hesitated. He had lived with the weight of his brother's death pressing into him for the last month. He couldn't bear the thought of adding to that load. All he could do was hope he'd been wrong about the symbols. There was a chance, however small, that the DW had chosen the paintings accidentally, not knowing about Dakine signs.

The boss's eyes narrowed into angry slits. He didn't like waiting for an answer.

"We had hoped," Joseph said slowly, gauging the man's reaction, "to meet someone who could help us. A doctor."

The boss's face hardened, and his voice snapped like electricity. "A doctor? The only ones who say that word are fanatics—sewer sludge that our city is scrubbing away."

Which meant that these people hadn't chosen the artwork accidentally. Joseph cast a glance at Sheridan to see if she had rethought her position. Her expression was firm, calm almost.

The boss's anger gained both momentum and volume. "Are the three of you fanatics?"

"No," Joseph said.

The waiter, now standing behind his boss, drew a black box from his belt and waved it in their direction. "Do we have some DWs we need to eradicate?"

"No," Joseph said again, louder. "We don't worship a doctor."

And they didn't. In Sheridan and Taylor's day, doctors were meds. No one worshipped them. He sent Sheridan and Taylor a look, telling them to deny it.

The waiter turned the laser box so it pointed directly at Sheridan. "You two didn't answer. Are you a worshipper of some higher being?"

As soon as the waiter phrased it like that, Joseph knew what would happen. He could hear the word before it even came off Sheridan's lips.

Not this. Not again. He wouldn't stand by and see Sheridan and Taylor shot.

They spoke in unison, their voices blending into an identical "Yes." Before they had finished the word, Joseph rushed at the waiter. It was almost as if he saw Echo's assassins before him, as if the replay he'd seen in his mind a thousand times was happening now. Only this time his feet weren't cemented, unmoving in horrified shock. Now his body jolted forward. He would reach the waiter and have one moment of vengeance before a shot cut through him.

The boss turned as Joseph went by, grabbing his arm and pulling him backward. The man was stronger than Joseph had expected but couldn't combat his anger. Joseph twisted, swung, and hit him across the jaw. The man stumbled, falling back against the cabinets with a crack. Joseph turned and saw that the waiter now had the laser box pointed at him. Time stopped. Joseph could focus on nothing except for the black box.

Then the shot came.

Sheridan screamed, or perhaps it was Taylor. He couldn't turn his head to tell. His muscles had frozen in place, as tense and unbending as ice.

It wasn't the burn of a deadly shot, just the shock of a stun setting. In a few seconds he would pass out. And then what would happen? Joseph struggled to breathe, felt himself falling backward, and the next second was caught.

The boss laid him on the ground while the waiter stood over him, still holding the laser box but now pointing it at the girls.

The boss pulled a restorer box from his belt and held it over Joseph's chest. Instead of sending out a large pulse that would have restored muscle function to his entire body, the boss sent out a directed pulse. Joseph could breathe easily again. The numbness left his face, and he could turn his head.

Sheridan had moved forward. "What are you doing?" she cried out.

The waiter took a step toward her, silencing her with a wave of his laser box.

The boss sneered down at Joseph. "You want to protect your Doctor Worshipping friends? I'm guessing that makes you a DW too, but then, maybe you're just the sentimental type. So I'll ask you: Is there anything you want to tell me before I decide whether to kill you? Any news you want to pass along?"

One of the phrases the Dakine used as a greeting was *The news is the thing*. The boss was waiting to hear if Joseph would say it.

Joseph knew how the Dakine worked too well, though. If he claimed to be one of them now, these men would have him kill Sheridan and Taylor to prove his loyalty. Joseph shook his head. "I have lots of things to say to you, but none that you want to hear."

The boss straightened and the sneer fell away from his lips. "All right then. You've passed our test. I suppose it's safe to help you." He pushed another button on the restorer box, and it sprayed out beams, pulsating warmth to Joseph's muscles, reversing his frozen state. Gradually, the tenseness that had clutched his body released its grip.

The boss rubbed his jaw where Joseph had hit him, opening and closing his mouth. To the waiter, he said, "Either you're getting slow or I am."

"They're just getting faster."

"Right. Next time I'll hold the laser box and you wrestle the wild ones to the floor."

Sheridan knelt beside Joseph, looking him over. "Are you okay?"

He pulled himself up on one elbow and nodded.

Taylor put her hands on her hips. Her glare bounced back and forth between the waiter and the boss. "You shot someone and this was just a test? You scared me to death!"

Fortunately, the men couldn't understand her. Joseph wasn't about to translate her complaint.

The boss held out his hand and helped Joseph up. Sheridan

stood as well. She wound her arm around Joseph's waist, helping to support him.

"Your feet are attached again?" the boss asked.

"I think so."

"You can call me Brother Navarone." He gestured at the waiter. "That's Brother Mendez."

"You're Doctor Worshippers?" Echo asked.

"That's one of our names." As Navarone spoke, he walked to a cabinet and unlocked it. "Sorry about that performance, but we have to make sure about people before we help them."

Mendez folded his arms and grinned at Joseph. "I was sure you'd fail. You seemed to know too much about our paintings."

Joseph's gaze returned to the painting and the twisting black Dakine symbol. "How did you get them, the secret symbols . . . ?"

"We have sources." Navarone took a tube of pain cream from the cabinet and applied some to his jaw. "It's surprising, but sometimes even the Dakine change."

Joseph ran one hand along Sheridan's back. "I need to explain about my friends. They don't speak the same as we do."

Navarone finished applying the pain cream to his jaw. "We know. Your friend Elise told us about the three of you." He tilted his head at Joseph, appraising him. "She neglected to mention that punch of yours."

"You've spoken to Elise today?" Joseph asked, feeling happier by the moment. "She's safe?"

Navarone ran a finger across his bottom lip, checking it for swelling. "She's already left the city. She wanted to meet you at Fairmore, but we thought it would be best if she wasn't around when the government assigned blame for its missing prisoners. We sent someone in her place. Couldn't find you, though."

"We ran into problems."

"She'll be happy to know you're safe." Navarone put the pain cream back in the cabinet. "What I don't understand is how you found us. Not even Elise knew of this place until we processed her out of the city."

"Sheridan found it. She recognized the religious symbols."

"Ah." Navarone nodded. "It's been a while since anyone has come to us that way. But if the government keeps bringing people from the past—we'll have to take that into consideration."

"We destroyed their machine," Joseph said. "They can't bring anyone else from the past."

Navarone's eyebrows hiked up in surprise. "You're certain?"

Joseph nodded.

"Good. Then we won't have to destroy it." Navarone turned, took a disk from his pocket, and unlocked several cupboards at once. He pulled out packs, put them on the counter, and checked through them. "We'll compile provisions for you so you can join the others. You didn't bring food with you, but we're a foodmart, so if you don't mind eating seconds, you won't starve. You'll have to change your clothes, hair color, and face dye. When we go outside, we do it in camouflage."

Navarone handed Sheridan and Taylor each a backpack. They looked through them, commenting to each other on the contents. Mendez hefted the last one from the counter and gave it to Joseph. "I'll hike you to our closest center. We have a facility there to safely remove your crystal."

Joseph gestured to the crystal on Mendez's wrist. "What if

someone tracks you and finds you're out of the city?"

"They won't," Mendez said, handing him a water pouch. "It's a fake."

Fake crystals? What other technology did these people have?

Navarone pulled two more water pouches from the cupboard and handed them to the girls. "After that, you'll leave with the others and travel to our city."

Joseph nodded. Everything was happening so quickly, but he was glad he didn't have time to think about what he was doing, what he was leaving behind. His father. His home. Every place he'd ever made a memory with his brother.

Joseph wished he could have seen his father again, said good-bye in person. Perhaps it was better this way, though. Jeth would've tried to keep him from leaving, and Joseph might have weakened and told him the truth. If Jeth knew that Echo had joined the Dakine, he would have been overcome with disappointment. And what would he think of Joseph for letting Echo die in his place?

It was better to leave quickly. "What is your city?" Joseph asked.

Mendez pulled a stack of pants and shirts from a drawer. They were a mishmash of greens and browns. "Santa Fe."

"Oh, of course," Sheridan said, and she smiled.

"Santa Fe, New Mexico?" Taylor asked.

Joseph shook his head. "That city was destroyed two centuries ago."

"But the religious built their own city," Sheridan finished for him, "and they named it after something they didn't find in their original cities: holy faith."

Mendez handed out the camouflage outfits. Navarone passed out sturdy boots.

Joseph pulled off his ruined shoes and took a pair. "I've never heard of a current Santa Fe."

"We call it Santa Fe," Navarone said. "Everyone else calls it Jackalville."

Joseph straightened. "I'm escaping to Jackalville?"

Navarone gave a deep laugh. "I've forgotten how little you know about us. I don't have time to tell you about our city, so I'll just tell you that it isn't what the government reports. You'll believe that much, won't you?"

"Yes," Joseph said. He knew the government lied about many things, but he was still uneasy.

Navarone pulled Joseph's electronics out of his pocket and gave them to Mendez to carry. As he handed over the disrupter, he said, "Our techs have never seen this device before. Is it some sort of bomb?"

Even though Joseph trusted the DW, or at least wanted to trust them, it was still hard to tell them the truth.

"It's a disrupter. Once it's activated, it deactivates any laser box that's within range."

Navarone's eyes went wide and his face brightened. "Our scientists will be eager to replicate this."

Yes, they would. He'd just helped the DW, shifted the balance of power. He hoped he wouldn't regret that later.

chapter

41

Mendez had said the DW med clinic was a three-hour hike outside Traventon. Joseph wished he had some sort of clock, but he'd left that function behind when he discarded his last comlink. Only Mendez had any electronics on him, and most of those were secured in his pack. Had they been hiking two hours or closer to three? He, Sheridan, and Taylor had been blind-folded, led through an underground passage, and driven in a vehicle that didn't run on the rails. Joseph knew it wasn't a rail runner because once they were dropped off and their blindfolds were removed, they were well away from the city. He supposed the DW had a tunnel that went underground for quite some way, and its door was camouflaged with a covering of rocks or bushes.

Mendez didn't speak as he walked, or offer any information

about their surroundings. Probably for safety reasons. Until Joseph's crystal had been removed, there was always the danger that the government could discover its mistake, turn his crystal back on, and track him. The threat of capture trudged along beside them as they hiked.

Mendez's head constantly swung left and then right, his braids sliding across his back as he surveyed the surroundings. He carried a laser box in one hand and a scanner in the other. Did he suspect they were being watched? Did he see anything, or was it only a precaution?

Joseph didn't ask. He didn't want to frighten Sheridan and Taylor in case Mendez gave the wrong answer.

The trees were greener, taller, than any he'd seen in wilderness programs at the VR center. They also smelled rich with some unfamiliar scent. Many of them lay on the ground, knocked over by—*pues*, what was strong enough to knock down such huge trees? All afternoon the group had to keep climbing over fallen ones.

When Joseph had asked about them, Mendez said, "They're pine trees. Storms come through every once in a while and pull some down." And then he wouldn't say more on the subject.

Sheridan, however, happily shared information about the outdoors. "Hear that chirping sound? That's bird language, which is something completely different from English.

"See those annoying little black things flying around? Those are bugs. They also don't speak English, and if you get too close, sometimes they fly up your nose. Actually, I was kind of hoping they were extinct."

Joseph reached over and swatted her with his half-empty

water pouch. "Do you remember how I said that if I got out of the city alive, I was giving up girls? I haven't changed my mind about that."

She laughed and took hold of his hand, swinging it back and forth as they walked. "You just hate to admit that I was right and you were wrong. Men haven't changed at all in the last four centuries."

He knew she was happy. Happy for perhaps the first time since he'd met her. The sadness had left her eyes, and in its place was optimism. And beauty. Like something you could look at and never grow tired of.

She squeezed his hand. The feel of her fingers in his was comfortable. Perhaps Jackalville wasn't going to be such a bad place after all.

Taylor was also excited about the city, laboring on her accent so she could ask Mendez questions that he refused to answer. He just smiled and said, "When you're safe inside, there will be time for questions."

So Sheridan and Taylor had to indulge their curiosity by talking to each other, guessing what Santa Fe might be like. Sheridan hoped they would have pets and a library filled with classics and novels that had been written over the last four hundred years. Taylor wanted parks with trees, a physics program, and at least one hot bath.

"I bet they don't have ranks," Sheridan said, already sounding relieved.

As they walked, the ground beneath them crunched and snapped in an unfamiliar way. Joseph had to constantly watch his feet so that he didn't trip over tree roots or the rocks that lay everywhere. That was another detail the wilderness program at the VR center had left out. Real dirt was so unstable.

Mendez stopped walking and held up one hand, the signal to silently wait. A minute went by. Not only Mendez's, but every head turned, searching the scenery for anything unusual.

Rocks. Trees. Shadows. A bird hopping from one branch to another.

Mendez put his hand down and motioned for them to start again. "A group of vikers is following us."

"How can you tell?" Joseph asked.

"When the wind is right, I can smell them."

Joseph took in a deep breath of air. He couldn't distinguish the stench of the vikers from the other smells around him. "They followed us all the way from the city?"

"It's a different group. Some of them live in the forest. They won't attack as long as I keep my laser box visible, but we'll need to hurry."

Taylor trudged behind Mendez, her boots making crackling sounds against the fallen pine needles. "Great. My legs are already killing me."

Sheridan shifted her backpack and increased her pace. "Better your legs than the vikers."

"We'd all be safer," Joseph said, "if you gave me back my laser box."

Mendez shook his head. "You're safe enough. We'll meet up with a group from the med clinic in about half an hour. They'll lead you the rest of the way blindfolded. But don't worry. The vikers never attack large groups."

"Even if part of the group is blindfolded?" Taylor asked.

Mendez didn't answer her.

Joseph watched the shadows the tree branches cast across their path. They shifted as the wind swayed through the trees. "How many of us will be traveling to Santa Fe?"

Mendez sidestepped a boulder, hardly making a sound as he trod across the brittle underbrush. "Enough. Elise and your father are waiting for us at the med clinic, so you can travel together."

"My father?" Joseph repeated, not sure he'd heard right.

"Jeth is your father, isn't he?"

"Jeth is with Elise?" Joseph asked.

Mendez glanced at his scanner. "I processed them together."

Jeth had left the city? Willingly? At that moment Joseph couldn't picture his father—all he could see was the office. The office full of old-twenties furniture and artifacts. The computer filled with research and theories and methods of study. Jeth's entire life was in that room.

And he had left it?

Mendez looked over his shoulder at Joseph. "You're not happy that your father went with Elise?"

"I didn't think he'd ever want to leave the city."

Mendez smiled and went back to scanning the area.

Joseph kept walking, vikers completely forgotten. Why had Jeth left Traventon? He wouldn't have been tagged with the blame for the time riders' release from their detention cells. That was clearly a Dakine operation. At most he would have been censured for leaving the girls alone before their first attempted escape.

Then the truth occurred to Joseph. It wasn't the government

Jeth was afraid of, it was the Dakine. They were looking for Echo and the time riders, and the first places they had searched were Jeth's apartment and the Wordlab. They'd probably threatened him.

So, not only had Joseph contributed to his brother's death, he'd endangered his father and forced him out of the city. *Sangre*, when Joseph made mistakes, he maximized them.

A few more minutes passed. Mendez stopped again, one hand aloft. He held out the scanner, turning it in a circular motion as he examined the area. He made an unhappy grumbling noise, then squinted through the trees behind them. "We have a problem. Someone from the city is tracking us."

The words hit Joseph hard, leaving him breathless. The government must have discovered he wasn't Echo and turned his crystal back on. "How many?"

"Seven. About eight minutes behind us. Usually the Enforcers won't come out this far. They must think you're important."

Not Joseph. The Enforcers wanted Taylor, and they couldn't be allowed to capture her. Joseph put his hands on his backpack straps, easing the pressure on his shoulders. "I'll leave the group and go in a different direction. That way the rest of you will be safe."

Sheridan took hold of his arm. "You can't leave now."

Taylor stared off in the direction that Mendez was still surveying. "I thought you said vikers were following us. How did they suddenly become Enforcers?"

"They're both following us," Joseph said. "Mendez's scanner can pick up other people's crystals. The Enforcers finally got close enough to register." To Mendez he said, "Are they on motor-walks?"

Mendez shook his head. "Machines can't make it over this trail. They're on foot like us." He slipped one side of his pack from his shoulder and drew Joseph's laser box and disrupter from a compartment. He handed them to Joseph. "Farther up, there's a dry creek bed that divides the hill into ridges. Go up the west side. I'll take the girls up the other. When the Enforcers follow your signal up the hill, I should be able to shoot out a few of their knees before they reach you."

It had to be their knees because the Enforcers wore helmets and deflector shields around their torsos, arms, and legs, as well as the palms of their hands. Only their fingers, joints, and small slits at their waists were left unprotected to allow them movement.

"What about the ones you don't manage to shoot?" Joseph asked.

"They're the reason I gave back your laser box. I'm hoping you know how to use it."

It wasn't the most encouraging of answers. "I know how to shoot," Joseph said. Since Echo's death, he had put in a lot of practice.

As they walked, Mendez kept scanning the forest. "Only use the disrupter if you have to. It won't do us any good to disable their laser boxes when ours will stop working too. Our best strategy is to shoot the Enforcers while we stay hidden. I've got camo tarps, so they shouldn't be able to find me or the girls unless they step on us."

The military used camo tarps made of a material that

reflected the color, shape, and texture of its surroundings so well that it could fool the human eye and most sensors. It wouldn't fool a sensor that had homed in on Joseph's crystal.

Mendez quickened his pace, and Joseph followed after him, gliding his thumb over the buttons of the laser box.

"I'm a good marksman," Mendez said. "And they won't expect to be shot from behind. They can't protect their joints forever."

Joseph's gaze went back to Sheridan. Her eyes were wide, frightened. "You'll be fine," he told her.

"I wasn't worried about me," she said.

No one spoke after that. They were listening to every rustle of the wind, every birdcall, concentrating on where to put their feet next. An urgency hung about them, pushing them forward. Joseph couldn't hear footsteps coming up behind him, but he could feel them.

The group reached the dry creek bed, and Mendez stopped walking. "This is where we diverge." He pointed left to a ridge on the hillside. "Hide in the bushes so the Enforcers can't shoot you from a distance. We want them to walk up that hill so I have a good shot at their knees. I'll do my best to stop them before they reach you."

"Thanks."

Mendez turned and headed toward the other hill, motioning for the girls to follow him. Taylor did. "Good luck," she called to Joseph.

Sheridan didn't move.

"Go," Joseph told her.

"What if . . . ?"

He bent down and kissed her quickly. "I may not have given up on girls after all, so you need to go now."

She took a reluctant step away from him. "I'm holding you to that."

"What does that mean?"

Another step, a smile. "You'll see when we're safe." She turned and took long strides to catch up with Taylor and Mendez.

EIGHT MINUTES. That's how long Mendez had said it would take for the Enforcers to catch up with them.

How far up the ridge should he go? He turned and looked at the opposite ridge. Through the collage of trees and bushes, he spotted splotches of greens and browns moving—the other three climbing. As Joseph watched, Taylor and Sheridan went behind a low-growing pine tree and didn't appear again. Mendez didn't join them. He positioned himself where he could get a clear shot of the other ridge.

Joseph had better hide soon too.

He walked a few more meters, then went up the biggest pine he could find. The lower branches didn't offer much cover, so he put his laser box between his teeth and climbed higher.

Trees in the VR center were always so sturdy. This one swayed as he climbed, the branches bending under his weight. He settled in one of the higher branches, hoping the brown-and-green clothing would hide him.

Then he waited, his laser box in hand.

Each chirp from the birds seemed especially loud. Bark and the needles of knobby branches dug into his legs. He kept as still as he could while he searched the forest floor for movement.

Nothing.

Nothing.

And then he saw them. The men hadn't taken the trouble to camouflage themselves, and they emerged from the trees like a trail of black shadows. Six Enforcers and one government official. Even from high up in the tree, Joseph recognized the black-and-gray-striped hair. Helix had come personally on this outing.

The Enforcers each held a laser box. Helix held something else. A large metallic contraption Joseph hadn't seen before.

The group stopped to get new scanner readings. Joseph pointed his laser box and waited. They would pick up the reading on his crystal, turn their backs on Mendez, and trudge uphill. He hoped Mendez had good aim.

The men spoke to each other, to Helix, then turned—but not toward Joseph. They began climbing up the other ridge, toward Sheridan and Taylor's hiding place.

For a moment Joseph didn't move, didn't understand what was happening. He waited for them to turn around again and walk back toward him. They couldn't know where Sheridan and Taylor were hiding. They couldn't. And yet they did. They were walking directly toward the place where the girls hid, and Joseph was too far away to help them.

chapter
42

chapter

Sheridan saw the men first. The large camo tarp that Mendez had put over them only had two small spots they could see out of, and those were blurry—like peering through scratched glass. But it was hard to miss seven men dressed head to toe in black. Helix was one of them, his black-and-gray-striped hair peeking out underneath an Enforcer's helmet. "Helix," she whispered to Taylor, and then added, "What's that thing he's carrying?"

The metallic device was the size of a pillow with a bowl-like bottom and a meter on top. Helix paused, consulting it, then turned away from the hill where Joseph hid and began hiking up the hill toward them. All six of the Enforcers followed, laser boxes held loosely in their hands.

"That wasn't supposed to happen," Sheridan said.

Taylor pulled herself closer to the hole on her side of the

tarp, then let out a punctured breath. "Oh no. They're not tracking Joseph. They're tracking us."

"How?"

Taylor shifted her position, still staring. "A QGP can identify and find a person's energy signals. They must have modified one to track us."

Sheridan wanted to shrink back but couldn't pull herself away from the view of the men marching up the hill. "I thought Reilly couldn't get those to work."

"Apparently the search apparatus wasn't the problem."

With each step the Enforcers took up the hill, Sheridan's heart beat faster. Where was Mendez? Where was Joseph? Did they see what was happening?

The ripping sound of shots cut through the air. Flashes of light sizzled around the Enforcers' legs like tiny fireworks. One of the Enforcers fell to the ground, then another toppled beside him. Both grabbed their knees, moaning.

"ALL down!" Helix yelled, and the remaining Enforcers knelt, their laser boxes pointed in front of them. Helix set the QGP on the ground and unclipped a laser box from his belt. "Stun setting only. I want no one killed until we have Tyler Sherwood bound." He pointed at one of the Enforcers. "Scan the area and find the sniper."

The man pulled a silver box from his belt and held it in the air, taking readings.

Sheridan expected the Enforcers to help their wounded, but the men kept their lasers up, surveying the area, seemingly unconcerned with the two who lay writhing and moaning on the ground.

The Enforcer with the scanner said, "I'm not getting any readings. The sniper either fled or has no crystal."

Helix grunted, as though the Enforcer had just admitted to being incompetent. He squinted at the forest. "They're here." He turned his head to the left and then the right, still searching. "Try every known scan until you find that sniper, then kill him."

Sheridan peered down the hill, wondering if Mendez had heard this pronouncement and if his covering would hide him from every scan.

Helix waved one hand in the direction of the wounded Enforcers. "Give them a pain eraser. Their yells will bring every viker from here to the city."

Two of the Enforcers took kneeling steps over to their companions. Instead of being relieved by the help, the wounded men seemed more nervous about Helix's command. "You're not going to leave us here?" the first asked. "The vikers will take us if we're unconscious."

"I don't need an eraser," the other said, pulling himself to a sitting position. "I'll be quiet."

No one answered them. The two kneeling Enforcers unsnapped a small box from each man's belt, took out syringes, and then inserted one into each wounded man's knee. The men went limp. The only sign they were alive was the movement of their chests rising and falling.

Helix motioned to his remaining men. "That should be warning enough for the rest of you. If you're stupid enough to let a sniper take you, you'll end up as dinner for the vikers. Now find Tyler Sherwood."

Step by kneeling step, the Enforcers moved up the hill. Each kept one arm straight down, the other straight out, swinging their laser boxes in front of them like sideways pendulums.

No more shots came from behind them. They weren't giving Mendez a target anymore.

How long would it be until they reached the hiding spot? Keeping her voice low, Sheridan said, "Can you think of any way out of this?"

Taylor gave an almost unperceivable shake of her head. "If we run, they'll shoot us. If we stay put, they'll find us. Joseph isn't around to use the disrupter, and even if he was, we're outnumbered and they're wearing armor. Mendez already shot at the QGP and nothing happened to it. They must have some sort of armor on it too."

"Taylor, you need to think harder."

Taylor scowled. "Now I know why you always got so mad when I told you that."

Sheridan didn't comment. She had just thought of the option Taylor wasn't mentioning.

Joseph had said that Traventon trackers couldn't distinguish identical twins from each other. They picked up whoever was closest. The same thing probably held true for the tracker on the QGP. Which meant that in order for Taylor to have a chance to escape, Sheridan had to be closest. She needed to draw the Enforcers to herself.

"I'm going to crawl down the hill and to the left," Sheridan whispered. "You crawl up the ridge to the right. When you get out of sight, run. You'll be able to get away while they're tracking me."

"I can't just—"

Sheridan didn't let her finish. "If you keep going east, you'll meet up with the group from the clinic that was coming for us. They must be close by now."

"No," Taylor said. "Maybe Mendez will—"

Sheridan didn't waste any more time arguing. "Go," she said. "Don't let my sacrifice be for nothing." Then she shimmied out from under the camo tarp, leaving it for Taylor.

Sheridan moved slowly, stayed low so as not to draw the Enforcers' attention too soon. Dry pine needles poked into her palms. Helix's men were halfway up the hill, moving only inches with every kneeling step they took. Still, each second brought them closer.

Sheridan kept crawling, ignoring the pain from the pine needles, twigs, and rocks that dug into her hands and knees. She tried not to wonder if she would ever see Taylor again, or Joseph. She couldn't let herself focus on anything but crawling. A minute passed. Maybe two. She looked up the ridge to see if she could spot Taylor moving. She couldn't. Good. That meant the Enforcers couldn't see her either.

"There! On the hill!" one of the Enforcers yelled. He was pointing to Sheridan.

She dropped to her stomach, flattening herself as much as she could. Shots ripped the air around her. She didn't dare move.

Down on the mountainside a man screamed. One of the Enforcers must have stood to chase her and had his knees shot. Either that or Mendez had been found.

The firing stopped. She lifted her head to peer down the hill. Through the foliage she could see black patches—Enforcers—three on the ground now and three still moving toward her on their knees. Helix took up the rear, glancing over his shoulder.

If she could slither away faster than they could move on their knees, they'd have to stand again, providing Mendez with a target.

She pulled herself along the ground, scraping across grass and rocks, pushing through clumps of weeds that caught around her arms. It was like swimming in dirt and not nearly fast enough. Her hands stung; the green dye on her skin was dotted with drops of blood.

More shots crackled around her.

Then a shot found her.

Her body was slapped with pain. Her muscles went so rigid, she couldn't breathe. She felt herself falling, rolling down the hillside, and couldn't put out her hands to stop herself, couldn't even shut her eyes.

She heard one of the men say, "We hit her."

And another said, "Finally."

She came to stop against a tree trunk, her face upward, staring into the sky. A few limp clouds floated forlornly above her. Below her, pine needles crackled. They were coming.

She needed air and couldn't draw it. The ache in her lungs grew into a sharp pain. She would pass out soon.

She concentrated, used all of her strength, and was able to gasp in some air. More pine needles snapped below her. She blinked. Some of her feeling was returning. Her back stung from where she'd rolled over rocks and sticks on the way down the hill.

She tried to move her fingers, but couldn't. Her hands felt as though they weren't connected to her body.

She heard one of the men call out, "I found someone else on the scanner."

"Take care of it," Helix said.

It had to be Joseph. He was probably in his hiding place on the other ridge, not even aware of what was happening to them. Sheridan jerked her head so that she could see the hillside. One of the Enforcers was creeping downward. Helix and the other two were taking kneeling steps toward her. They were only a dozen feet away.

"She's moving," Helix called. "She didn't get a full stun. Shoot her again."

An Enforcer raised his laser box, pointing it at Sheridan.

Nothing happened.

"Shoot her," Helix shouted.

The Enforcer's thumb pressed down on the black box.

Still nothing.

"Are you waiting for a moving target?" Helix yelled.

"It won't fire," the man said.

Which meant Joseph was nearby. He had used the disrupter. Sheridan smiled. The feeling had come back to her lips. She looked down the hill to see if she could spot Joseph. She saw someone in camouflage coming up the hill but couldn't tell if it was him or Mendez.

Helix set down the QGP and aimed his laser box at Sheridan. He gave her a daggered look as his thumb came down on the button. He was close enough now that she heard it click.

Nothing happened.

"*Sangre!*" Helix took the laser box in two hands, pressing the button so hard, he could have snapped the box in two.

"Sangre! Sangre! Sangre!" He threw the box to the ground, his face flushed with rage. On hands and knees he came toward Sheridan like an angry, black-and-gray-striped dog.

Sheridan glanced downhill again. Joseph—she could make him out now—was still far away, but rushing up the ridge. Relief and fear mixed together inside her. He was coming to help her. They were still outnumbered, though, and one of the Enforcers was headed straight toward him.

Off to Sheridan's left side, the pine needles crunched. A moment later Mendez appeared in her view. Instead of a laser box, he held a large stick.

Helix looked at him, unconcerned. "Rossmar, Graham, kill the sniper while I bind our prisoner. We need to find the other girl and return to the city quickly."

The first Enforcer lowered his head and ran toward Mendez like a football player going in for the tackle.

Mendez sidestepped him. As he went past, Mendez brought the stick down on the back of his neck. A sharp crack sounded, and pieces of bark flew through the air. The Enforcer was knocked to the ground. Mendez turned to face the next man.

Sheridan didn't see more because Helix knelt in front of her. He pulled a silver rope from his belt, tugging it outward like a spider laying a web. "You've cost me time and men. I'll see to it that you suffer before your memory wash. I'll shatter you a hundred times." He rolled her over so she was facedown in the dirt, then yanked her arms backward to tie them. She tried to move away from him, but her limbs were as motionless as the stones beside her. "Then when your memory is erased," he said, giving her arms another tug that shot pain across her shoulders,

"I'll tell you that you're my daughter." He turned her over and took hold of her chin so that she was forced to look into his cold eyes. He smiled to let her know he was enjoying this. "You'll do everything I tell you to do then."

chapter
43

Joseph had spent several minutes crawling up the ridge on his hands and knees to avoid being seen. His coming up the hill that way was perhaps more dangerous than helpful.

As long as the Enforcers knelt, their shields protected them from his laser fire. The coverings diffused energy and scattered it with a harmless flash. But if the Enforcers detected Joseph, he'd be shot. He didn't even dare use his disrupter, because even without laser boxes, the Enforcers would be hard to beat. Their armor had a stiffness to it that could take several more blows than Joseph's unprotected head and torso.

Joseph needed to wait until he and Mendez could bring down the Enforcers' numbers before he used his disrupter.

Joseph kept moving forward. He was breathing in dust and dirt. It coated the inside of his mouth. He watched as the

Enforcers discovered and stunned one of the girls. He couldn't tell which. . . . No, that wasn't right. Even though he couldn't identify her from this far away, he knew it was Sheridan. She had come out of the camo tarp to lead the Enforcers away from Taylor.

He crawled faster, the disrupter gripped in his hand. He had to keep reminding himself that they wouldn't kill her.

And then he heard one of the Enforcers yell out, "I found someone else on the scanner!"

Joseph couldn't wait any longer. He switched on the disrupter, left it there pulsing on the ground, then stood and ran up the hill toward the group.

One of the Enforcers headed downhill toward him, but Joseph had the element of surprise. The man held out his laser box and pushed Fire. Nothing happened. In the time it took him to push it again, Joseph picked up a rock and heaved it at the man. It hit him squarely in the chest, and he staggered backward.

Out of the corner of his eye, Joseph saw that Mendez had appeared from behind the trees, a thick stick in his hand. A stick, yes. They would have to fight like vikers now, with any weapons they could find. The armor might shield the Enforcers, but it made them move slower too. If he could get in enough hits, he might be able to stop the Enforcers long enough to rescue Sheridan.

Joseph spotted a low-growing tree branch. He would rip it off and use it like a club. He reached up and grabbed hold of the branch, trying to use his weight to tear it off. It didn't tear. It only swayed downward. He pulled harder. How could a tree branch that was smaller than his arm support his weight this way? He didn't have time to ponder the physics; the Enforcer ran toward him.

Still holding on to the tree branch, Joseph swung both his legs forward and kicked the Enforcer's chest.

The man sprawled backward, hitting the ground. Joseph didn't wait for him to get up. He leaped on top of him, wrestling like he'd wrestled Echo a thousand times. Only this time it mattered who won. In a few swift moves, Joseph pinned him facedown. Joseph's arm wound around the man's neck in a move that had always been illegal. Too much pressure, and you could break someone's neck. The man's armor protected him from that, but the Enforcer knew he was at a standoff. He called out for help.

Joseph glanced up. Mendez had just thrown an Enforcer to the ground. Taylor was with him, trying to fend off the second Enforcer with a stick. The Enforcer who Mendez had thrown on the ground stood up and headed toward Joseph.

Pues, that would help Mendez and Taylor take care of the other Enforcer, but it meant Joseph had to work fast.

Keeping his weight on the man, Joseph used his free hand to unsnap the Enforcer's med kit from his belt. He shook out the pain-eraser syringe, then thrust it into the slit where the helmet attached to the shoulder armor. As the liquid went in, the man stopped struggling. With a full dose, not only could he not feel pain, he couldn't feel his limbs either.

Joseph released him, just in time for the second Enforcer to reach him. The man yelled as he dived toward Joseph. Joseph rolled out of the way, and a second wrestling match began.

People who wrestled in armor didn't have the advantage.

It occurred to Joseph, the way one calculates any contact game, that if Helix had left Sheridan alone and fought alongside his men, the Enforcers would have overpowered Mendez, Taylor, and him. But Helix hadn't left Sheridan. He was so obsessed with capturing Tyler Sherwood, he hadn't even thought to help fight. Helix tied her hands, then heaved her over his shoulder. It was only after he had secured her that he looked to see the progress the Enforcers had made.

And by then it was too late.

chapter 44

While Helix lifted Sheridan, she caught sight of the fight. Joseph was on the ground struggling with one man. Another man lay unconscious on the ground beside him. Mendez had a stick across an Enforcer's throat in a choke hold. And Taylor—when had she joined the fight?—was taking something from the Enforcer's belt.

After Helix flopped Sheridan onto his shoulder, she couldn't see anything except the center of his back. She struggled against his grasp, twisted, but her efforts did little more than make her bump against his shoulder. If Helix disappeared into the forest, the others wouldn't be able to find her. She wanted to yell out, but she didn't dare distract anyone while they were fighting.

Helix took a few steps, then cursed. She could tell it was cursing by the way he spit the words out: sharp and full of hatred. He slid Sheridan from his shoulders so that she stood in front of him. She couldn't feel her feet. She didn't have any strength in her legs and thought she would topple to the ground again. Helix wrapped one arm around her waist and the other around her neck, keeping her upright and trapped against him. She tried to press her chin down so that his arm wouldn't cut off her air supply, but she didn't have the strength for it.

"It won't result," Helix yelled, taking a step backward and dragging her with him. "You can't have her."

Mendez and Taylor stood over the last of the Enforcers, checking to see if he was completely unconscious. Joseph strode toward Helix, halting only when Helix tightened his arm around Sheridan's neck, making her gasp for breath.

Joseph stood still, his hands clenched into fists. "You'll never make it to Traventon with her. Let her go, and we won't hurt you."

Helix shook his head. "Both girls will come back with me, or this one dies here."

No deal. Sheridan looked firmly at Taylor, saying with her eyes what she'd already said in words. *Don't you dare let my sacrifice be for nothing.*

Taylor understood her. She covered her mouth with trembling hands and shook her head.

Mendez wiped the dirt and pine needles from his hands. "Even if we let you go, you won't make it back to the city. Not with vikers around. Once they realize you're more unarmed than they are, you'll be their next menu item."

Helix tugged Sheridan closer. His breath brushed against her cheek. "Then the only way you save this girl's life is by coming back to Traventon with me to guard us from the vikers."

Mendez took a measured step toward Helix. "Without lasers, a couple of guards won't keep them away."

Helix turned his head, his gaze darting around the surrounding trees. "I see the rest of your men. I know you're not alone."

And then Sheridan saw them too. A half dozen men painted in camouflage greens and browns were scattered among the trees on the hillside, moving toward them. She couldn't tell at first—he looked so different without his maroon hair and green circles—but on second glance she was sure one of them was Jeth.

Helix watched them, then turned around and pulled Sheridan so hard, her feet twisted and dragged across the dirt. Several more men had been coming up from behind, surrounding him.

"Don't come closer!" Helix shouted, his head swinging from side to side. He tightened his arm against Sheridan's throat. She struggled to free her hands but couldn't.

Joseph walked to where Helix could see him. His voice was a controlled calm. "If you try to take her back to the city, the vikers will kill you. If you hurt her now, I'll kill you. If you let her go, we'll make sure you reach Traverton safely."

"No," Helix spat out. "If she doesn't help us, she doesn't help anyone."

Joseph slowly stepped toward him. "You don't even know if you have the right twin."

Helix tensed and jerked his eyes in Taylor's direction, but after a moment's thought, he relaxed. "I have the right one.

Otherwise you wouldn't be here bargaining for her. You would have taken Tyler Sherwood and left."

Joseph took another step. "You only think that because you don't know anything about twins."

The pressure on Sheridan's throat increased. She couldn't breathe. It would take Helix only a few seconds to break her neck, and Joseph was still too far away to help.

She wanted to call out to Taylor—to tell her it wasn't her fault. Some problems didn't have good solutions no matter how much you thought them out.

Sheridan fought against the pain in her throat, fought to fill her lungs. The world around her was dimming—Joseph rushing toward her was just a blur—and then a blast shook the trees. They flew up all around her, though she couldn't understand why. She didn't realize she was falling, and not the trees, until she hit the ground. A slap of pain went through her, then Helix's weight pressed into her back. He'd fallen on top of her.

Joseph yelled, "Sheridan!"

She took deep breaths, couldn't get the air into her lungs fast enough.

Footsteps ran toward her. Taylor called out, "Are you okay?"

Sheridan wasn't sure. She wanted to roll over and push Helix off, but couldn't move.

Someone heaved Helix off of her. Jeth's voice was directly above her. "Is she alive?"

"I don't see any blood." Joseph turned her over, and then she understood.

Jeth, with trembling hands, was holding the handgun from her century. He had shot Helix.

Sheridan smiled up at him. "I thought you said the gun didn't have bullets." Her words slurred because her tongue was still partly numb.

Jeth slipped the gun into his pocket. "I lied."

Joseph smoothed her shirt out, looking for a wound. "The bullet didn't pierce you anywhere?"

"I don't think so." Her body was still half numb, and what wasn't numb hurt from falling.

One of the men from the clinic had joined them. While he and Joseph cut the rope from her hands and feet, Jeth kept inspecting her for wounds.

"I was expecting the bullet to knock Helix over," he said. "I didn't know it would go through his armor. If it had gone through twice, it might have killed you. I should have thought of that."

In a wave of emotion and gratitude, Sheridan threw her arms around Jeth. "You saved my life. Thank you."

He patted her back awkwardly instead of returning the hug. "*Pues* . . . I . . . yes . . . of course."

Joseph watched her. "I saved your life too."

She released Jeth and flung her arms toward Joseph. He pulled her into an embrace. Held her. She shut her eyes and tried not to think about Helix's arm on her throat. She shuddered anyway. "Joseph, I was so—" She never finished the sentence.

"Joseph?" Jeth said, his eyes registering shock. "Joseph?"

Sheridan felt Joseph stiffen and wished she could take back the words, hide them. How could she have given away his secret so easily?

Joseph released Sheridan and turned to face his father. His

eyes were rimmed in pain. "I wanted to tell you, but there were things I couldn't explain."

"Tell me now," Jeth said.

Joseph swallowed hard. His gaze remained on his father. "Allana recruited Echo into the Dakine. She told me about it, and when the Dakine found out, they ordered my execution. Echo switched places with me to save my life." Joseph's words wavered, stumbled under the weight they'd carried. "How could I tell you I let him die for me? How could I tell you that Echo had joined the Dakine?"

Jeth's expression crumpled and tears filled his eyes. His shoulders heaved. He reached out and gathered Joseph into his arms. "You didn't need to carry the secret alone. I knew Echo had joined the Dakine. His rank suddenly went so high. He wouldn't ever tell me where he was going. How could I not know? But I have you back, Joseph." Jeth lifted his head, held Joseph away so he could look at him. "I have you back."

"But you've lost Echo now," Joseph said softly. "We both have."

"If he died for you, then in part we got him back too. He defied the Dakine. He became himself again before he died."

Joseph nodded, letting this thought sit with him. "I'm sorry all of this forced you to leave Traventon."

"Forced?" Jeth straightened. "I went willingly—as soon as Elise told me you were going. My work in Traventon—what is that compared to my son?"

The man from the clinic held a black box over Sheridan. "This will restore your nerve function."

She saw no light, no sign that it was doing anything. Still, the feeling rushed back into her body. She stretched out her fingers and toes, enjoying the sensation of movement. "Thanks."

The man then turned to Jeth and held out his hand. "You'll need to submit your weapon."

Jeth reluctantly took the gun from his pocket and handed it over. The man stared at the gun, holding it between his thumb and forefinger like it was a poisonous snake. "It won't fire if I put it in my pack, will it?"

"No. It only had one bullet."

The man carefully slipped the gun into his pack. "We wouldn't have let you bring it if we'd known it was a weapon. You said it was a relic; it looked so harmless."

"That's the problem with people now," Jeth said. "No one knows history. Those relics controlled the world for centuries."

The man closed his pack. "The other antiques you took from Traventon—are any of them dangerous?"

"Dangerous how?" Jeth patted the man's shoulder. "History is a dangerous thing if we don't learn from it. At our first opportunity, I'll give you lessons to explain the function of each of my antiques."

"When we reach the city, I'll be happy to hear about them." The man then turned to where Helix lay. A group had congregated around him, working to stop the flow of blood. Gauze and syringes lay scattered beside his body.

Sheridan couldn't feel anything about Helix's state yet; she was still upbraiding herself for calling Joseph by name. "I'm sorry I told your secret," she said.

"It's all right. It was time." The relief in his expression was evident, tangible. A shadow had left him.

Taylor broke into the conversation. "Why didn't you just tell Helix that *I* was the one they were looking for, not you?"

Sheridan had forgotten that Taylor was sitting on her other side, and now she turned to her sister. Taylor's arms were wrapped around her knees. Her cheeks were wet from where tears had been. Taylor never cried. Not since they were little.

"It was more important to keep you safe," Sheridan said.

"More important?" Taylor repeated. "How is that supposed to make me feel?"

Sheridan shrugged. "It's not such a bad thing to die in the place of someone you love."

"That's exactly what I'm talking about." Taylor's breath caught in her throat. "It's so easy for you to be noble, but what does that make me? I didn't ask you to die in my place. So stop it. Don't pretend to be me anymore." Her gaze fell on Joseph and she let out a choked cry, realizing what she'd said. "I'm sorry," she told him. "I'm so sorry."

Sheridan could see it, almost as though it were a physical thing, the bond forming between Joseph and Taylor. His brother had died in his place, and now Taylor understood how that felt.

He nodded at her, an acknowledgment of her pain, but didn't say anything.

Mendez walked over to them, holding the QGP. "Do any of you know how this tracking device works? How did it find you without crystals?"

Joseph stood, then helped Sheridan and Taylor to their feet. "It's not a tracking device," he said. "But apparently it can be used as one if you know someone's energy signal."

Taylor wiped at her face and took the QGP from Mendez,

examining it. "If Traventon gets it working right, it can also turn people into energy waves." She squinted down at its interface while Joseph translated her words.

Mendez took the QGP back from her. "We should destroy it then."

Joseph said, "We should study it first."

It hurt Sheridan to say the next words, but she knew if she didn't, someone else would think of it soon enough. "We can't go to Santa Fe. We'll be tracked there. Traventon might attack the city if we're there."

Joseph translated, but Mendez didn't look concerned. "The other governments already know where our city is, and it's been attacked many times. It will stand."

Sheridan glanced at Taylor to see her reaction, but she and Joseph were staring at each other.

Taylor ran a weary hand through her hair. "We need to find a way to sabotage or destroy the QGPs' data—all of it—before Reilly figures out a way to make them functional."

Joseph nodded, and it seemed to be a pact between the two of them. "We'll work on it in Santa Fe."

Mendez didn't comment, just turned to the group of men still huddled over Helix. "We need to leave. What's his status?"

One of the men looked up. "The bleeding is too deep and too heavy for the blanchers in the med kit to fix. He's alive now, but that may pass by the time we reach the clinic."

"We'll have to carry him anyway," Mendez said. "We can't leave him here for the vikers."

"What of the others?" another man asked. "Do we carry them to the clinic too?"

"We'll take them as close to Traventon as we can. When they regain consciousness, use their comlinks to signal someone in the city to reclaim them."

As soon as he spoke, several of the men retreated into the forest. Not long afterward they came back, leading nearly a dozen horses.

Horses. Sheridan smiled despite everything. One of them was a palomino like Breeze. Even the saddles didn't look very different—thinner, lighter, but the same concept. She turned to Joseph and saw him staring at them openmouthed. "I think you'll like Santa Fe," she said, taking hold of his hand. "I think we all will."

Together, they walked over to meet the animals. And despite everything that Sheridan had said about animals not talking, she spent several minutes stroking her horse's mane and whispering to him.

Acknowledgments

A lot of people should be in my acknowledgments because they helped inspire this story, even if they didn't know it.

To all the Brits I met in England. I was fairly certain they were speaking English, but sometimes it was hard to tell.

To MC Hammer for his song "U Can't Touch This." I still have no idea what it means, even though he is definitely speaking English.

To whoever put the ichthys in the original Jack in the Box logo. I mean, how covertly cool is that?

And of course to my family for all their love and support.

Also a big thanks to my editor, Sarah Shumway; my agent, George Nicholson; and his assistants, Erica Silverman and Caitlin MacDonald. You guys helped me turn coal into diamonds . . . or at least into words with considerably more shine.

A 2140 592237 2